"What does it take to ruffle your feathers?"

Sam asked.

"You're the most polite woman I've ever known," he added impatiently.

"Is being polite against the law out here?" she asked, politely.

"No. But there's not much that *is* against the law out here." He sighed. "It'll be a rough ride tomorrow. Get a good night's rest."

She started to close the door on Sam, but his hand came out and stopped her. Their eyes met. Elizabeth couldn't look away from the velvet eyes glowing with mischief.

"Let me give you a little advice, Liz." He paused, as if savoring his next words. "You'll be a lot more comfortable if you leave off that damn corset. No one out here gives a hoot in hell if your waist is two inches smaller, your stomach sticks out, or your breasts are shoved up a little higher."

Sam pulled the door closed, but not before he saw her eyes widen with shock and a flush cover her cheeks. He grinned and ambled down the

Dear Reader,

This month we bring you the promised second half of the very special miniseries that began last month. In Kristin James's *The Gentleman*, you met Sam Ferguson, older brother of hero Stephen Ferguson. This month, Sam has his own story, *The Hell Raiser*, written by bestselling author Dorothy Garlock, writing here as Dorothy Glenn. Sam is rough and tough where Stephen was smooth and polished. In fact, Sam epitomizes the West itself—so it's a real surprise when the one woman who can tame his heart turns out to be a polished Eastern belle. *The Gentleman* and *The Hell Raiser*, two very different heroes—and two equally perfect books!

This month also introduces a new author for the line, Mollie Ashton. And in coming months, look for favorites Bronwyn Williams, Caryn Cameron, Kathleen Eagle and more. The past has never been more alive—or more romantic—than it is every month, right here, in Harlequin Historicals.

Enjoy!

Leslie J. Wainger
Senior Editor and Editorial Coordinator

The Hell Raiser

Dorothy Glenn

Harlequin Books

TORONTO • NEW YORK • LONDON
AMSTERDAM • PARIS • SYDNEY • HAMBURG
STOCKHOLM • ATHENS • TOKYO • MILAN

Harlequin Historical first edition May 1990

ISBN 0-373-28645-7

DOROTHY GLENN

is one of several pseudonyms for award-winning Iowa author Dorothy Garlock. Often known to contemporary-romance readers as bestselling Johanna Phillips and Dorothy Phillips, Dorothy has previously written many historical novels under her own name. Perhaps best loved for her action-packed, authentically flavored Westerns, the former newspaper columnist makes her exciting Harlequin debut under the Dorothy Glenn name with *The Hell Raiser*. And this particular debut is dramatic in more ways than one: it also marks a unique publishing event. Working closely together, Dorothy and her friend and fellow writer Kristin James crafted two stories about two dynamic—and dynamically different—brothers. Each novel stands solidly on its own merits and plot; together *The Gentleman* and *The Hell Raiser* create an intriguing, inventive, jigsawlike duet.

Prologue

Montana Territory 1866

Run up to the house and fetch that little leather pouch of nails, Sammy."

Sammy, engrossed in pulling long, wiggly worms from the soft, damp earth, didn't hear his father's deep voice because he spoke softly, absently. Nor did the father look to see if his son obeyed.

Joe Ferguson grasped the curved handle of a big wooden plane and began shaving the rough edges from the plank he had cut. For Joe work was a way to relieve his troubled mind. His wife, Eleanor—Nora—more precious to him than life, had defied her affluent family in Saint Louis to come to the Montana wilderness with him. She had become more and more withdrawn during the past few weeks, and he was worried. She seldom spoke to him, or to their sons for that matter, unless it was absolutely necessary. A nagging dread had been eating at Joe for weeks, and he worked every minute he could spare, hoping to make life easier for her.

Today he was building a platform for his wife to step onto to dip water for her wash pot. Nora had never washed her own undergarments until she married him. Now she scrubbed the family's clothes in a tub beside the creek in the summer and hung them on the bushes to dry. In the winter she scrubbed in the kitchen and hung the clothes over the cook stove.

While he worked, thoughts tumbled around and around in Joe's mind. If he made it easier for her to draw water for her washing, if he trapped enough mink to make her a coat, if he took her to visit the neighbors more often, if he told her that he knew how much she had given up to become his wife, if he told her how much he loved her...

"Sammy!"

"Yeah, Pa."

"Run fetch the nails, son."

"Then can I go fishin' down by the flat rock?" Sammy scooped up a handful of worms and crammed them into the pocket of his britches.

"Sure, but fetch the nails and tell your ma where you're going."

"Look at this'n, Pa." The boy pulled a thick worm from his pocket. It wiggled out of his small, dirty fingers and fell on his bare foot. He quickly retrieved it. "It's a mean one, Pa. I'll catch a big'n with this'n, and Ma'll cook it for supper."

"You might at that."

"I'll take Stevie fishin' with me. He likes to fish."

"You'd better ask your ma about that. Stevie's only five, and he needs watching."

"I'm ten," Sammy said as if it was something he had accomplished all on his own. "I'll watch him."

"Ask your ma."

Sammy picked up the long wooden plane Joe had inherited from his grandfather, who had been a master craftsman. Unser Ferguson could build anything and build it better than anyone else, or so his grandson thought. Joe had a wooden trunk Unser Ferguson had built. It was grooved on the ends and pegged—truly a work of art.

"You said I could use this sometime."

"Aye, I did. But not today, son. Be gone and fetch the nails."

"Why are nails square, Pa?"

Joe paused and looked at this son of his who always had a headful of questions and who liked working with his hands.

"Because they're hand-forged. That means they were made by a blacksmith."

"You used these before, didn't you? You pulled 'em out of the old cellar door."

"Aye, and I greased 'em so they wouldn't rust."

"I'm goin' to grease my nails like you do, Pa."

That brought a smile to Joe's craggy, weathered face. He cupped his big hand around the boy's head and hugged it to his side for a brief instant.

"And I'm going to grease your bottom with my hand if you don't fetch the nails."

Sammy broke away and grinned. "You gotta catch me first." It was a game they played in the winter when the ground was covered with snow. "Catch me, Pa. Catch me," Sammy would scream as he raced into the woods with Joe in pursuit. When Joe caught him, he would roll him in the snow, then throw him over his shoulder and tickle his ribs as he carried him home.

"Not today, son. I've got work to do."

The boy turned up the path toward the comfortable three-room house set amid tall pines. He dragged his bare toes in the dirt and wiped his nose on his sleeve. He wished his pa had time to play and go fishing. Stevie never sat still long enough to catch a fish; he just wanted to play with the worms. Sammy decided on the way to the house that when he grew up he was going to be just like his father and build things with that big plane that made wood as smooth as doeskin. He was going to be a logger like his father, too. His father could cut down a lodgepole pine quicker than any man in all Montana Territory, Samuel thought proudly.

At the back of the house he stopped to pick up the fishing pole, then stepped carefully around his mother's wildflower garden. He pursed his lips and whistled a gay Irish tune. When he heard a horse stamping and a harness jingling, he instantly forgot fishing, forgot everything in his belief that someone had come to visit.

At the corner of the house, the grin left his freckled face. It wasn't a neighbor's wagon. It was *their* wagon and *their* horses hitched to it. Stephen sat on the wagon seat. Sammy smiled again, then frowned; he'd have to wash up. They were going visiting. Why hadn't Pa told him?

When he heard a small cry behind him, he turned to see that his mother had come out of the house. She was wearing her hat and carrying a valise. Her startled eyes were on his face, her hand over her mouth.

"Where we goin', Ma?"

Eleanor tore her eyes from her son's face and hurried to the back of the wagon. It took all her strength, but she managed to throw the valise in over the gate. She turned and caught Sammy's face in her hands and kissed him. Then she pulled up her skirts and climbed the wagon wheel to the seat.

"Come on, Sammy! We're goin' to see Grandpa. I'm takin' my whistle," Stephen yelled.

"Ma!" Sammy ran to the side of the wagon. "Where'er you goin'? Can't I go?"

His mother looked at him, mumbled something and shook her head. He could see tears on her cheeks.

"I want Sammy to go!" Stephen wailed, and began to cry.

Eleanor took up the reins and slapped them against the backs of the horses. "Giddyap!" Her voice came out in a screech.

Sammy began to panic. Something was wrong. Suddenly he knew—his mother and brother were leaving and were not coming back!

"Sammy come! Sammy come!" Stephen screamed as the wagon turned to leave the yard and head down the trail through the thick pines.

"Ma...ma! Don't...go!" Samuel ran after the wagon. "I got worms, Stevie. See..." He dug his hand into his pocket and brought out the fistful of worms. "Don't go, Stevie! I'll take you fishin'..." The wiggly, wet worms slipped through his fingers, but Sammy didn't notice, didn't care.

"Sam...my..." Stephen cried between sobs, turning to watch his brother run behind the wagon. "Sam...my..."

Eleanor whipped the horses into a trot, and Stephen had to cling to the seat.

"Come...back, Ma...ma—" Sobs burst from Sammy's throat as he ran. "Mama...come back!"

Although the wagon pulled ahead, Sammy ran as fast as he could. Through the blur of his tears he could see his mother's straight back and his brother's hand stretched toward him.

The boy ran after the wagon until he was weak and gasping for breath. When his legs would no longer hold him, he dropped on the dirt track, buried his face in his arms and sobbed his anguish. Somehow he knew that his life would never be the same.

He lay in the dirt for an hour or more and cried as though his heart was breaking. Then his father was kneeling beside him, lifting him. Sammy wound his small arms tightly around his father's neck.

"Ma . . . ma's gone," he sobbed.

"I know." Joe held his son, and they cried together.

Later, a long time later, he lifted Sammy in his arms and carried him to the house.

Chapter One

Montana Territory 1888

The logging camp, high in the mountains above Nora Springs, was quiet in mid-September. Only a handful of men were in the camp. Soon the five-month cutting season would begin. A half a hundred men would descend on the camp and stay until the ground thawed in the spring. To some of the loggers one bunkhouse or another was as much of a home as they wanted. They decorated the walls with pictures from the *Police Gazette* and stored their belongings beneath their bunks.

Awakened at dawn by the cook ringing a cowbell and shouting "Roll out! Breakfast on the boards," the woodsmen would tumble out of bunks, dress in the freezing temperature and hurry to the cookshack. Grub at the Ferguson logging camp was famous among the lumberjacks. The owners, Sam and Joe Ferguson, believed a well-fed man made a contented, productive worker.

Evenings at the camp would be spent at the grindstone, as the men prepared their axes for another day's work. The double-bitted ax was used by expert choppers who commanded the best wages in camp. No work was done on Sundays, and those who were sober did their laundry or cut one another's hair. Some even shaved, although most of the men allowed their beards to grow until spring. When these tasks were over, time was spent in horseplay or hazing a newcomer.

Sam Ferguson stood in the doorway of the camp headquarters and gazed at the soaring lodgepole pines surrounding the camp. This was his life, and he had never given a thought to doing anything else.

Soon the swampers would arrive to prepare the roads. For the past few years he had used the Michigan lumbermen's idea of driving tank sprinklers along the trail to insure a heavy coating of ice in the ruts made by the sleds. Great loads of logs then could be slid along the ice-coated ruts.

Each year Sam looked forward to the start of cutting season, and each year he looked forward to the end. He was like all the other lumberjacks: a creature of the forest. He grumbled and swore about the isolation, but by autumn the call of the forest was in his veins, and he was as eager as any lumberjack to put in thirteen hours a day in weather twenty below zero.

Sam was tall. His arms and shoulders were thick with muscles from years of swinging an ax. He handled the cutting end of the lumber business he and his father had started twelve years ago when Sam had finished his schooling in Missoula. Joe Ferguson ran the mill in Nora Springs. They had prospered during the past twelve years and had put all their profits into the mill.

Sam watched Burley Owens come toward him from the cook house. The cook had told Sam at breakfast that the old man had come up from Nora Springs the night before, eaten and gone straight to the bunkhouse.

"You sick or something?" Sam called as Burley approached.

"Hell, no, I ain't sick. Do I look sick?"

"You're usually in here complaining about something the minute you hit camp, so naturally I thought you were sick."

"Well, I ain't."

Burley sat on a bench and leaned against the side of the building. Sam lifted a booted foot to the bench, rested his elbow on his thigh and waited. He had no doubt that Burley had made the trip for a reason, and Sam could wait to find it out.

"Hot, ain't it?" Burley said.

"We have a hot day now and then up here."

"Yore just dyin' to know the news, ain't ya?"

"Yes, Burley, I'm just dying to know the news, but I know you're not going to tell me until you're damn good and ready."

"Well, I'm ready. First off, Joe said he'd got word 'bout the new saw blade. It'll be in Missoula in a couple of weeks. He thinks ya ort to go with me an' Jim to get it, that is if'n there's somebody here ya can leave in charge."

"Someone should go with you two lunkheads." Sam smiled at the old man affectionately. "You grizzly old buzzard, you're not fit to be turned loose in town by yourself."

"I whipped yore hind oncet, boy. I can do it again."

Sam laughed. "Does Pa think he'll have time to finish the contract?"

"He's thinkin' so. 'Twas a hell of a time ta break the big blade. I'm thinkin' he ought not to be givin' a cut in price if he don't fill the bill in time."

"Well, he will. He'll fill it in time and pay off the loan to the bank. Any news from town worth repeating?"

"Yeah, a dab. Yesterday the stage come in with Jessie ridin' on top. She'd been visitin' down south a ways. It pulled up big as ya please, and two dressed-up city fellers got out." The old man shook his gray head, and his rounded shoulders shook with laughter. "Lordy mercy! They was so sissy-lookin' me 'n' the boys was makin' bets that they'd squat ta pee. Well...it 'ppears that one of 'em was a val...et to the other'n. Anyways, that's what the driver says. The val...et set about waitin' on the other fancy dude hand 'n' foot. While he was bowin' 'n' scrapin', Henley from the livery pipes up 'n' asks if we reckon that valet wipes the dude's butt." Burley laughed until tears came to his eyes.

"Why didn't you ask him?" Sam laughed with him. Because he knew how much Burley enjoyed telling a story, he listened attentively.

"Like I said, Jessie was on the stage. The dude thought she was a boy. She had on them britches she's always wearin', 'n' totin' her rifle. The dude says, 'Hey thar, boy, carry my trunk.'" Burley stopped to laugh again. "Jessie's eyes spit fire. She flung off her hat, 'n' that red hair came fallin' out. She flew into him like a scalded cat." Sam had to wait for Burley to stop laughing. "Well, that dude backtracked a-plenty. The val...et loaded himself up with stuff, but he warn't no stronger than a pissant."

"What did Jessie do?"

"She bent over 'n' grabbed up them bags. The dude 'n' the val...et got a eyeful of her rear in them britches."

"Jessie's been wearing britches too long. She shouldn't have toted the dude's bags. Amanda should've put her in a dress and taught her to sew and knit instead of packing a gun and spittin' like a man."

"She was only showin' up the dude."

"That's another thing. She's too old to be showing off. She needs her butt whipped."

"Why don't ya do it? She's been runnin' after ya like a hound dog after a bone since she was dry behind the ears," Burley said dryly.

Sam watched the old man. Burley had been pushing Jessie at Sam for the past couple of years. Beside his pa, Burley, along with Jessie and her mother, Amanda, were the closest things to a family Sam had known since the day his mother had left with his brother, Stephen. Amanda's husband, Jessie's father, had been killed in an accident at the logging camp, and Sam and Joe had been looking after the two women ever since. Now nineteen years old, redheaded Jessie had given up everything feminine to try to prove she could take care of herself and her ma without help from anyone.

"What's the dude doing in Nora Springs?"

"I never got around ta findin' out. Joe wanted me ta come on up here. Ya got any decent coffee? I could make better coffee out of shoe leather than that cook ya got."

Sam sat at the table working on his maps while Burley snored on a bunk, but his mind was not on his work. It was on Jessie. It was time she started wearing a dress and acting like a woman. He had snatched her out of enough scrapes. Sam was thinking that her shapely little butt in britches had invited comments from every newcomer in town. Suddenly the object of his thoughts stuck her head in the door.

"Howdy, Sam."

"What the hell are you doing up here?" He got to his feet, suddenly fearful she was bringing bad news. "Is Pa all right?"

"Uncle Joe is fine. I brought someone to see you." Jessie stepped into the room, followed by a stranger.

"Jessie, you know I've already hired the crew."

Burley reared up off the bunk. "Hellfire 'n' brimstone! If it ain't the...dude!"

Sam met the man's brown-eyed stare. Something about him stirred old memories. The two men looked at each other for a long while as the silence wore on. A strange feeling started in the tip of Sam's toes and worked upward. His heart pounded in his chest, sending weakness instead of strength throughout his body.

Both men were tall, brown-haired, brown-eyed. Sam was just a bit taller and heavier. His features were rougher from days and weeks spent outside in all kinds of weather, and he had a slash of silky mustache on his upper lip. His hair was streaked from the sun and grew long on his neck. The face of the man who stared at him was smooth. His hair was glossy, neatly cut and just a shade darker than Sam's. His clothes were obviously new, from the general store in Nora Springs, and his hands looked as if they had never done a hard day's work.

"Hello, Sammy."

The words almost knocked the legs out from under Sam. No one had ever called him that but...

"Stephen?" He didn't know how he managed to say his brother's name.

"My God!" They both said at the same time.

Stephen stepped forward and offered his hand. Sam took a step to meet him, seemed to hesitate, then took his hand in a formal handshake.

"It's been a long time."

"Yes, it has. Twenty-two years."

"More than a lifetime for some people. I suppose you've seen Pa," Sam said.

"Of course he's seen Uncle Joe," Jessie said, looking from one man to the other. "He was determined to come up here. I had to bring him. Uncle Joe was afraid he'd get lost in the woods and the bears would eat him," she added dryly, and waited for a reaction from Sam. He ignored her.

"I've seen Father," Stephen said. "I was anxious to see you."

The silence was awkward. Unaware of his movements, Sam went to pour coffee into a graniteware cup and found the pot empty. Moving restlessly, he went to his worktable and shuffled papers. Years ago he had blocked his mother and brother from his mind. It was unnerving to be suddenly thrust into a past he wanted to forget.

"Sit down," he said, suddenly remembering his manners.

Stephen remained standing. "Mother died a few weeks ago."

"Really?" Something inside Sam's throat began to swell until it almost choked him. "Is that the reason you came to see Pa?"

"One of them. I came to see both of you. I thought you'd want to know."

"Don't expect me to mourn," Sam said harshly. "She means no more to me dead than she did alive."

"Ya durn clabberhead!" Burley exclaimed. "That's a mean thin' to say 'bout yore ma."

"Shut up, Burley. You're butting in where you have no business." Sam had never spoken so harshly to the old man and was immediately sorry when he saw the stricken look on Burley's face.

"I had another reason for coming." Stephen's voice filled the embarrassing silence. He reached into his inside coat pocket and pulled out a small packet of letters tied with a narrow ribbon. "Mother left these for you. She did some things that were wrong, but she wasn't a bad person. She loved *both* her children."

Stephen held out the letters until Sam was forced to take them. He tossed the bundle onto his worktable without looking at it.

"I'm not much of a reader," he said curtly.

"Mother let me believe that you and Father had died," Stephen said, looking his brother in the eye. He pulled an envelope from his pocket. "While she lay dying, she wrote me a letter. I'd like for you to read it."

"No, thanks."

"Suit yourself." Stephen's voice carried a hint of irritation. He put the letter in his pocket.

It was hard for Sam to believe that this tall, well-spoken man was his younger brother, yet the resemblance to his father was there. Too much time had gone by for Sam to greet this stranger with open arms. He remembered him, but he remembered more his father walking the floor those first few weeks when they were alone. He remembered the tears on his face, remembered seeing him age prematurely from grief. Joe had never ceased to love the woman who had deserted him and their son. He had named his town Nora Springs after her. Sam hated the name; it was a constant reminder of a mother who did not want him.

Sam thought about how he had put his own hurt behind him and tried to make up to his father for his loss. It had not been easy. Now, on seeing his brother, all the old resentment boiled up inside him.

"We'd better be going. I told Uncle Joe we'd be back before dark." Jessie edged toward the door.

"I plan to be here for a while, Sam. I want to get to know you and Father before I return to Saint Louis."

"Well, enjoy yourself at the local saloon. It's about all we have in the way of entertainment, unless Jess takes you to the spelling bee at the school. There'll be a hurrah over at Gogg's Flats, Jessie. I hear they've got a fiddler now that's got more than two strings on his fiddle."

"Sam Ferguson, you make me so mad I could...spit!" Jessie tossed her mane of red hair and glared at him.

Stephen stood beside the door with his hat in his hand. He had a puzzled look on his face.

"Goodbye, Sam. I'll see you again before I leave."

"No doubt you will. I'll be down in a few days. I make sure I see Pa every week or so," Sam said pointedly.

After they left, Sam sat at the table and stared at the clenched hands in front of him.

"Well, ya shore do know how to make a ass o' yoreself, don't ya?" Burley exclaimed.

Sam looked up. "Get yourself gone, old man. I don't want to talk about it."

Sam was scarcely aware of Burley's leaving. He picked up the bundle of letters. His first impulse was to toss them in the fire. His second impulse was to hide them from his father. Joe had been hurt enough. Sam took his saddlebags from the peg on the wall, buried the letters in them and tried his best to forget them.

He stayed in the cabin all evening, not bothering to go to the cook house for supper. His thoughts were a jumble. He thought of his brother and how it had been twenty-two years ago. Times had been hard for the family. The country had been sparsely settled when he had last seen Stephen. For the first time in years, Sam heard in his mind the small, sobbing voice of his brother on that morning his life had changed forever. *I want Sammy to come!* He remembered the small hand that had stretched out to him as he ran behind the wagon, and how his mother had ignored him.

Hell! Stephen had been only five years old. He had been a victim of their mother's callousness as much as Sam had been. Stephen was not responsible for breaking up the family and for ruining his father's life. Stephen had suffered the loss of his father and his brother. But he had grown up surrounded by wealth, had been educated in the finest schools and stood to inherit a shipping business from his grandfather.

Stephen had wealth and education, but Sam thanked God that he had been left with his father. He loved his life amid the trees, the cold, fast-moving streams, the snowy winters and the warm, fragrant summers. His life was here where he had worked alongside his father building the Ferguson Lumber Company from scratch.

Sam rode down the mountain to Nora Springs on a bright autumn day. As he approached the mill, he could hear the whine of the powerful spinning saws as the steel teeth bit into the butt of a log. The metallic scream of the blades was as familiar a sound to Sam as his father's voice. He left his horse at the stable and walked into the office.

Joe got to his feet, a broad smile splitting his face. He was a big man, like his sons, but the years had thickened his middle and streaked his thick black hair with gray. The shoulders of his plaid flannel shirt, which was tucked into his duck trousers, were sprinkled with sawdust. Joe closed the door to muffle the sound of screeching machinery.

"How's things going at camp?"

"All set. I left Gordy Sunner in charge."

"Sunner's a good man."

Father and son looked at each other. Both men knew that things were not the same. It was no longer the two of them. A stranger who was son and brother had appeared and rocked their world.

"I suppose you heard about Stephen?" Joe sat on the end of the desk.

"Jessie brought him up to the camp, but you know that. She said you sent her with him."

Joe's face took on a puzzled frown. He got to his feet. "You haven't heard that...he was shot after he and Jessie left camp?"

"Shot? What the hell!"

"He's all right. A bushwacker shot him out of the saddle, would've killed him if not for Jessie. She fired a few shots and chased him away, then got Stephen back in the saddle and brought him home—that is, brought him to Amanda. He was hit high in the chest. They dug the bullet out and have been taking care of him."

"Who would have a grudge against Stephen?" Sam asked.

"Damned if I know."

"He could have been mistaken for me. I turned away a few soreheads while I was hiring for the winter's work."

"I couldn't believe my eyes when I saw that boy, Sam. Twenty-two years is a long time."

"He's hardly a boy, Pa. He could have gotten in touch with us a long time ago if he'd wanted to." There was a sharp edge to Sam's voice.

"Don't blame him, Sam. I've spent many hours getting reacquainted with him. He's told me all about his and Eleanor's life since they left here. She told the boy we were dead, thinking it would be easier for him."

"Eleanor thought it would be easier! Hell, Pa—"

"Don't say a harsh word about your mother," Joe said quickly. "That's all over and done with. She suffered, too."

"Bull! While she was *suffering*, she was sleeping on a feather bed and being waited on hand and foot."

"Samuel!" Joe thundered, then softened his voice. "Meet your brother halfway, son. The two of you are all I have."

It had been more than five years since either man had mentioned the woman who had left them. Joe was just as forgiving as ever, and Sam was just as resentful. It was a subject better left alone. Both men were grateful for Jessie's interruption.

"Hello, Sam."

Jessie stood in the doorway, slim and boyish and smiling. She had never understood why she was expected to wear cumbersome skirts when she could wear the simple boys' clothing she bought at Swenson's Mercantile. Britches and flannel shirts were comfortable and warm. She saw little advantage in dressing like a woman. It was the men who had the adventure and the fun.

"Hello, squirt."

"Did Uncle Joe tell you that Stephen wants you to meet his fiancée when you go to Missoula?"

"Meet his...what?" Sam's eyes snagged his father's before Joe could look away. "All right. Spill it, Pa."

"I told Stephen you were going to Missoula to get the blade coming in on the train, and I said I was sure you wouldn't mind escorting the woman back here."

"Hellfire!" Sam sputtered. "What do you mean... escort? Didn't you tell him there was a stage?"

"He knows that," Jessie put in. "He came in on it. He says that Miss Elizabeth Caldwell is a gentle-born woman—whatever the hell that means—"

"Hush up your swearing, child," Joe said gently.

"Sorry, Uncle Joe." Jessie mouthed the words but didn't look one bit sorry.

"I'll put her on the stage," Sam said. "She can't ride the freight wagon with Burley and Jim Two-Horses."

"Stephen says he'd rather *dear* Elizabeth travel under your protection. *He* made the trip by stage, and *he* don't think that a woman of *her* upbringing should be subjected to that mode of travel. She's been sheltered all her life." Jessie's voice was heavy with sarcasm, and in spite of himself, Sam had to grin.

"If she wants to ride the freight wagon with Jim Two-Horses, Burley can ride horseback."

"He knows you're here," Jessie said. "I told him I saw you ride into town."

"Just a regular little know-it-all, aren't you, squirt?" Sam teased Jessie while a worried frown covered Joe's face.

"I've spent every evening with him, son. Your brother understands your bitterness, but he wants to be friends."

"Settle down, Pa. I don't hold anything against Stephen. I'll admit I was taken aback at first. Lord! It's been twenty-two years. Did he expect me to greet him with open arms?"

"Why not?" Jessie said. "Uncle Joe did."

"Someday I'm going to paddle your butt for mouthin' off, squirt." Sam jerked a strand of bright red hair as he left the office.

Sam went up the stairs at Amanda Randall's boardinghouse and knocked on the door of his brother's room. It was opened by a man in a white shirt, black tie and coat. The man raised his brows in question, and for a moment Sam stared at him stupidly.

"Yes?"

"Yes, what? Who the hell are you?"

"Charles, who is it?"

"He has not given his name, Master Stephen."

"It's Master Samuel Ferguson of the Nora Springs Fergusons," Sam said sarcastically. "Do I need an appointment to see my brother?"

"Come in, Sam. Charles, this is my brother, Samuel."

"Pleased to make your acquaintance, sir."

"Likewise, I'm sure," Sam said dryly, and tossed his hat onto a chair.

Stephen lay propped up by plump pillows, a writing table over his lap and papers scattered on the bed.

"I'll not need you, Charles."

"Very well, Master Stephen." The servant went out and gently closed the door. Sam thought of a comment he'd like to make about the val...et, as Burley called him, but stifled the urge.

"Sit down, Sam."

"I'm sorry about the ambush. Someone may have thought it was me riding with Jessie."

"Does this sort of thing happen often out here?"

"Not often, but occasionally."

The second meeting between the brothers was less strained. In the next few hours they talked of many things, carefully skirting any mention of their mother.

"I got a wire the other day from my fiancée, Elizabeth Caldwell, Sam. She's on her way to Nora Springs and will arrive in Missoula a week from tomorrow. There's no way I can go to meet her. I'm sorry to have to ask, but I would greatly appreciate it if you would meet Elizabeth and bring her here. Father told me you were going to pick up a blade for the mill. Something extremely important must have happened to cause Elizabeth to make the journey. She's not a flighty woman.''

''We're taking a heavy freight wagon to get the blade and other supplies. Burley and Jim Two-Horses are going with me. I'll meet her and put her on the stage. That way she'll get here a couple of days before we will.''

''I'd rather you didn't do that. Hire a carriage in Missoula with a top and good springs. If you can't find one for hire, buy one, regardless of the cost.''

''That isn't necessary when there's a stage that runs from Missoula to Nora Springs.''

''I don't think you understand, Sam. Elizabeth isn't used to being in a situation where she must cope with ruffians and the like. I expect to pay you for your trouble. Charles will give you money for the buggy.''

Stephen realized he had said the wrong thing when he saw Sam's eyelids half cover his eyes and his lips thin. When Sam spoke, his voice was so cold, so angry, that Stephen realized this brother of his was a dangerous man when crossed.

''This might come as a surprise to you, but out here money doesn't solve everything. No amount of money will buy a favor if the person doesn't want to give it.''

''Good Lord! I didn't mean to insult you!''

''Pa and I aren't rich, but we're not poor, either. You might say that we've got more pride than money. I'll meet your prissy-tail woman who's too good to ride the stage, and I'll bring her here.''

''I'm sorry, Sam. I'm used to paying for everything. People in the East expect it.''

Sam shrugged. His manner was casual, but he was still angry and seething with resentment, as his next words indicated.

"I don't think Nora Springs has accommodations suitable for such a high-toned *lady*."

Stephen met his brother's eyes steadily. "You took my meaning wrong. Elizabeth is a *lady* through and through. She's intelligent, sweet and kind. We grew up together, and our families have always planned that we marry, and we will before the year is out."

"Why couldn't she wait for you in Saint Louis? Why is such a woman coming to the wilds of Montana Territory? You of all people should know that *gentry* don't adapt to this country." There was heavy sarcasm in Sam's voice.

"Elizabeth said she would explain. I know her well enough to know that she does not act impulsively." Stephen was determined not to let his brother rile him.

"Maybe she's so in love she couldn't wait a few weeks to see you again." *Maybe she wants you to bed her. Maybe she's like an ordinary woman under those fancy skirts.*

"Regardless of her reason for coming, I'm responsible for her. And I know she will be safer with my brother than with anyone else."

"Thanks for the confidence, but it's not saying much for your judgment. You don't know a damn thing about me."

"Oh, but I do. Father has told me a great deal about you."

Sam snorted. "A father's not likely to tell one son the other son is a no-good son of a bitch!" He slammed his hat on his head. "I'll see you before I leave for Missoula."

Sam left the room. He didn't see the look of regret on his brother's face.

Chapter Two

Jehoshaphat!"

"What's griping you now, old man?"

"Ya'd think that was the last bottle o' whiskey in Missoula the way yore guzzlin' it. I ain't never seen ya down the stuff like that before."

"This might surprise you, Burley, but there are a lot of things you haven't seen." Sam's voice had an edge. "And that's pure gospel."

"Yore right as rain 'bout that. I ain't seen much, but you ain't seen much, neither."

The old man eyed the younger man, affection and disapproval competing in the expression on his lined face. He had seen Sam in this mood before. He was in his don't-cross-me-or-I'll-twist-your-tail mood—and had been ever since they'd left Nora Springs to come to Missoula. Before the night was over, Sam Ferguson would be in a hell-raising mood.

Sam pushed his hat to the back of his head and poured another drink. His face reflected boredom, but that didn't fool Burley. He had known Sam since he was knee-high to a duck. The shock of seeing his brother after twenty-two years had drawn Sam's nerves as tight as a bowstring. One of two things could happen. The whiskey was going to loosen him up or he was going to turn mean and hurt someone.

"How long have you known Pa, Burley?"

"Long time. You know that."

"You knew . . . *her*, didn't you?"

"If yore meanin' yore ma, you know I did."

"She was a bitch!" Sam's voice was low and hard. He spit the words out as if they were nasty in his mouth.

"She warn't no such thin'. She was a nice, pretty woman."

"Nice? Bullshit!" Sam snarled. "She ran off and left me and Pa. She took Stephen and told him Pa and me were dead." Sam emptied his glass in one gulp and poured another drink.

"She had her reasons. Yore pa don't hate her. Why do you?"

"I've not thought about her enough to hate her. She wasn't that important to me." Sam's words were cold and hard as an icicle to hide his hurt. Burley had no desire to argue with Sam about his mother. That was a subject he and Joe left alone.

Sam's thoughts turned to one of the two reasons he and Burley and Jim Two-Horses had come to Missoula. The big saw blade at the mill had been damaged, and they had been forced to use a smaller blade to try to complete an order that would pay off their bank loan, which was due in a month. The new blade they had ordered from the steel mill back east had come in on the afternoon train. It was already loaded on the freight wagon.

Joe had assured Sam that things were going along well at the sawmill and that, with the new blade, they would finish the contract in plenty of time. Sam did not like Frank Grissom, the mill foreman, although Joe insisted Frank did a good job. Frank had his eye on Jessie. She had made it plain to the man she was not interested. If that bastard bothered her while he was away, Sam thought, he'd take care of Grissom when he got back.

Suddenly Sam got to his feet and went through the batwing doors of the saloon. He walked with a steady, easy stride. One would never guess he had consumed almost a full bottle of whiskey. He stood on the porch, leaned casually against a post and looked up and down the rutted street of Missoula. He wondered what Stephen, who had lived in a city the size of New York and had gone to school in the East, had thought of Missoula when he stepped off the train.

He wondered, too, what that prissy, high-toned woman of Stephen's would think when she arrived. She was too persnickety to ride the stage. Damn Stephen! He should be here to meet his woman.

As Sam stood on the porch of the saloon, the conversation with Stephen played over in his mind. Remembering only made him more curious about the highfalutin Miss Elizabeth Caldwell. *She was not used to ruffians.* A cocky grin widened Sam's mouth. Maybe he should give the hoity-toity baggage a trip with a real, honest-to-God Western hell raiser. It would give her something to talk about while serving tea to the garden club after she returned to the mansion in Saint Louis.

Sam looked up the street toward the hotel where he had a room, down the street toward the tin shop, the mercantile and sundry other shops that made up Missoula, a railroad town that serviced the logging camps and ranches in Northwest Montana Territory. It was dusk, suppertime. Soon things would liven up. The town had its share of saloons and whorehouses. Sam thought about going to one but realized he wasn't drunk enough...yet.

He went into the saloon, picked up a bottle from the bar as he passed it and headed for the table where Burley sat.

Mike, the bartender, ran the wet cloth over the bar and watched Sam Ferguson. Sam had first come into the Emporia Saloon with his pa when he was a stripling. He took no pushing, drunk or sober, and was known to jump into a fight among strangers just to even the odds. He was drinking more than usual this trip, and before the night was over, he just might take it into his head to let off steam.

Sam hooked a chair with his booted foot and sat.

"Where in the hell is Two-Horses? I told him to see about getting a rig to carry Miss Prissy-tail."

"He'll be along." Burley pounded on the table with his empty beer mug, and the bartender brought him a full one.

"When? Next week?"

"Soon as he sees to the wagon and the mules...and the rig," Burley said patiently.

"When's the next train?"

"From the east?"

"Of course from the east. Dammit, Burley, are you awake?"

"Four days. Why?"

"If Miss Prissy-tail's not here, she can find her own damn way to Nora Springs. I'm not waiting here four days."

"Have ya checked the hotels?"

"I'll do it in the morning."

"I thought we was leavin' in the mornin'."

"We are. If she's not here, we go without her."

"Hellfire! You can't do that."

"Who's going to stop me?"

"Oh, bull fiddle!" Burley exclaimed. Sam had consumed his limit of whiskey and was no longer reasonable. From here on it was hell-raisin' time.

Jim Two-Horses was part Sioux, part Mexican and part something else that no one had bothered finding out about. He was small, wiry, of undetermined age, and extremely loyal to the Fergusons as they were to him and Burley. He came to the table, pulled out a chair and sat down.

"Mike," Sam shouted. "Bring Jim a whiskey or a beer. Bring him the whole damn barrel if he wants it."

Jim's bright, dark eyes met Burley's. They looked at each other and shook their heads as Mike made his way to the table. He stood close to Sam and spoke in low tones.

"Now, Sam, you know we can't serve Indians."

"Then don't serve the Indian part of him, damn you! Serve the Mexican part."

Jim got to his feet. "I got ta go see—"

"Sit!" Sam placed a heavy hand on his shoulder and shoved him down in the chair. He poured whiskey into a glass and set it down so hard in front of Jim that it splashed on the table. He glared at the bartender threateningly. "*I'm* serving him. You got something to say about it?"

"No. I don't reckon I do."

As Mike passed Burley on his way to the bar, he gave the older man a nudge. Burley got the message. If Sam caused trouble, Mike would call in the marshal. It wouldn't be the first night Sam had spent in jail. Burley remembered the time Sam had gotten in a fight with a town tough because of a remark the man made while they watched an Irish funeral procession pass. The man had said something about dirty mick. Almost as soon as the words left his mouth, they were followed by a few teeth, courtesy of Sam's rock-hard fist. The fight that erupted between the mourners and the bystanders resulted in broken windows, broken porch posts, broken noses, several broken arms, one broken leg and two runaway horses. Sam had had to dig up a hundred dollars to pay his share of the damage.

Burley filled a glass from the whiskey bottle and waited for Sam to look the other way. He set the glass in front of Sam, and Sam picked it up. The sooner Sam became so drunk that he was manageable, the sooner Burley and Jim would be able to get him to the hotel room, and maybe, just maybe, they would avoid trouble.

Elizabeth Caldwell wondered if she had taken leave of her senses when she left the security of her hotel room and ventured onto the street alone. She had seen quite a few new towns on the journey west, and Missoula was no more primitive than the others: a hodgepodge of painted and unpainted buildings strung out along a dusty street. Feeling more lonely and more frightened than she had felt in her life, she walked sedately down the boardwalk to the restaurant. The rigid training of her school years and the required behavior of the daughter of a socially prominent family forbade her to show her fear. She had to eat; her stomach had been complaining for hours.

At the restaurant she was served a huge slab of partially cooked meat, fried potatoes and onions, cold biscuits and bitter black coffee. The sight of blood from the meat on her plate had almost turned her stomach. After forcing herself to take a few bites of the potatoes and biscuit, she had placed her fork on the edge of her plate and taken a few sips of the coffee.

When the woman came to take away the dishes, she looked so concerned that Elizabeth had forced a smile.

"The long train trip, the smoke and all, has taken my appetite."

"It does that, dearie." The raw-boned woman clicked her tongue sympathetically. "But don't you fret none. In a day or two you'll be hungry as a bear. Just passin' through?"

"Yes."

The woman lingered, plainly curious. The sight of such a fancily dressed woman alone in Missoula was rare. The top of Elizabeth's high-necked gray suit fit perfectly over generous breasts and a waist that looked no wider than a man could stretch his two hands. A row of tightly spaced pearl buttons ran from neck to waist, where the bodice flared over curving hips. The soft kid gloves that lay on the table were decorated with a row of small pearl buttons, miniatures of those on the suit. The serving woman's eyes kept returning to the pink silk rose, nestled in a cluster of gray veiling, attached to the brim of Elizabeth's hat. It was the most beautiful thing she had ever seen.

"Waitin' fer the eastbound? It'll be comin' Saturday." When Elizabeth gave her a noncommittal smile, the woman said, "Well, you come back, hear? We'll have steak 'n' eggs 'n' biscuits in the mornin'."

"Thank you." Elizabeth took some money from her purse and placed it on the table. "Is this enough for the meal?"

"Yes, ma'am, it's aplenty."

Thinking about the supper as she hurried toward the hotel, Elizabeth didn't think she would ever again be hungry enough to eat meat.

She was a woman of medium height, and she appeared to be perfectly confident as she ignored the stares of the passersby who turned to gawk at her. Dressed all in gray, from the soft, high-buttoned shoes to the felt hat that set on her high-piled dark curls, she looked as out of place as a rose in a patch of dandelions. Back straight, chin held high, she continued on her way, her skirt swaying gracefully as she walked.

It was almost dark. From inside a saloon she was passing she heard a woman's tinkling laughter, then crude, slurred words in a loud male voice. The woman laughed again, and Elizabeth felt the blood rush to her face. How could the woman laugh at that lewd suggestion?

Music from an out-of-tune piano drifted across the street. Light streamed from open double doors. Two couples were galloping around the plank floor while shouts of encouragement came from the men lined up at the bar.

Most of the porches in front of the businesses were lined with benches, which were occupied by an assortment of men of all ages and, by their attire, all occupations. Indians with long braids and black flat-crowned hats watched as she passed. There were drovers with spurs on their boots, and railroad workers wearing heavy work shoes. Elizabeth avoided looking directly at any of them, but some tipped their hats as she passed. It was all very frightening to Elizabeth—this newness, rawness, wildness.

She stepped off the boardwalk, crossed the dusty street and climbed the split-log steps to the porch of the hotel. A handsomely dressed man in a dark frock coat lifted his bowler hat. His eyes roamed her figure boldly, and when he smiled, white teeth showed beneath a trim black mustache. He moved to approach her, but she entered the hotel, quickly crossed the lobby and started up the steps.

On the first landing she stopped and looked back. The lobby was clear. The man had not followed her in. She sighed with relief as she slowly retraced her steps to the desk where a young man in a white shirt with a stiff celluloid collar and black sleeve bands stood watching her. As she approached, he lifted his palms and smoothed his already slicked-down hair. It was parted in the middle with a flat curl on each side of the part.

"I'm expecting my fiancé, Mr. Stephen Ferguson from Nora Springs. When he comes in, will you tell him I have arrived?"

"Your... fiancé? But, ma'am, he arrived this afternoon, shortly before you did." The clerk moved his finger along a line on the register. "S. Ferguson, Nora Springs, Montana."

"Oh, but that's wonderful! Did he ask if I was here?"

"No, ma'am. But this isn't the hotel the train passengers usually stay in. They stay in the one nearest the depot."

"The conductor said the Baltimore House was the nicest."

"It is. But most passengers want something cheaper."

"What room is Mr. Ferguson in?"

"Room 208."

"Thank you." Relief caused her to forget herself, and she allowed her shoulders to slump momentarily. She smiled at the young man and turned to go up the stairs.

"He went out."

Elizabeth paused. "He went out to dinner?"

"He went out this afternoon just after he arrived."

"Oh? When he comes in, please tell him that I'm here and that I'm anxious to see him."

The train conductor had recommended the hotel, saying it was the best in town. Even at that, it was lacking in the accommodations Elizabeth was used to having. She unlocked her door, leaving it open so that she could see to light the lamp in her room, then closed the door and locked it. She removed her gloves, pulled the hat pin from the crown of her hat, removed the hat, replaced the pin and set the hat in a hatbox. She was meticulous with her person and her possessions. Elizabeth patted her hair into shape with her fingers before she removed her suit jacket and hung it in the wardrobe.

The small number of bags, boxes and a small trunk was evidence of her hasty departure from Saint Louis. Glory! What had possessed her stepmother, Netta Caldwell, to act as she had? Stephen would understand why Elizabeth had come when he heard about Netta's latest scheme. Dear Stephen. Only two years older than she, he had grown up with her. Her father had considered Stephen the son he never had. Papa and Eleanor, two of the dearest people in the world to Elizabeth, were gone. Only Stephen remained. Knowing that he was in Missoula, Elizabeth no longer felt so alone.

Elizabeth pulled back the window curtain and looked at the street, searching for Stephen's familiar figure. He would be wearing his black bowler, and Charles would be with him.

Her attention was drawn to a building across and down the street from the hotel. A woman had come out onto an upper porch and was calling to someone on the street. The light from the window shone on her bright yellow sleeveless dress. She had yellow feathers or ribbons—Elizabeth couldn't tell which—in her hair. A man stood on the sidewalk with his hands on his hips and called something to the woman. She turned, bent over and flipped up the back of her dress before she flounced inside. The man on the walk laughed and slapped his thighs with his hands. He was joined by some other men. They all laughed and looked up at the empty porch.

This was a strange new world for Elizabeth. She had seen a side of life, during her trip, that she had not known existed. The people in the West seemed to enjoy life to the fullest. They took an uncommon interest in their fellow man. The serving woman at the restaurant was concerned because Elizabeth hadn't eaten her food. The conductor on the train found someone to take her and her bags to the hotel. In a way, they were as uninhibited as children. She thought of the cowboy on the train who had suddenly burst into song. No one had seemed to think it strange. He sang about "dogies" and "mavericks" and the girl he left behind him. The other passengers applauded, which encouraged him to sing song after song. Elizabeth had to admit she had enjoyed the diversion.

A half hour went by while Elizabeth watched the activity on the street. Finally she pulled up a chair and sat by the window. During the next hour only a few people came into the hotel, and none of them was Stephen or Charles. Finally her attention was drawn to a trio coming down the boardwalk. Two men were helping a third, who seemed to be very drunk. The drunk was a good head taller than his companions, and every so often he refused to take another step. Elizabeth giggled in spite of herself when the three staggered up the split log steps. Then the tall man backtracked and stood in the street laughing at the other two.

She looked up the street to where a crowd had come out of a saloon. One man had been thrown into the street. Several men jumped on horses, fired their guns in the air and raced out of town. When she looked back, the drunk and his companions were not in sight.

Elizabeth heard people going down the narrow hallway, doors slamming and the low murmur of voices. She was tired. She looked longingly at the bed and suppressed a yawn. She couldn't imagine what Stephen would be doing at this time of night, unless he had found someone who enjoyed a game of chess as much as he did. When he was playing chess, time meant little to him.

She would write a note and slip it under his door. They could meet in the morning for breakfast, and she would tell him the news. The decision made, Elizabeth opened her small trunk and took out her writing materials. She wrote Dear Stephen, then paused and thought about him.

Stephen had been excited when he left Saint Louis. He was eager to meet the father and brother he hadn't seen for twenty-two years. Elizabeth had known Stephen for all that time, although she was too young to remember the first few years. She thought her father might have been in love with Eleanor Ferguson in his younger days. But she was sure that Eleanor had considered him a friend and nothing more. What had caused Eleanor to leave one son and bring the other home to her parents? Eleanor had refused to talk about that part of her life.

Stephen had taken Elizabeth to her first party and given her her first kiss, even if was a mere peck on the cheek on her sixteenth birthday. Heavens! That was almost ten years ago. Could she be twenty-five years old, going on twenty-six? No wonder Netta was anxious for her to marry and leave home. It made Netta seem older having a spinster stepdaughter living in the house. There was no one Elizabeth would rather marry than Stephen. She loved him, had always loved him. It wasn't the kind of passionate love she had read about in novels. It was a comfortable love. They understood each other, liked the same things, knew the same people.

"Oh, shoot! I'm so tired I'm thinking in circles," she muttered, and covered her mouth to hide another yawn.

After penning the note in neat script, she folded it, picked up her drawstring purse and unlocked the door. She went out, relocked the door, dropped the key in her purse and looped the strings over her arm as she went down the hall in search of room 208. She turned, went down a short hall and found the room on the right. The light in the hall shone on the brass numbers. As Elizabeth stooped to slip the note under the door, she heard a sound inside the room. She stood and listened. Had Stephen returned while she was writing the note? She heard another sound, crammed the note in her purse and gently rapped on the door.

No sound came from the room. She rapped harder. "Stephen?"

The door was suddenly flung open.

Elizabeth gasped and backed up a step. The man who stood there was...*shirtless*. He stood on legs that were not quite steady. His face had a growth of dark beard, his hair was in wild disorder and his shoulders seemed a yard wide.

"I beg...your...pardon," Elizabeth stammered. "I thought...this room—"

"S'all right, swee'heart—" He reached out, grasped her wrist and yanked her into the room. "Guess I'm drunker'n I thought. Don't remember tellin' Bertha ta send me a woman, but I sure am glad she did."

"Oh..." Elizabeth shrieked in fear and pain. Her arm had almost been yanked from her shoulder. A red tide of fear washed over her. She tried to jerk free of the hand holding her. "Let go!"

"What's your name, honey?" The man dragged her to the bed, sat down and jerked her onto his lap. "Hellfire! You're stiff as a board—"

"Help! Help!" Elizabeth shrieked, and hit him on the head with her purse. "Let go of me!"

"You wantin' to get right at it, hon? I don't know if I can, just yet. Let me kiss ya a little, then we'll..." His arms wrapped around her waist so tightly she could hardly breath.

"Help!"

"Gimme a kiss—"

"Help!"

"You're strong for a skinny woman. Stop wigglin'—"

"Help!"

"Hell, woman! You got on a corset!"

Elizabeth worked her arm free, and with strength brought on by desperation, jabbed him in the stomach with her elbow.

"You...beast!"

Abruptly the man stood, dumping Elizabeth off his lap and onto the floor. For a second she was stunned and lay there, looking up at the giant. He towered over her, holding his stomach with his two hands. Suddenly he reached for the bowl on the washstand and retched as she tried to scramble away. On her hands and knees, screeching her revulsion, she tried to crawl to the door, but the man took a step, and his booted foot was planted firmly on her skirt, pinning her to the floor.

"Dear God!" Elizabeth closed her eyes briefly. The odor of vomit filled the room. Fear churned her stomach so that she was afraid she would swoon before she could get out. She tried to call for help again, but only a squeak came out of her tight throat.

The door was jerked open, and Elizabeth saw two booted feet take two steps into the room and stop. On her hands and knees, she looked up through the hair that tumbled over eyes that were blurred with tears of frustration, rage and fear.

"Help me!" she pleaded, and burst into loud sobs.

"Jehoshaphat! Sam! What the thunder are ya doin'?" Burley looked at the woman, then at Sam, bent over and holding his stomach.

"Get 'er out. I never called for a . . . woman—" Sam's stomach erupted again.

"Oh, dear God!" she wailed.

Burley stepped over Elizabeth and shoved Sam, onto the bed.

"Dammit, yore standin' on her dress. Lordy! Look what ya've done. Let me help ya up, miss. I ain't never seen him so drunk he couldn't hold it afore." Burley helped Elizabeth to her feet. "What'd ya come in here for anyhow? Who sent ya?"

"Nobody *sent* me!" She didn't understand what he was talking about. Then the meaning of his words hit her like a brick. *He actually thought that she was a whore!*

She had to get back to the safety of her room. In a sudden movement she darted for the door and ran into a man who stood there. This man's hair was black and hung to his shoulders. *He was an Indian!* She cowered and looked wildly for a way out.

"We ain't goin' to hurt ya none, miss." Burley didn't know who she was, but he was certain she wasn't who Sam thought she was. "This's Sam's room, ain't it, Jim?"

"That's his saddlebags, ain't they?"

"Please . . . let me go—"

"Ma'am, we ain't keepin' ya. We're plumb sorry—"

"My purse! It's got my room key."

Elizabeth looked for her purse and saw it on the floor, where she had lost it when she fell. She looked helplessly at the short man with the sparse gray hair. She saw the concerned look on his wrinkled, weathered face. Then she looked at the big shirtless man sitting on the bed.

This was a nightmare. It had to be.

The bare-chested giant who had dragged her into the room sat with his head in his hands. The drunken, low-life, worthless creature had not even the decency to apologize.

Sudden anger washed away Elizabeth's fear and humiliation. How dare that vulgar man do this to her! She took the steps necessary to reach her purse and picked it up. Then she picked up the large crockery water pitcher from the washstand and carried it to the bed and calmly poured every last drop of water in it on the drunk's head. He sat there as if nothing was happening. He didn't move a muscle. Elizabeth glared at him, hating him, then threw the empty pitcher on the bed beside him.

Miss Elizabeth Caldwell of the Saint Louis Caldwells had never done such a thing in all her life, but then she had never been in such a situation before. With all the dignity she could muster, she turned to face the Indian and the short, gray-haired man.

"For what it's worth to you," she said with her chin in the air, "your drunken friend dragged me into this room when I rapped on the door, thinking it was my fiancé's room. I am not a loose woman to be insulted by the likes of . . . him! Room 208 is the number the clerk downstairs gave me. Now stand aside and let me pass or I'll scream my head off. Even in this uncivilized place there must be someone within hearing distance who has some decency."

"That clerk made a mistake, and that's sure, ma'am. This is Sam Ferguson's room. Ya can't be a blamin' him fer—"

"Sam Ferguson?"

"Yes'm. He's here to meet his brother's betrothed and take her to Nora Springs."

"What's his brother's...name?" Her voice sounded small and weak. She felt small and weak.

"Stephen. Stephen Ferguson, a fine—"

"No! Oh, no!"

"Do ya know him? Oh, Lordy—"

Elizabeth pushed past Jim and walked rapidly down the hallway.

"What's she in a snit for?" Jim asked.

"Whadda ya think, ya dunderhead? It's *her*! Stephen's woman. Go after her," Burley urged.

"You crazy?"

"Hellfire!" Burley ran after Elizabeth and caught up with her as she was fumbling to open her door. "Miss," he called. "Are ya...are ya Stephen's woman?"

"I'm Mr. Ferguson's fiancée." Her voice trembled with the effort not to scream at him.

"I'm shore sorry, miss—"

"You said that."

"Yeah, well...My name's Burley Owens. I been with Joe and Sam Ferguson since Sam was no bigger than a...well, I been with 'em a long time."

Elizabeth looked him straight in the eyes. "Why did Stephen send that...inferior piece of humanity to meet me?"

"Piece a...what? Well...we was comin' ta pick up a saw blade 'n' he asked Sam to fetch ya 'n' carry ya back."

"And that's all? Stephen is all right?"

"Right as rain!" Burley said cheerfully. No sense in telling her that her man had been shot, Burley thought. Sam had already scared the life out of her.

"Mr. Owens, is Stephen aware that his brother is...that sort?"

"Sam ain't like *that* all the time."

"Well, that's a relief. Regardless, I'll stay in Missoula until Stephen comes. Good night."

"Ya can't do that, miss. Ah..." *Bang.* The door slammed in his face. "Damn!" Burley stomped down the hall to the stairs. "I'm too old fer this," he muttered. "Too damned old ta be messin' with drunks 'n' high-toned women."

Chapter Three

I did what? Stop mumbling, Burley.''

"Ya nearly puked all over her."

"Don't shout." Sam gritted his teeth. "I thought you said I puked on someone."

"Almost—on Miss Caldwell."

"Damn! My head feels like someone was beating on it with a hammer."

"I wish they was," Burley muttered.

Sam stood at the washstand, splashing water on his face with his cupped hands. His head hurt, his mouth tasted like the bottom of a cave and his stomach lurched, but there was nothing more to come up.

"What the hell was she doin' in here?"

"Ya dragged her in. I'm guessin' ya thought she was a whore."

"Damn!"

"The clerk told her S. Ferguson was in this room. She thought it was Stephen."

"I didn't . . . hurt her?"

"She was on the floor. Ya was standin' on her dress, pukin' into that bowl."

"Oh, Lord!"

"She's the high-toniest woman I ever did see, but she's spunky. Afore she left she dumped the water pitcher on ya."

"I'm relieved to know that. I thought I'd wet the bed. Phew! This room stinks. What time is it?"

"Six."

"That late? Go tell somebody to shag their butt up here with some hot water. I've got to clean up. We're leavin' here in an hour. Knock on that woman's door and tell her to be ready. See that Jim brings the rig around."

"She said she warn't goin'. Said she'd wait for Stephen."

"She's goin' if I have to hog-tie her. Tell her that."

Sam began to dig clean clothes out of a carpetbag as soon as Burley was gone. *Puked right in front of his brother's future wife!* He didn't care about the woman, but he wondered what Stephen would think. The first and only thing his brother had ever asked him to do, and he had to go get drunk and make a fool of himself. What the hell happened? He never puked when he was drunk. The last thing he remembered was Burley and Jim helping him up the steps to the hotel porch. He had raised a lot of hell in this town, but this was the first time he'd drunk himself senseless.

Burley said the woman was really peeved. In a way he didn't blame her, and in another way he thought it was her own damn fault. He would apologize in time, but he'd be damned if he'd grovel at her feet. It would depend on her attitude. He didn't owe her anything. Hell, he was entitled to let off steam once in a while. She just happened to be in the wrong place at the wrong time.

Burley returned with a bucket of hot water.

"Did you tell her?"

"Yeah."

"Well . . . what did she say?"

"She said to tell ya that she wasn't goin' on the say-so that ya was Stephen's brother. She said that Stephen was a gentleman 'n' couldn't possibly be related to an *atrocious degenerate* such as ya be. What does them fancy words mean?"

"It means she doesn't like me much. Hell! I forgot the letter." Sam dug into the carpetbag again, found an envelope and held it out to Burley. "Take her this. Tell her to be downstairs in half an hour, or I'll be up to get her."

"Take it yoreself. I ain't yore delivery boy." Burley stood with his hands on his hips, his chin jutting stubbornly. He had not had much sleep, and he was in no mood to play nurse.

"Come on, Burley. I know I gave you and Jim a bad time and I'm sorry for it. I'm not making excuses, but things just piled upon me and I acted the ass."

Burley snatched the letter from Sam's hand. "Ya did, fer a fact. That woman's a nice woman. She don't have nothin' ta do with yore feelin' for yore ma. Ya best treat her right, or ya'll hear from me." He stomped off down the hall.

While he shaved, Sam thought about what Burley had said. His mother had been a high-toned woman who had everything she wanted until she married his pa. His pa had given her his all, worked his fingers to the bone, but it wasn't enough. It was a good thing Stephen had his business in Saint Louis to go back to. This woman wouldn't last out here as long as his mother had. Within a year she would be running back to the soft life in Saint Louis.

Sam dressed and packed his bag. He looked around the room. Hell. He'd never left a room in such a mess before. Burley and Jim had cleaned up some of the mess, but there was plenty left. He would give the clerk an extra dollar for the cleaning woman when he paid his bill. Before he went out, he paused to look at himself in the mirror above the dresser. He assessed himself critically even though his head pounded so hard he could scarcely focus. He looked tired, and his eyes were bloodshot, but otherwise he looked his usual. He picked up his bag, closed the door gently and walked down the hallway, trying not to jar his head.

Elizabeth folded her nightdress and packed it in her trunk. She was wearing a maroon gabardine traveling suit and a soft pink blouse. Matching gloves lay on the bed beside a pink parasol and a small travel bag. Pink silk roses adorned the narrow brim of the maroon fedora that sat atop high-piled inky black curls. Elizabeth inspected herself carefully in the mirror. She was satisfied that the hat pin held her hat firmly in place and that she was neatly and properly dressed for travel.

Just before she was ready to leave the room, Elizabeth read for the third time the note Burley Owens had handed her.

My dearest Elizabeth,
This letter will introduce you to my brother, Samuel, whom I told you about before I left Saint Louis. At the present time, due to a slight accident to my shoulder, I am unable to come to Missoula to meet you. Samuel is coming to pick up a blade for his sawmill and will escort you to Nora Springs. He will see to your needs. You will be perfectly safe with him.

I am looking forward to seeing you and showing you this beautiful country. I trust you are well and that the long journey has not been too tiring.

Your devoted Stephen

Elizabeth wondered how well Stephen knew his brother. *Perfectly safe, my hind foot!* She snorted. She would be about as safe in a bed of rattlesnakes as she would be with him. Thank goodness she wasn't totally at his mercy. The little pistol in her travel bag might persuade him to behave like a gentleman and treat his brother's intended wife with respect. She would keep the bag close at hand. Stephen would not knowingly put her in danger, but obviously he did not know his degenerate brother very well. She felt the long hat pin in the crown of her hat and smiled. She had two means of protecting herself. If Samuel Ferguson as much as laid a hand on her arm, he would get something he would not soon forget.

Carrying her hatbox, travel bag and parasol, Elizabeth went to the hotel desk. The clerk was older and fatter than the one she had spoken to the night before.

"I'm Miss Caldwell, room 201. I'd like my trunk and two valises brought down."

"I get 'em."

Elizabeth had not noticed the Indian she had seen the night before in Samuel Ferguson's room until he spoke. Already he was taking the steps two at a time.

"Does he work here?" she asked.

"An Indian work here? Heaven forbid! This is a first-class hotel."

"Oh?" Elizabeth lifted her brows and gave the man a haughty stare.

"He's Sam Ferguson's man."

"What do I owe you?"

The clerk backed up a step or two and looked at her. "Mr. Ferguson paid for your room."

Elizabeth was shocked into silence by his words. Was that a smirk on his fat, pasty face? Damn and double damn! This stupid fool thought . . . thought . . . that she had . . .

Denying the anger that bubbled up in her, she kept her features calm and pleasant as she gave the clerk one of her sweetest smiles.

"How very nice of Mr. Ferguson." She placed the room key on the counter, went to the door and out onto the porch, muttering threats of torture and death to the louse, reprobate, blackguard—

"Ya say somethin' ta me, ma'am?" Burley jumped from the bench where he had been waiting.

"Good morning, Mr. Owens. Yes, I said that I'd like to break Mr. Ferguson's unwashed body and feed it to the buzzards." Elizabeth was shocked by her own words. What was this uncivilized country doing to her? "Do I have time to eat something before we leave? I don't wish to disrupt your schedule."

"Yes'm. Sam said feed ya. He ain't stoppin' till noon."

The street was almost deserted. A heavy freight wagon, filled to capacity and covered with a tied-down canvas, was on the street. The four mules hitched to it waited patiently. In front of the hotel was a light buggy with a red and white striped top edged with a fringe of red balls. The seat of the buggy was black, the base and footboard apple-green. Hitched to it was a big-footed sorrel that looked as if it could pull a locomotive. The whole outfit was disgustingly tacky, garishly ugly, the gaudiest rig Elizabeth had ever seen. She turned her back on it and handed her hatbox to Burley.

"Excuse me. I'll go have some breakfast."

Burley scratched his head and watched her as she made her way down the walk to the restaurant. She was the proudest, most high-flown woman he'd ever seen. He scratched his head again. He wasn't sure if she was just putting on airs, or if she was really the way she seemed. Was she going all the way to Nora Springs dressed like she was going to church or to wherever rich, grand women went when they got gussied up like a trussed-up turkey ready for Thanksgiving? Fiddle and be damned! 'Bout the first time they splashed across a creek, or she stepped out on a fresh cow pile, she was going to be fit to be tied. Pink gloves! Lordy! Pink roses on her hat! Fiddle! A pink parasol! Holy hell! Was this what they called civilization? Sam was going to laugh himself sick.

Sam was surprised that he could eat. After he downed two cups of strong black coffee, his stomach settled and he ate a plate of eggs and biscuits. With something in his stomach, his head eased and he was able to move it without groaning. He kept trying to think of what he had drunk last night. He had started out with good Irish whiskey. After that he'd had beer. He must have had a hell of a lot of both.

Sam was mopping his plate with his last biscuit when he heard one of the serving women hiss to the other.

"Psst! That's her. The one I told you about."

Sam looked over his shoulder to see who they were talking about.

"Ain't them the fanciest clothes you ever did see? She ain't got on nothin' she had on last night."

The woman who stood inside the door, waiting to see if she should seat herself or if someone would come to seat her, looked like a picture from *Godey's Lady's Book*.

"Last night it was gray gloves, shoes, everything. She's got a pink rose on this hat, but it ain't as big as the one on the gray hat."

Sam looked Miss Elizabeth Caldwell over as she pulled off her gloves, one finger at a time. He looked at *her*, not at the clothes that so impressed the serving women. Her hair was black and shiny and pulled to the top of her head. The skin on her face was porcelain white, making her eyebrows and lashes appear to be black as coal. Her eyes were the only beautiful feature on her face when he looked at each feature individually. Her eyes were green. God, they were green, large, tilted up at the corners. They gleamed from between rows of thick, dark lashes like new oak leaves in the spring. They were beautiful. When he looked at them, he didn't notice that her mouth was a trifle too wide, her nose a trifle too short, her chin tilted too high. *Elegant* was the way to describe her. Elegant and confident. So this was Miss Prissy-tail Caldwell, the one he had mistaken for a whore last night.

Head held high, looking neither left nor right, she passed Sam and went to a vacant table in the back of the room. He caught a whiff of sweet-smelling perfume that, for some reason, only added to his dislike of the fancy woman. He got to his feet as soon as she passed him, placed some coins on the table and hurried out.

Holy hell! Stephen had picked himself a straightlaced, stiff-necked prude of a woman who looked like a clotheshorse in a dressmaker's window. Stephen said she was two years younger than he was. That would make her twenty-five or twenty-six, long past the age when most women married. It was no wonder the grande dame was an old maid. She would put off any red-blooded man who came near her with that hoity-toity attitude of hers.

The devil inside Sam began to jab at his sense of humor with his tiny pitchfork. The prissy-tail woman thought he was a hellion. It wouldn't do to disappoint her, now, would it? It was time she knew a little of the hardships the women in this country endured—that is, those who had the guts to stick to their men. She would learn that out here people took each other at face value. She could put on all the airs she wanted to, but they wouldn't mean doodle-dee-da!

There was a chance, a slight one, that by the time they reached Nora Springs, she might unbend a little, settle down and act like a soft, honest-to-goodness woman. Sam grinned when he thought of what Jessie would think of her. Jessie was a woman to winter with, as the old-timers used to say. She was worth six of this prissy old maid.

When Sam saw the buggy and Jim strapping trunks and cases on the back, he laughed heartily.

"God almighty, Jim! Where did you get *that*?"

"Wagon shop." Jim continued to work at the straps.

"Is that all they had?"

"Nope. Storm surrey with three seats 'n' a funeral wagon. Ya said good springs 'n' a top." Jim finished tying a canvas over the luggage and stepped onto the walk.

"What did you do? Take parts from two buggies and put them together?"

"Purty, ain't it?"

Sam reached out and shook the frame. The buggy was sturdy and the springs were strong, even if it did look like a buggy the circus would use to carry the fat lady. Sam couldn't keep the grin off his face, and when he saw the heavy, big-footed horse, he laughed out loud again.

"You done good, Jim. Real good."

The Indian's usual stoic features creased with a smile. He reached out and flipped some of the red tassel balls with his forefinger.

Burley came from around the building, stopped and swore. "That's the gawdawfullest lookin' thin' I ever did see. That ain't no fit rig fer Miss Caldwell."

"I like it. Do you want to drive this morning or do you want Jim to do it?"

"I ain't drivin' that thin'!" Burley made a complete turnabout, went to the freight wagon and climbed the wheel to the seat.

"That leaves you, Jim. Burley will drive tomorrow."

"Not me!" The Indian tried to wiggle past Sam, but Sam dropped a heavy hand on his shoulder.

"Yes, you! I'm boss, remember?"

"You ain't that much boss." Jim ducked under Sam's arm and darted across the walk to the freight wagon. "You boss, you drive snotty woman."

"Cowards!"

Burley unwound the reins as soon as Jim was aboard, slapped them against the backs of the mules and yelled, "Hee yaw!" The heavy wagon with the saw blade and various other supplies for the mill pulled away, turned in the street and headed out of town.

"Cowards!" Sam yelled again.

Elizabeth took her time eating breakfast. The biscuits and honey were delicious. The eggs were another matter. She had asked for soft eggs and was served eggs that resembled shoe leather. The coffee was freshly made, hot and strong. She sipped at it and dabbed at her mouth with her handkerchief. She had not been supplied with a napkin.

"I see ya et more this mornin'. Stomach not actin' up as much?"

The serving woman had edged over to the table after pouring another patron's coffee from a big graniteware pot. A rag was wrapped around the handle of the pot, and she rested the smoked bottom on the table.

"No. I feel fine. The honey is the best I've ever had, and the biscuits are delicious."

"I'm proud to know it. Made 'em myself." The woman flushed with pleasure. "Leavin' today?"

"Yes. Would it be possible for you to pack a few biscuits, buttered and spread with honey? I see you have apples. I'd like one of those, too."

"Why, shore, hon. Ya just sit right there and I'll fix ya up a bait to carry along with ya. Anythin' else I could fix ya to take?"

"No. That will be all."

Elizabeth had noticed the glances cast in her direction. Surely she wasn't the only stranger here. This was a railroad town, and strangers must stop here all the time. Maybe they were just curious because she was alone. As she waited for the woman to bring the biscuits, she thought about Samuel Ferguson. She would accept his apology—for Stephen's sake—if he had the decency to offer one. The two brothers had been raised at opposite ends of the earth, and that accounted for one brother being an uncouth hell raiser, the other a perfect gentleman.

After paying her bill, Elizabeth left the restaurant and walked leisurely down the walk toward the hotel. She was late, but after the way Samuel had treated her, he deserved to wait. The gaudy-looking rig was still parked in the street. Now, however, it had a saddle horse tied behind it. The porch of the hotel was empty. She paused.

They would not dare go off and leave her. She took a few steps inside the hotel lobby. There was no sign of Mr. Owens or her luggage. She went back to the porch and looked up and down the walk, her brow wrinkled with concern.

"Hey, Liz!" The male voice came from somewhere close by. "Shake your butt, gal, we got miles to go."

Elizabeth turned toward the voice. A man leaned out of the buggy and looked at her. His hat was pulled low on his forehead. His knees were spread, his booted feet on the footboard. The cigar between his teeth was tilted upward.

"Were you speaking to me?" she asked with a lift of her brows.

"Ya don't see nobody else, do ya? C'mon, honey bunch, we ain't got all day. Shake your pretty little fanny, girl, and climb in."

Elizabeth took a deep, unsteady breath. She was incensed that he dared speak to her in such a crude, familiar manner, but she was determined not to give him the satisfaction of knowing he had offended her.

"And who are you?" she asked even though she knew he was Stephen's less than desirable brother. He was as disgustingly crude this morning as he had been last night. The brown eyes, lashes and brows and the shape of his face were like Stephen's. The hair was the same texture, only a shade lighter. His voice held the same deep tone as Stephen's. But he was *nothing* like Stephen.

"Samuel Ferguson at your service, ma'am." Sam saluted cockily and grinned around the cigar. "But we already met. Remember?"

"How could I possibly forget?" Her eyebrows rose. "Where is my luggage?"

"Tied on the back."

Elizabeth went to the back of the buggy and checked her luggage. Then she placed her traveling purse, the package from the restaurant and her parasol on the floorboard. Ignoring her, Sam looked down the street as if there was something that held his attention.

Lifting her skirt, Elizabeth placed her foot on the highstep and grasped the seat to pull herself into the buggy. She didn't make it on the first attempt. She tried again, and this time Sam reached for her arm and hauled her onto the seat with such force that she fell across his thighs. Her hat tilted over her ear when her head slammed into his chest.

"Now, now, Lizzie, babe. If you're wanting to ride on my lap, you'll have to wait until we get out of town. I got my reputation to think of." Sam held his cigar to the side and tapped off the ashes.

Elizabeth righted herself, knowing that her face was scarlet, hating it . . . and hating him. She moved as far as possible from him and repinned her hat. Sam sat hunched over, his knees spread so far apart that he took up two-thirds of the seat. He held the reins loosely in his hands.

"Ready, hon?" He looked at her, grinned, then turned and lifted the reins. The horse lifted her tail. "Yupsy! We'll have to wait for the old gal to do her business. Isn't that just like a woman?" he muttered as if to himself. "They always have to go at the wrong time." The horse held her tail high and big globs of solid waste came tumbling out while Sam took a couple of puffs on the cigar. "Didn't see any reason to scatter it down the street." A wide grin split his face as he looked at Elizabeth's flushed cheeks. He spoke to the horse in a confidential tone. "Finished, girl? Then let's go." He stung the mare on the rump with the whip. "Giddyap!"

The horse took off so suddenly that Elizabeth's head was jerked back. She grabbed the side of the seat to keep from tumbling out. The buggy sped down the middle of the main street, bumped across an intersection, careened around a corner and headed for open road.

The miles down the narrow green valley stretched before them, and in the distance jagged mountain peaks were muted by a soft purple haze. To Elizabeth, the mountains seemed a million miles away.

"Whee!" Sam shouted, and flicked the reins. The horse settled into a fast, lumbering pace. "Ain't this great, Lizzie? There's nothing like a good fast buggy ride to clear the head after a wild night of whiskey and fast women." He slapped her knee with the palm of his hand. "Right, Liz?"

They hit a rut in the road, and Elizabeth's head hit the side of the buggy. Her hat went askew again and tilted over her eyes. She gritted her teeth. For the first time in her life she muttered an obscenity, one she had heard used by a stable hand when he smashed his thumb.

I hate him! I hate him! When I get out of this buggy, I'm going to kill him!

Chapter Four

Sam kept the horse moving at a fast pace until they caught up with the freight wagon, moving up close. The dust stirred up by the wagon settled around them like a cloud. Sam appeared to be unaware, but Elizabeth, choking on the dust, loosened her hold on the side of the seat long enough to pull a handkerchief from the tight sleeve of her jacket and cover her nose so she could breathe.

The big horse pulling the buggy had begun to sweat. Sam was sure this plodding animal had not had a good run in months. His horse, tied behind, was not even winded. He glanced at the woman beside him. Sitting stiff as a board, looking straight ahead, she had not uttered a single word since they left town. He suspected that she was wearing one of those corset things women laced themselves into that cinched their waist and pushed their breasts up. He had seen pictures of them in the catalogs and wondered how the hell a woman could stand to be in such a contraption.

"Dust bothering you, Liz? Up ahead there's a place where we can go around. By whoopee damn! Here it is. Hold on, we'll give 'em our dust!" He flicked the mare's rump with the tip of the whip and swung around the freight wagon. "How about a race?" he yelled when he was even with the lumbering wagon.

"You crazy or somethin'?" Burley shouted angrily. He looked down, then gave his attention to holding the suddenly excited mules. The buggy pulled ahead and put distance between them. "Crazy half-sloshed clabberhead!" Burley yelled once he had the mules under control. "Ya ain't got the brains of a pissant. Yore actin' like a drunk hoot owl! If'n ya turn that buggy o'er 'n' hurt that thar woman, I'll take a whip ta yore butt!"

"Boss gone loco." Jim Two-Horses spoke matter-of-factly and hunched his shoulders in resignation.

"He's got a burr under his tail, that's certain," Burley grumbled.

Sam slowed the horse to a walk, turned and grinned at Elizabeth's set profile. She sat as still and as straight as a statue. Thick dark curls had come loose from the pins and now lay curled against her cheeks. She lifted a gloved hand and looped them over her ears. The wind had whipped some color into her cheeks.

"I've got to walk the old girl for a while or she'll give out on us."

Elizabeth turned a calm face toward him. "How far is it to Nora Springs?"

"Miles or days?"

"Either."

"Six or seven days."

"Is that all? I thought it would take longer." Proud of the unconcerned way she answered him, she stuffed the handkerchief in her sleeve, folded her hands in her lap and looked straight ahead toward the mountains.

Behind the calm facade her thoughts were filled with turmoil. Besides the physical torture, she didn't know how she would be able to endure the presence of this crude creature for six or seven days. How could Stephen have done this to her? She would have spent weeks or even months waiting for him in Missoula rather than spend six or seven days in the company of his brother.

Elizabeth moved slightly to tilt some of her weight to her left buttock. She had first noticed a sore spot when she sat on the hard chair at the restaurant. Even now, on the soft buggy seat, she felt some discomfort. Her corset strings may have come loose and the metal end worked into her drawers. Elizabeth had worn a corset every day since she was thirteen years old. She was absolutely certain that the whalebone stays had never dug into her flesh as they were doing now.

And she was hot. If not for this poor excuse of a man beside her, she would remove her gloves and suit jacket. She simply would not give him the pleasure of knowing how hot and miserable she was, or that the dread of the days ahead was settling like a rock inside her. On the train coming out, she had been told that it was cold in the mountains, that sometimes it snowed in late September. It certainly wasn't cold in the foothills. Elizabeth decided that she would bear up until they stopped, which surely they would have to do by midmorning in order to water and rest the horses.

They met two horsemen heading for town. Both men gaped in open-mouthed amazement as the buggy approached. They reined in their horses and gawked.

"Howdy." Sam lifted a hand in greeting.

"Howdy." The two men spoke in unison, then whooped with laughter after the buggy passed. "I ain't never seen nothin' like that in all my born days!"

The loud words drifted to Elizabeth. Embarrassment sent waves of heat to her already hot face. She had no doubt that Sam Ferguson had hired this gawdy rig to humiliate her. She glanced at him. He had removed his hat, revealing thick, light-brown hair that waved back from his forehead. The deep opening of his shirt showed hair darker than his mustache. His brows and lashes were dark and thick, and no shadow of a beard lay beneath his sun-browned skin. The thought came to her that he was not unpleasant to look at, but looks were only skin deep. Some of the most atrocious crimes had been committed by handsome men. After all, John Wilkes Booth had been a fine-looking man.

Sam pulled a gold watch from his pocket and pressed the top of the winding stem to flip open the lid. Could it be only a quarter till ten? It had been one of the longest two and a half hours of his life. An hour ago, when he failed to get a rise out of Miss Prissy-tail, he had given up trying. Now, lolling against the side of the seat, he had loosened the reins. The animal was used to pulling a buggy and stepped along at an even gait without being prodded. The buggy was so comfortable that Sam had almost forgotten how ridiculous it looked until he heard the remark.

Overhead a lone eagle soared, its screech audible in the midmorning silence. As Sam watched the magnificent bird, he envied its untamed freedom, its ability to fly, to go where it chose to go. The golden bird screamed again and plummeted from sight behind a dense stand of spruce, its talons outstretched as it prepared to scoop up its prey and carry it away for a feast.

For a split second Sam wanted to share the drama with his companion. He turned to see her looking at him with a haunting wariness in her wide green eyes. Then quickly her expression changed as if a shadow had suddenly crossed her face, leaving her finely sculpted features without any indication of what she was feeling or thinking. What a poker player she would make, Sam thought when she had turned away to give him a view of her profile once again. He forgot about the eagle, forgot about needling her as he watched her soft mouth compress into a taut line and her chin tilt a fraction higher because she knew he was looking at her.

If Sam had one redeeming quality, it was that he was exceedingly fair-minded. Damn! he thought, this can't be easy for her, either. He analyzed his actions, and decided he had played the fool because he was embarrassed about what had happened the night before. Seldom had he been so drunk that he didn't remember anything. He had to take Burley's word for it that he had grabbed her, dragged her into his room and... Damn it to hell! What would Stephen think when she told him?

Burley was right when he said it was not Miss Caldwell's fault that his mother had deserted him and his father. Why was it that he was compelled to blame her for something that had happened twenty-two years ago? Elizabeth Caldwell and Eleanor Ferguson were as alike as two peas in a pod, that was why. They were cut from the same cloth, his inner self told him. But, he reasoned, Elizabeth Prissy-tail Caldwell wasn't his problem; she was his brother's. His job was to get her to Nora Springs all in one piece, so to speak. With that in mind, he tried to think of something to say to her that would make the journey a little more pleasant.

"We'll stop soon. You can get out and rest awhile."

She nodded.

"There's a creek up ahead that comes right down out of the mountains. You can get a cool drink while we water the horses. We'll not stop again until noon."

She turned her cool, green eyes on him and nodded politely.

"The noon stop is halfway between Missoula and the first stage station, where we'll stop for the night."

Again she looked at him and nodded, then turned to look toward the mountains.

Hell! He wasn't good at carrying on a conversation with a woman, much less a one-sided conversation. His thoughts turned dark again. Prissy-tail, highfalutin old maid! She could sit there like a dummy in her tight corset with her mouth buttoned up like a miser's purse all the way to Nora Springs and it would suit him just fine. Even if she wasn't his brother's intended, she'd have nothing to fear from him. He liked women who were soft when they were supposed to be soft, attentive and amusing women who acted as if they enjoyed a man's company instead of looking down their hoity-toity noses at everything and everybody.

What was he up to now? Elizabeth wondered. If he thought for one minute that she'd be a friendly traveling companion, he was sadly mistaken. Uncomplaining, *yes*. Friendly, *no*. Definitely *no*, after the way he'd acted last night and this morning. His actions were a reflection of his character, and a person's character did not change in a matter of a half hour or so. She vowed silently that she would die of thirst, swelter in the heat or freeze to death before she would utter a single complaint. With that resolve firmly in mind, she shifted her weight slightly to ease her left buttock, which had gone numb, and winced when she put her weight on the sore spot.

Sam pulled off the main road onto a trail that led to a crop of aspen along a creek bank. The leaves were turning yellow. A birdcall rang clearly from across the creek, the shrill notes seeming to float on the crystal-clear air. Reflectively, Sam puckered his lips and imitated the call.

Startled, Elizabeth looked at him and was surprised to see the intelligence and humor that gave depth to his coffee-colored eyes. His smile faded when she failed to respond.

Sam stopped the horse and without a word climbed down, walked up the creek and disappeared. Elizabeth sat in the buggy, not knowing what to do. She needed privacy, but didn't know how she was going to manage it. She saw the freight wagon pull in. The men climbed down, unhooked buckets from the side of the wagon and went to the creek for water. They returned and set a bucket in front of each mule.

Elizabeth removed her gloves, then her hat and jacket. The cool breeze felt wonderfully refreshing. She watched Sam approach. It was the first good look she had had of him. He was taller and heavier than Stephen, and he moved differently. His long body seemed to flow over the uneven ground, and one look at his sharp eyes gave testimony to his alert state. She wondered how often he used the gun that was strapped to his lean waist, if there was a woman who loved him, if he was a father of children . . . and if Stephen really knew him.

"Climb down, Liz. I scouted the creek bank. There's no Indians hiding in the bush to carry you off and no bears to eat you for dinner. If there were, you'd have nothing to worry about—bears are fond of sweets." He grinned wickedly. He had not intended to be brash, but the disapproving look on her face as she'd watched him approach had goaded him into it.

His words were no surprise to Elizabeth. They were what she had come to expect from him. It also was no surprise that he went to the back of the buggy and untied his horse without offering to help her down. She waited until he was leading the horse away before she carefully backed out of the buggy and eased herself to the ground. After waiting a minute or two for her legs to steady, she hooked her small travel bag over her arm and walked a distance along the creek bank before she paused and looked over her shoulder to see if she was out of sight.

Elizabeth looked around her. It was hard to believe that two weeks ago she'd been home in Saint Louis where she had only to walk down the hall from her room to use the water closet. Now she was traveling with strange men in the wilds of Montana, getting ready to squat in the bushes to relieve her aching bladder.

She lifted her skirt, feeling inside the split in her drawers to find the loose corset string she had been sitting on. Surprised to find there was no loose corset string, she searched her buttock with her forefinger and found a hard knot beneath the skin that was sore to the touch. She wondered if she had been bitten by a spider. Knowing that there was nothing she could do about it, she relieved herself, straightened her clothes and walked along the path.

Sam had taken the buggy to the creek so the horse could drink. Burley Owens came to her with a canteen of water.

"Drink, ma'am?"

"Yes, thank you. I have a cup in my travel bag." Elizabeth dug into the bag and brought out a small tin circle that telescoped into a drinking cup.

"Well, ain't that fancy," Burley exclaimed. "Are ya sure it won't leak?"

"I'm sure. Try it." She smiled at him while he filled the cup then drank the cool water gratefully. "I'll have more, if you don't mind."

"Any time ya want a drink, jist reach for the canteen. I'm leavin' it with ya."

Sam led the horse to the track leading to the road and handed the reins to Burley. Without a word, he mounted his horse and turned toward the road.

"It seems that Mr. Ferguson has washed his hands of me. I can drive, Mr. Owens, if you lead the way."

"I'd not hear of it! Let me help ya on up in there." He went around to the other side of the buggy, held out his hand and gently pulled her up. "Jist let me get my rifle. Dang young pup," he muttered as he walked away. "He ain't got no manners at all no more."

They reached the open road. Sam was riding slowly up ahead. For the first time since they left Missoula, Elizabeth relaxed and could appreciate the view of the mountains.

"How far away are they, Mr. Owens?"

"The mountains. 'Bout twenty miles. The goin'll slow down when we get there. Ever little bit we got to rest the mules on the uphill."

"Will we be there by night?"

"Yup. We stay at the stage station. Sam's got it mapped out where ya can spend the night. He don't plan for ya to have to sleep in the open."

"That's nice of him," she said dryly. "Do you know the nature of Stephen's injury, Mr. Owens?"

"Yup. Somebody shot him."

"S-shot him? Oh, my word!"

"It ain't nothin' to get in a lather over. Jessie and Amanda dug the bullet out 'n' are fussin' over him like a hen over a chick."

"Who are Jessie . . . and Amanda?"

"Well . . . Jessie is Amanda's girl. They run a boardin' house 'n' Jessie works for Joe some. Joe, that's Sam 'n'

Steve's pa. Joe 'n' Sam got a sawmill 'n' lumber business. That Jessie is somethin'. Feisty as a cat on a hot stove. She got the reddest hair ya ever did see. Purely looks like a sunset." Burley grinned and spit tobacco juice over the side of the buggy. "Anybody messes with Jessie's got Sam to reckon with, that's certain."

"Is she his wife?"

"Wife? He ain't got no wife. But women's chasin' after him right along. Hell! He's always a gettin' pie, cake 'n' offers for washin' 'n' ironin' 'n' stuff like that. Jessie'd like ta be his woman, ta my way of thinkin'. I figger they'll marry up someday. She's growed up right under his nose 'n' thinks he's 'bout the grandest thin' ever hatched."

"Poor, misguided girl," Elizabeth said softly, but Burley's sharp ears heard the words.

"She ain't poor. She 'n' her ma's doin' fine. Joe 'n' Sam see to it."

"Who shot Stephen?"

"Don't know. Sam thinks 'twas somebody turned down for a job. Jessie had took Stephen to the loggin' camp to see Sam. Jessie got in a few shots."

"Sam Ferguson is certainly nothing like Stephen."

"I reckon not. About what happened last night. Sam carouses some when he comes ta town, but he ain't never been that drunk afore. Me 'n' Jim poured the drinks in ta him, so's ta get him outta the saloon afore all hell broke loose. He's ashamed of the pukin'. Course I don't reckon he's goin' ta say so."

"Why not?"

"It's cause yore the same kind of a woman as his ma was."

"He could not give me a higher compliment than to compare me with Eleanor Ferguson," Elizabeth said staunchly. "She was a dear, sweet person."

"Sam's hurtin'. Been hurtin' fer a long time. Him 'n' Joe went through a bad time after his ma left."

If Burley thought to dredge up sympathy for Sam and make excuses for his behavior, he failed. Elizabeth felt not one ounce of pity for the man riding ahead on the buckskin horse. The man was a bore, an uncouth bore, and the sooner she saw the last of him the better. She and Stephen would be married, leave this uncivilized place together and go to Saint Louis. Elizabeth was so caught up in her thoughts that she unconsciously shifted her weight to her right buttock and winced.

At noon they stopped beside another stream. Burley explained that water was plentiful in this country.

"In places there's too dang many rivers ta cross. Course, waterways is what loggers need. Ya just ort ta see them logs comin' down river ta the mill when the gate's lifted. Sam's the best log herder I ever did see. He'll dance over them buckin' logs, a pushing 'n' a bumpin' till he gets 'em sucked into the current 'n' on their way—"

"Sounds dangerous," Elizabeth said, because she felt she had to say something.

"'Tis. A man can slip away real fast on a rollin' log. Lose a few ever' year."

Not waiting for assistance, Elizabeth backed out of the buggy and reached for her jacket. It was surprising how fast the air had cooled.

"No bears, no Indians," Sam said softly as he rode past Elizabeth and looked down on the lustrous black swirls pinned atop her head. Without the silly hat she looked softer, more like a real woman. He wondered what she would do if he combed her hair with his fingers, scattered the pins and let the hair tumble around her face and down her back. He grinned. She would probably be outraged. Poor Stephen. Sam didn't envy Stephen marrying such a prude.

When Elizabeth returned from taking care of her bodily needs, Burley was staking out the mules and horses to munch on the grass, and the Indian was squatting over a small fire. A smoked coffeepot sat over the blaze. Elizabeth went to the buggy for the biscuits and apple she had brought from the restaurant.

Sam came from the creek, where he had dunked his head. He combed water out of his hair with his fingers, slammed his hat on the grass and squatted beside the fire.

"What are we eating?"

Jim handed him a hunk of bread with a piece of meat on it, and a tin of peaches.

"Is this all?" Sam glanced at Elizabeth, who was leaning against the buggy. "Ever had smoked possum, Liz?"

Jim snorted. "Ain't possum."

"What is it? Rattlesnake?" Sam's eyes, filled with a mischievous light, stayed on Elizabeth's carefully controlled features.

"Elk. You loco?"

"Tastes like rattlesnake to me," Sam said between mouthfuls. "Want to try it, Liz?"

"No, thank you." Elizabeth poured water from the canteen into her cup, carried it to a deadfall and sat. She opened the packet and took out one of the biscuits, determined to get it down, although she had never felt less like eating. She had a splitting headache and her bottom hurt.

Burley flipped back the top of the coffeepot to see if the coffee was boiling, then removed it from the fire and poured in water from a tin cup to settle the grounds. He waited a minute or two then poured coffee into a graniteware cup and carried it to Elizabeth.

"It's not the best, but it's hot 'n' it's strong."

"Thank you."

"Ever had camp-fire coffee, Liz?"

"Dang bust it, Sam. Yore pa didn't raise ya ta be disrespectful to women folk."

"What's the matter, Burley? Don't you want me to call her Liz? She's going to be family. After she hooks...after she and my brother are married, I can't be calling her Mrs. Ferguson, can I? I think Liz suits her."

"It's all right, Mr. Owens. Don't fuss. I'm used to being called Liz. My father had a brother who was a rotter, a drunken ne'er-do-well, an insensitive man who lived on other people's charity without a considerate thought for anyone. He called me Liz...too."

Burley failed to get the thrust of her remarks. He nodded agreeably and went to pick up the bread and meat Jim had laid out. Sam, however, understood exactly what she meant. He kept his eyes on her face. When she looked at him, he didn't look away, nor did she. Brown eyes and green ones did battle for several long seconds. Then she calmly looked away from him as if he was of no consequence. That, more than her words, infuriated him.

Sam ate and drank in silence. When he finished, he walked out of the clearing and was soon out of sight behind the thick growth of brush that grew along the creek bank. Jim put out the camp fire, then he and Burley hitched the mules to the freight wagon and the horse to the buggy.

Elizabeth was hoping that Burley wouldn't leave her at the mercy of Sam Ferguson. He didn't. He assisted her into the buggy and climbed in beside her. They led the freight wagon out of the clearing and onto the trail.

A half hour went by before Sam rode past and took up a position ahead of the buggy.

Chapter Five

It was twilight when they finally stopped. As soon as the sun went behind the mountains, the air became cool. Elizabeth was chilled to the bone. She had looked forward to a warm, cozy inn, and was keenly disappointed when Burley stopped the buggy in front of a long, low building made of logs and rough timber. It squatted along the roadside among tall pines as if it had grown there. Smoke rose from a stone chimney, but no light shone from the open door.

Sam was waiting for them. He stood beside the doorway with a heavily built bearded man in loose, baggy pants held up with wide suspenders. He was so short he had to tilt his head to look at Sam. When Sam motioned to Burley, the old man grumbled.

"Sit right here, ma'am, 'ppears that somethin' ain't quite up ta snuff."

Burley, then Jim, joined Sam and the other man. Sam stood with one shoulder against the building. Elizabeth waited impatiently in the buggy. She sensed that whatever they were talking about was important. Her anxiety goaded her to ask Burley when he came to help her down.

"Is something wrong?"

"Bridge is out up ahead. The stage won't be runnin' till it's fixed."

"Then we can't go on?"

"We'll go 'round. It'll take a mite longer is all."

Burley untied her luggage and set it on the ground. The bearded man, his hands on his hips, looked at the buggy then at Elizabeth. She suspected that behind the beard he was laughing, but she was so miserably cold she didn't care. She lifted her hatbox and fixed him with an icy stare.

"I would like a room for the night."

"Sam's already told me, ma'am. Sorry I am that my woman ain't here to meet ya. She went down to Missoula to visit her ma, thinkin' we'd have no lodgers till the stage run again. Come in. Come right on in."

Elizabeth followed him into the building, passing Sam without a glance. She waited beside the door while the innkeeper lit a lamp. The room he led her through, according to the tall counter along one side and several tables with chairs along the other, was used as a barroom. The floor was slabs of warped plank that made walking perilous for one used to smooth floors. The air was fouled by the odor of stale ale. They passed through a wide doorway and into a newer part of the building, which served as kitchen and dining room in one. The stove was shiny black, the long table scrubbed, the floor even. A delicious aroma came from a pot on the cook stove. This was a woman's domain.

They entered a short walkway and then stepped into a small room. The landlord placed a lamp on a shelf beside the door and flattened himself against the wall so Burley and Jim could bring in her luggage.

"Bed's clean, ma'am. My woman keeps the mattress clear o' bedbugs with a regular dose of coal oil." He turned to follow Burley and Jim out, then turned back. "I'll get ya a fresh bucket of water and rustle ya up some supper."

"Thank you."

Elizabeth waited for him to leave. She didn't know what she was going to do if there wasn't a chamber pot under the bed. As soon as the plank door closed, she lifted the patchwork quilt and there it was—a low, squat china pot with a tin lid. Relieved that she no longer had to worry about that, she looked around. The room was a ten-foot square. The window was shuttered and fastened on the inside with an iron clasp. The door had a bar to drop across.

Elizabeth gripped the end of the iron bedstead. It seemed to her that she had suddenly been transferred to another world. Wanting only to sink on the bed and rest, she set about doing what had to be done. She shook the dust from her jacket and put it away, brushed the dirt from her hat and placed it in the hatbox with the gray hat and a flower-decorated one she planned to wear at her wedding. From her trunk she took a washcloth, a towel and an ivory box that held a bar of scented soap.

The rap on the door and the innkeeper's voice came simultaneously.

"I got ya some water, ma'am. A bucket o' warm 'n' a pitcher o' cool spring water."

Elizabeth opened the door and stood aside. The man carried the bucket and the pitcher to the washstand.

"Thank you."

"Stew's on the stove, ma'am. It'll be ready when ya want some."

Elizabeth nodded, closed the door and dropped the bar.

It was good to be alone, and it was heaven to take off her dusty clothes, remove the tight corset and wash in the warm water using the fragrant soap. She dried herself on a soft towel and dusted her body with fragrant powder. Then she pulled on a soft flannel gown with a high neck and long sleeves, relishing the warmth as it fell to her ankles. Sometime during the past half hour she had decided that she would rather do without eating than get dressed again. That decision was made before she heard the sound of running horses and loud male voices coming from the front of the building.

Elizabeth removed the pins from her hair. The heavy mass of dark curls fell to her shoulders and down her back to her waist. She massaged her scalp with her fingertips then picked up her brush. The long, even strokes through the cloud of thick dark hair were soothing. Curly hair, she had been told, was a blessing. At times like this, when it curled around her fingers as if it was alive, sprang up from her forehead, thick and lustrous, she thought it was. At other times, when she wanted to wear it slick and neat, it was a curse.

The sore spot on her bottom worried her. She had tried to see it in her hand mirror, but the angle was not right. It felt hard and hot to the touch. *Please, God, don't let it be a boil.* She had not had a boil in years, but she remembered the agony she had endured as a child when, one hot summer, one appeared beneath her arm.

Elizabeth lifted the bed covers and inspected the sheets. The landlord was right: the bedding was worn and mended, but it was perfectly clean. A wave of fatigue washed over her. She lay on her stomach on the bed. She heard the murmur of male voices and occasional loud laughter as if they came from a great distance.

A knock on the door jarred her out of near sleep. She slid off the bed and called, "Who is it?"

"Sam. Open the door."

"Ah... what do you want?"

"Open the door."

"I'm not dressed, Mr. Ferguson."

"Then dress, dammit. I'm not going to attack you."

"Just a moment." Elizabeth took a heavy wool robe from her trunk, slipped it on and belted it. Before she lifted the bar she looked to be sure she was completely covered. "Yes?"

Sam, shocked speechless, gazed at the pretty black-haired woman. This couldn't be the stiff-necked Miss Prissy-tail Caldwell who had sat so prim and proper beside him, who had compared him to her drunken, good-for-nothing uncle. She looked young, terribly young and defenseless, with her hair hanging over her shoulders, curling around her white face.

He watched her lift a hand to brush away a curl that was stuck to her cheek. Inquiring green eyes merged with inquiring brown ones. Was it fear or uncertainty that clouded her eyes? Whatever it was, it jerked at Sam's conscience, and he pulled his brows together into a frown. *My God!* He couldn't take his eyes off her. She was the epitome of all that was soft, sweet and feminine. The fragrant scent of her body drifted up to him. He felt something begin to coil in the pit of his stomach as the memory of his treatment of her came back to haunt him.

"Yes?" Her inquiring voice came from softly parted lips.

"I just wanted to tell you not to come out to supper. A bunch of rowdies rode in and are boozing it up in the barroom. It may be... unpleasant."

"I wasn't coming out."

"They were pretty well liquored up when they got here and the barkeep says they're a fighting, cussing bunch—"

"I wasn't coming out," she said again.

"I'll bring your supper. Burley's getting it ready."

"You don't need to. I've got a biscuit and an apple left from this morning."

"A biscuit and an apple? You've got to eat more than that," he said gruffly, then spun on his heel and walked away.

Elizabeth closed the door and leaned against it. *The pot was calling the kettle black.* The irony of it, she thought, laughing softly. One reprobate protecting her from other reprobates!

She could still see the surprised look on his face when she opened the door. Why had he stood gawking at her? She looked at herself again. She was completely covered; not a line of her body showed beneath the thick robe. He couldn't have been shocked by her lack of covering.

She *was* hungry, and she was grateful for this temporary respite of thoughtfulness on the part of Stephen's brother. Sam was handsome when he was behaving himself. He exuded strength and something that was primitive and . . . sexual. Lordy! Where in the world had that thought come from?

Abruptly Elizabeth sat on the bed and leaned over to take her weight off her buttock. With gentle fingers she felt for the sore spot on her bottom and wished the innkeeper's wife was here so Elizabeth could ask her for something to put on it.

Sudden boisterous laughter came from the front of the building, followed by a crash, thumps on the floor and yells from the innkeeper.

"Outside! Fight all ya want, but ya'll do it outside! Ya break up my place ya'll pay! Hear?"

This was a raw, violent land, and the men in it were even more raw and more violent. Elizabeth wondered if she would have left the security of home had she known what she was getting into. Yes, she decided, even this was better than what Netta had planned for her. She shuddered at the thought being held against Judge Thorpe's big belly and being touched by his pudgy, soft hands.

Elizabeth went to the door when she heard a thud near the bottom of the solid slab. "Yes?"

"It's me. Sam."

When she opened the door, he stood with a plate of food in one hand, a small pitcher of milk in the other. He smiled into her eyes. It was not the sarcastic grin she had seen so often today, but a friendly smile that crinkled his eyes and tilted his wide mouth. She returned the smile, admitting she had been more than correct about him being a handsome man.

"I had to kick the door since I have only two hands."

"Most people do."

"Haggerty's wife cooked before she left. Where do you want this?"

The heavy china plate he was holding was filled with small chunks of meat, potatoes and carrots all swimming in rich brown gravy. It looked and smelled delicious. She smiled into his eyes.

"It looks a lot better than what I had at the restaurant in Missoula." She stood back and swung the door open wide so he could angle his large frame through the doorway. "Over here on the bureau. It's the only place."

"I didn't bring a glass for the milk. I remembered you had that folding thing you used today." Sam set the plate and pitcher down, reached into his shirt pocket for a spoon and a three-tined fork and placed them beside the plate. "The coffee has been sitting on the back of the stove for a week. It tastes worse than boiled acorns."

"I'm glad you brought the milk. Thank you."

Sam went to the door, passing so close to her that his arm accidently brushed the robe she was wearing. In the confines of the small room, the air was filled with the scent of her—the sweet, woman scent of her. With his hand on the door, he looked back. Their eyes meshed. She seemed small, standing there . . . alone.

"You're the most polite woman I've ever known. What does it take to ruffle your feathers?"

She studied his face and realized that he looked amazingly like Stephen at this moment, yet different. The thought left her as the most incredible warmth washed over her. A sheltering warmth. With Stephen, a woman need never fear anything.

"Is being polite against the law out here?" she asked, scarcely realizing what she was saying.

"No. But that doesn't say much. There's not much that's against the law out here."

"I appreciate your bringing me the food. I wanted to rest more than I wanted to eat. I'm sure that I'll get used to the travel in a few days and not be so tired."

"It'll be a rough ride tomorrow. We've got to make a detour around the bridge that's out. Eat and get a good night's rest."

"Thank you. Good night."

As Sam turned to go, she started to close the door. His hand came out and stopped it. Their eyes met. Elizabeth couldn't look away from velvet eyes glowing with a mischievous light. He smiled, and creases appeared in his cheeks. *Why had she not noticed them before?*

"Let me give you a little advice, Liz. You'll be a lot more comfortable if you leave off that damn corset you wore today. No one out here gives a hoot in hell if your waist is two inches smaller, if your breasts are shoved up a little higher, or if your stomach sticks out a bit."

Sam pulled the door closed, but not before he saw her eyes widen with shock and a flush cover her cheeks.

He couldn't keep the grin off his face as he went through the walkway to the kitchen, climbed over the sturdy bench and sat at the trestle table where Burley and Jim were eating second and third helpings of stew.

"I ain't likin' that look on yore face one bit, ya young scutter," Burley said, making jabbing gestures at Sam with his spoon. "Ya done somethin' mean ta that woman, didn't ya?"

"No, I didn't, so don't get high behind, old man. I was very nice to the lady up to a point, then I told her a simple fact for her own good." Sam reached for the bread then dug his knife into the butter crock.

"Well," Burley had stopped eating, but Jim continued to eat as if he was going to be hung come morning and this was his last meal. "What'd ya say to her? Spit it out."

"I said—" Sam took a bite, deliberately chewed a long time and swallowed before he continued "—that she'd be more comfortable if she left off that bone-crushing contraption she laces herself in."

"God almighty, if ya ain't the limit! Ya ain't been talkin' ta that lady 'bout her...corset?"

"Why not? It's true."

"True or not," Burley sputtered, "it ain't yore place ta be sayin' it."

"Pass the salt."

"Yore brother'll think yore dumb as a stump."

"Pass the bread."

"But maybe she won't tell 'im."

"And the butter."

"That's a nice woman! Dad burn it! She's been raised up gentle like, 'n' ya got no business talkin' ta her 'bout her corset."

"I'll have more coffee."

"Hellfire! Ya ain't listenin'!"

"What are you getting all riled up for, Burley? Settle down. We've got more important things to discuss."

"Bridge didn't just fall down." Jim spoke.

"We know that." Burley gave Jim a disgusted look. "Haggerty thinks someone's got it in fer the stage line."

"We can go around this one, but I'm wondering how many more are out. What if the one is out up around Bitterroot?" Sam mused.

"It'll snow any day," Jim said.

"What'd you say?" Sam asked, turning concerned eyes on the Indian.

"Said it'd snow soon."

"Well, now, ain't that jist fine 'n' dandy," Burley exclaimed, taking what the Indian had said without question, knowing that if Jim said it would snow in the mountains, it was almost sure to snow. "It ain't goin' ta be easy getting that wagon up them mountain roads when they're slicker'n goose grease."

"Then we've got to make every hour count." Sam took a sip of coffee. "We'll start at dawn and go till dark."

"Ya mean forget 'bout stoppin' at the stage stations?"

"There won't be any stage stations if we leave the main road. You know that, Burley. We'll go as far as we can each day and camp."

"What 'bout Miss Caldwell?"

"What about her?"

"Good Lord! She can't camp out!"

"She'll have to. She can't stay here with Haggerty's wife gone."

"We can take her back to Missoula, is what we can do."

"Burley, you know as well as I do that we've got to get that blade to the mill. It's going to take twenty-four-hour shifts to complete that order as it is. I mean to disappoint that old bastard at the bank if he thinks we're not going to fill the contract and pay back the loan."

Two men came reeling into the room, laughing and pushing each other. They grabbed tin plates from the stove and filled them so full of stew it sloshed onto the table when they sat. They laughed as if it was a great joke and began to shovel quantities of food into their mouths. The one nearest Sam reached across him and speared the loaf of bread with his skinning knife without as much as a by-your-leave. Their clothing, hands and faces looked as if they had not seen soap and water for months. Neither man had bothered to remove his hat.

They slurped the food in silence, then refilled their plates before one of them spoke.

"Hey, Pete, did ya see that fancy buggy out back with them little red balls hangin' on it?"

"Yeah. Looks like a Injun's rig ta me."

Jim's spoon hesitated for a fraction of a second on its way to his mouth, then he continued to eat.

"Shore does. Injuns like them little red balls goin' flip-flop, flip-flop." The man who spoke stood, poked his knife into the butter crock and dragged it across the table toward him, grinning at Burley and Sam.

"That yore rig out there, Injun?" Pete asked.

"Don't reckon the Injun talks white man's talk," his friend said when Jim remained silent.

"I'm talkin' to ya, Injun. I ain't likin' ta be ignored by no blanket-ass," Pete said angrily.

"Don't get riled. Maybe he ain't hearin' ya. Maybe he's deaf as a stone."

"And maybe he ain't."

"Reckon we ort ta find out?" Pete's friend cupped his hands around his mouth, leaned toward Jim and yelled, "Boo!"

Pete laughed so hard, he spit food onto the table. "Ya scared the blanket-ass!"

Sam nonchalantly placed his palms on the edge of the table and pushed himself to his feet. He moved behind the men on the bench as if he was heading for the door.

"I ain't likin' ta be eatin' with no dirty redskin bast—"

An arm, roped with muscles, whipped around Pete's neck, choking off wind and words. Sam jerked the man's head back, knocking his hat onto his plate. Pete arched his back and clawed at the arm that, with a simple twist, could break his neck.

"When talking to my friend, you call him *Mister* Two-Horses." Sam spoke softly, pronounced each word clearly. "Do you hear me, or are you deaf as a stone? And . . . I don't care to eat at a table with dirty slobs who stink like they've been rooting with the hogs. Get out until we've finished."

As Sam loosened his arm, he fastened his other hand round the other man's wrist.

"Touch that knife and I'll break your arm and his neck," he said quietly. "Now get out."

"We paid to eat—"

"So did I. But I didn't pay to eat with hogs. I'll say it for the last time—get out."

The men got to their feet. The one Sam had nearly choked picked his hat out of the stew, glanced at it and shoved it on his head.

"Ya ain't heard the last o' this," he mumbled threateningly.

"If you want to take it further, I'm ready," Sam said, steely-voiced and calm. "I'll take on both of you at once, if that's the way you want it."

"C'mon, Pete. Don't make sense ta get kilt over a Injun."

The men stomped out.

"Them fellers is bad medicine." Burley slipped his six-shooter into its holster. He had been holding it beneath the table, and Jim had palmed his knife.

Sam shrugged. "All they've got is whiskey courage."

"Guess me 'n' Jim'll be sleeping in the barn with the freight wagon," Burley growled, as if it was Sam's fault.

"Where did you expect to sleep, old man?" Sam retorted as he straddled the bench, sat and reached for his coffee. "On a feather bed?"

"Don't be givin' me no sass, Sammy boy. It might be a spell since I boxed yore ears, but I can still do it."

A loud string of profanity came from the barroom, followed by a crash.

"Here now! Here now! Hell, boys! Stop it!"

Burley chuckled. "'Ppears like Haggerty's got his hands full tonight."

"Buffalo gun'd speak louder," Jim muttered. He got to his feet and walked silently out the back door.

"What do you have in the freight wagon in the way of blankets and camp supplies, Burley?"

"The usual. Not thin's for a woman like Miss Caldwell."

"What do you suggest I do with her? I sure as hell can't leave her here. I've got a hunch that our Miss Caldwell has got more grit than we're giving her credit for and that she'll make out just fine. She was worn out tonight, but did she complain?"

"Not to me," Burley said staunchly. "She jist barely made her legs hold her when she got down outta the buggy, but she didn't squawk 'bout it none at all."

Sam got up and stretched. "I'll get more blankets, another lantern and some coal oil from Haggerty in the morning. Damn! I hope Jim is wrong about the snow."

"Don't count on it. Get a canvas or two from Haggerty. The only ones we got cover the freight. Ya don't reckon Haggerty's got a tent, do ya?"

"I doubt it. If he did, it would be a ragtag thing. We can throw up a brush shelter for Steve's woman. This'll be something she can tell at tea parties when she gets back to Saint Louis. She'll tell how she roughed it in the wilds of Montana Territory with an Indian, a crusty old mountain goat and a handsome lumberjack."

"Which one's the goat?"

Sam grinned. For all his ribbing of Burley, Sam thought almost as much of him as he did his pa.

"I'll bed down out there in the walkway." Sam dropped a hand on Burley's shoulder and gave it an affectionate clasp. "We don't want anybody busting in on our Miss Caldwell, now, do we?"

Sam threw some blankets on the floor beside the door to Elizabeth's room. He was tired, but he didn't go to sleep immediately. He thought of the treacherous downhill trail they would take tomorrow. He thought of Jim's prediction of snow and of a green-eyed woman who belonged to his brother.

Chapter Six

The rap on Elizabeth's door a half hour before dawn awakened her, and she rolled onto her back. A small cry escaped her lips at the unexpected pain. She turned onto her side and pushed herself out of bed as the rap came again, heavier this time.

"Are ya awake, ma'am?" It was the gravelly voice of Burley Owens.

"Yes. I'm awake."

"We be leavin' soon."

"How soon?"

"Soon's ya can get ready."

"All right. I'll hurry."

Shivering with cold, Elizabeth lit the lamp and blinked at the light. She used the chamber pot, then carefully felt for the sore spot on her buttock. She couldn't tell if it was any larger, but the slightest touch was painful. She dreaded to think that it was a boil. A knot of fear caught in the back of her throat, and she almost panicked at the thought of sitting in the buggy all day. She backed up to the bed and eased herself down, winced, then shifted her weight to her left buttock. Cautiously she crossed her right leg over her left, testing to see if it would lift the pressure off the sore spot. It did.

But it was not proper for ladies to cross their legs except at the ankles. How many times had she heard that? *Proper,* be damned! Her main concern was just getting through this day.

She allowed herself a moment of self-pity, then washed her face in the cold water and dressed quickly. The night before she had laid out the clothes she would wear today. She had chosen a heavy black skirt, stockings and high-lace shoes, a white blouse and a light hip-length coat.

At the last minute she put her corset into the trunk, not because Sam Ferguson had suggested it, she told herself, but so she could bend sideways at the waist. He wouldn't know if she had worn it or not. The waistband on her skirt was a bit snug, but the loose coat would cover it. She pulled her hair to the top of her head and pinned it securely. Then she put a few things she would need during the day, including a long scarf, in her small travel bag and closed the trunk.

Sam was coming down the walkway when she opened the door. In the dim light she could see that he wore a sheepskin vest over a flannel shirt. Forcing herself to stand and face him, Elizabeth could feel the heat that rushed to her face at the thought of his parting words the night before. Sam, however, seemed not to be in the least embarrassed. Rather he was cheerful.

"Morning. Sleep well?"

"Yes, thank you."

"Go on out to the kitchen and eat. Burley is there. I'll load your things."

The kitchen, when she reached it, was warm compared to the room in which she had slept.

"Morning, Mr. Owens."

"Morning, ma'am. Sit 'n' have a bite." He set a bowl of mush and a pitcher of milk on the table. "Coffee's fresh made."

"I think I'll stand. I'll be sitting all day."

Elizabeth smiled at the old man and poured milk on the hot mush. Sam came through the kitchen carrying her trunk. She looked up, and their eyes caught. When he hesitated, Elizabeth quickly lowered her eyes to the heavy trunk he carried so easily. Then she slowly raised them again. His eyes had not left her. A sudden smile arced the corners of his mouth. She thought he was going to speak, but his eyes shifted to the doorway when the innkeeper called to him.

"Here's the blankets, Sam."

"Bring them out and total up what I owe you."

"Mr. Ferguson—" Elizabeth opened her travel bag "—I'll pay for my lodging."

The dark eyes that caught hers were no longer friendly. They held a hint of contempt and bit of anger.

"The Montana Fergusons are not rich like the Saint Louis branch of the family, but we're not dirt poor, either. I think we can manage to pay for temporary quarters for a guest coming to visit, especially one that will not be staying long." The sneer in his voice angered her.

"Very well. But I'm sure Stephen will reimburse you."

"Oh, yes. I'm sure he'll try." His faint smile was as cold as his eyes.

Sam carried the trunk into the crisp, cold morning and strapped it to the back of the buggy. Haggerty had piled blankets on the buggy seat. Sam spread them out to sit on, leaving one on the floor to lay over Elizabeth's lap, then returned to the inn for the rest of her luggage. He didn't as much as glance at her when he passed through the kitchen. He returned with the valise and hatbox.

Dawn was lighting the eastern sky when Elizabeth came out of the inn. The freight wagon, with Jim on the seat, was waiting on the road. Sam's horse was tied behind the buggy.

"Let me help ya, ma'am." Burley came to take Elizabeth's arm.

"It's all right, Mr. Owens. I can get in by myself. I want to tie my scarf over my head. My, it's cold."

"Shore is." Burley watched her loop the scarf over her head and wrap the ends around her neck.

"Are you going to ride with me this morning?"

"No, ma'am. I'll ride with Jim and work the brake."

"Oh." The sound that came from her was low, but not low enough.

"Disappointed?" Sam asked from behind her. "Well, it can't be helped. You'll have to make do with what's at hand." He walked past them and went to speak with Jim.

Elizabeth pulled herself into the buggy, sat carefully and looked at Burley.

"Pay him no mind, lass. He's got a burr under his tail for certain. It'll take a day or two ta work it out."

"Don't worry, Mr. Owens. I can stand most anything... for a few days."

Later in the morning she was not so sure. She sat tilted on one side, holding the bar that supported the buggy top. Sam had climbed into the buggy and without a word had unfolded a blanket and covered her. She welcomed the warmth and the concealment, which allowed her to cross her legs. Even at that, when she did let her weight press on her buttock, the pain was so bad that she almost cried out.

Moving slowly, they followed the freight wagon down a rocky tree-lined track. The sky was overcast with gray clouds, the wind sharp. They reached a level, smooth path that allowed Elizabeth to free one of her hands and pull the blanket up to her chin. Suddenly the wagon ahead moved faster. The trail plunged sharply down a steep incline.

"That's why Burley's riding the freight. He knows when to brake and when not to." Sam spoke as if they had been carrying on a congenial conversation for the past two hours, when, in fact, not one word had been said.

"And you don't?" As soon as the words left her mouth, Elizabeth regretted saying them. It had not been her intention to belittle his ability, and she was relieved when he did not appear to be offended.

"I can, but Jim and Burley each know what the other will do in any given situation. They've been together a long time. This is a dangerous trail for a heavily loaded wagon, and I don't want to take any chances. Working together, they're the best drivers in the territory."

"Do they own a freight line?"

"They work for me and my father. In the summer they freight in supplies. In the winter they bring logs down to the mill on skids after the ground freezes."

"I suppose you've known them a long time."

"Burley was here in the territory when Pa first came. Jim showed up about fifteen years ago."

This was the most normal conversation she'd had with him, and Elizabeth wished to prolong it, but the only way was to ask questions. Because she didn't want him to think that she was prying, she remained quiet.

As the ground leveled off, the horse began to trot. Sam glanced over to see that Elizabeth, turned so her back was to him, was holding on with both hands. He immediately reined the horse to a slower gait.

"You needn't be afraid. She's not a runaway horse."

"I'm not afraid." She looked at him over her shoulder, her face white and strained.

"Then sit back and relax. Are you warm enough?"

"Yes, thank you." She turned her face away, but her gloved hands still clutched the rods that supported the buggy top.

Sam didn't know much about women, especially this kind of woman, but he knew enough to know that this one was miserable and doing her best not to let it show. He kept seeing her in his mind's eye as he had seen her last night with her hair around her shoulders. She'd looked young, alone and scared.

"Would you like a drink of water?" Sam reached for the canteen at his feet.

"No, thank you. I'm fine." Elizabeth turned to look at him and forced her lips to curl upward in a smile, but Sam was looking at her eyes. They were as bleak as a rainy sky.

Sam let the canteen fall to the floorboard. He felt an emotion he was afraid to acknowledge for fear it was admiration for the lady. She wasn't complaining, but she wasn't giving out any information about herself, either.

"Are you and Stephen going to wait until you get back to Saint Louis to be married?"

"I won't really know until I talk to him."

"Do you love him?"

The question came so unexpectedly that her head swiveled and her startled eyes met his.

"Of course. I've always loved Stephen. He's like a bro—" She cut off the word, not wanting this strange, wild man to know the feelings she had for his brother.

But Sam wouldn't let it go. "Are you saying that you love him like a brother?"

"I'm saying I love Stephen Ferguson."

"Are you *in* love with him? Wildly, passionately in love with him?"

"I'm saying I love him. And it's no business of yours how much or what kind," she said in a frigid tone.

"You're right about that. Are you looking forward to going to bed with him?"

"You are the most insensitive boor I have ever met! I don't see how you can possibly be Stephen's brother."

Sam shrugged. "How long have you been engaged?"

"Before my father died, he spoke to Stephen. That was a few years ago."

"Why didn't you get married then? Lord! You're old enough to wed. Most women have three or four babies by the time they're your age."

For endless seconds their eyes held. Hers had a green, glacial light, his were unperturbed. The reference to her age hurt. In Saint Louis she'd had to endure Netta's constant harping on the fact that at twenty-five she was still unmarried.

"You are unbelievably bad-mannered! I'm under no obligation to answer your rude question. However, I will. Stephen has been in the East. He returned only a few months ago, and we set our wedding date."

"And you decided that you couldn't wait for him? Or were you afraid he'd not come back?"

"My reason for coming is between Stephen and me."

"Why didn't you marry him and come with him in the first place? That would make more sense to me."

"It is only proper that we should wait a reasonable time after his mother's passing."

"Ah . . . yes, dear Eleanor. Even after she's dead she's arranging people's lives." His voice was heavy with sarcasm, and Elizabeth's already strained temper flared hotly. Green eyes clashed with brown.

"Don't you dare speak of her in that tone of voice. She was like a mother to me."

"To you maybe," Sam sneered, "but not to me."

"You don't know how she grieved. My father told me—"

"Poor, grieving Eleanor. She left a brokenhearted husband and a child who couldn't understand what he had done to make his mother hate him so much that she'd go off and leave him. Years went by without a word from this poor grieving soul who chose a soft, easy life rather than honor her marriage vows. My heart bleeds for her."

"We never talked about it, but I know she didn't want to leave you—"

"Bullshit!" Sam yelled.

"Just . . . shut up!" Elizabeth shouted in a voice she hadn't used since she was a child. "You're a mean, vulgar man without an ounce of sensitivity. And . . . I don't even want to talk to you." She stared out the side of the buggy, surprised how good it had felt to yell at him even though tears of frustration blurred the trees they were passing.

"So Miss Prissy can get her little prissy tail over the line after all. It's nice to know you're human, Liz, and not one of those plaster dolls they dress up and stick in a dressmaker's window."

"Don't call me that!" Elizabeth turned and glared at him. "You don't know anything about me, and you have no right to judge me or my reason for coming here. I didn't ask to be your *guest*, and I will no longer endure your insults."

Her face was filled with vulnerability, and tears made her eyes silver-green pools. Her mouth trembled, yet her voice was strong. Sam felt as if someone had kicked him in the stomach. Gutsy. He'd be damned, the woman was gutsy!

"No, I don't have the right to judge you. And I was rude and crude. I apologize . . . for everything."

Elizabeth had turned her back to him. All he could see was the side of her face. A lone tear came from the corner of her eye and slowly slid down her cheek. That lone teardrop pierced Sam's heart like nothing had done in a long, long time. Suddenly he wanted her to understand what had been eating at him for so long.

"My problem is that I've had all this resentment bottled up inside me since I was ten years old. I thought I had learned to live with it. But the sight of you, the kind of woman you are, brought out a flood of unwanted memories," he said, speaking to her, to himself. He took a deep breath and slowly exhaled. "You . . . remind me too much of *her*. I resented her intrusion my life, in my thoughts, and took my resentment out on you. I'm . . . sorry." It was a blanket apology, covering everything, and as much of an apology as Sam had ever made in his entire life.

"I . . . accept your apology." Her soft voice trailed off to a whisper.

Sam's words tore at Elizabeth's heart. This big, angry man had offered her a glimpse of his soul, and she didn't know what to say to offer him comfort. Words and phrases came to mind. She discarded them in favor of silence. It was better to say nothing at all than to say the wrong thing and break this fragile thread of civility strung so suddenly between them.

Sam followed the freight wagon into a clearing beside the narrow track and stopped. While he was busy setting the brake and looping the reins over the brake handle, Elizabeth dabbed at her eyes with the end of her scarf.

"Jim must have seen something up ahead and pulled over to let it pass," Sam said quietly. "I'll be right back."

He climbed down and checked his horse, which was still tied behind the buggy. He walked to the wagon, checked the ropes holding the canvas over the bed, then made his way to the front. Elizabeth watched as his steps took him out of sight. She felt she understood him a little better now. She thought of him as he must have been as a small boy, feeling hurt and rejected, grieving over a beloved mother who was still alive. Had she died, he could have put his grief behind him. Instead, he had protected himself the only way he knew how: by denying his love for her.

Elizabeth carefully uncrossed her legs, threw off the blanket and backed out of the buggy. Her legs were wobbly, and she held tightly to the buggy. It seemed to her that the soreness was not localized in one spot, but that the whole side of her bottom throbbed. She wanted to cry. Her only hope was that wherever they stayed tonight there would be a woman she could confide in, one who would help her with hot packs or a poultice that would bring the wretched thing to a head.

A big wagon pulled by three teams of mules had stopped up ahead. Sam was talking to the driver, bracing his tall frame on spread legs, his hands in the back pockets of his britches. The gun that lay against his thigh was like a part of his clothing. Elizabeth had never met a more masculine man than Sam Ferguson. It was men like Sam who had settled this vast country beyond the Mississippi.

The horse tied behind the wagon whinnied, bringing Elizabeth's head around. Two riders were approaching, both rough-looking men. She looked toward Sam. He and the driver of the other wagon had moved out of sight.

The riders came to within a few feet of her before they stopped their horses. Elizabeth had never seen two more unsavory characters in her life. The one closest to her was a grossly fat man, wearing dirty, shapeless clothing and a greasy leather hat. A crooked nose that shone red at the end sat askew on his unshaven face.

"Ain't that the fancy buggy we saw back at Haggerty's?"

The other man had a black patch over one eye. The other eye was bloodshot. He spat brown tobacco juice from thick, slobbering lips that wore a lustful leer as he eyed Elizabeth up and down.

"Can't be more'n one like that'n in the whole world." The fat man's voice was hoarse. "The old nag pullin' it ain't much, but that'n tied on behind is a horse 'n' a half. That yore horse, honey?"

Elizabeth could have answered, but she said nothing. Her throat was too dry to talk, and she was too busy trying to hide her fear behind a bland expression. She had the feeling that if she turned her back on them to look for Sam they would pounce on her.

"Cat's got her tongue, Vernon. I'm thinkin' she don't take ta ya. Maybe she'd take ta me." The one-eyed man grinned a snaggletoothed grin, and tobacco juice dribbled from the corner of his mouth. "You travelin' with that freighter, purty woman?"

Elizabeth lifted her chin and met his gaze silently.

"Mighty fine buggy. Be my pleasure ta ride in it with ya, ma'am." The fat man was eyeing her trunk and the boxes ties to the back of the buggy with a greedy glint in his eye.

"Do ya reckon she's with the Injun that was sleepin' in the buggy at Haggerty's?"

The fat man didn't answer. His eyes were on the tall man in the sheepskin vest running toward them.

"She's with me." Sam's voice came from somewhere behind Elizabeth. Seconds later she felt his hand on her shoulder and leaned into it gratefully.

For a moment the good eye of the one-eyed man shifted to his companion, as if waiting for a signal. The fat man settled back in the saddle, took off his hat and scratched his head.

"Jist offerin' help ta the lady," he said in a pious tone.

"The lady doesn't need or want your help," Sam replied in a cold, no-nonsense tone. "Move on."

The fat man slapped his hat on his head and nodded to Elizabeth. He moved past, his eyes never leaving her face. The one-eyed man followed. They rode around the two freight wagons and were out of sight.

"Where did they come from?" Sam asked.

"I don't know. I turned around, and there they were."

"They probably came down through the woods from that upper trail. Get in the buggy. I've a few things to say to Jim and Burley."

Elizabeth pulled herself into the buggy as soon as he left her. She quickly rolled the end of one blanket into a cushion of sorts, and moving slowly, carefully, until she found the position that gave her the least discomfort, she sat. The mountain wind was bitingly cold. She shivered as she covered herself with another blanket, pulling it up to her shoulders.

The men on the freight wagon heading in the opposite direction tipped their hats as they passed. She acknowledged their greeting with a nod, then watched Sam lope toward the buggy. Burley's wagon had moved onto the trail by the time Sam released the brake and slapped the reins against the horse's back.

The buggy jarred across the ruts and onto the track. Elizabeth's hand pressed down on the seat between her and Sam to brace herself. Even at that, the pain was severe. She gritted her teeth and tried desperately to keep her mind off her misery.

It was autumn in the mountains, and the leaves were turning. The gusty wind blew golden yellow, dark crimson and mottled orange leaves at them. At any other time Elizabeth would have been excited about traveling through this wild, beautiful land and would have loved every mile. Now, she was sick with pain and worry. She scarcely heard Sam when he spoke to her.

"Another bridge is out up ahead."

"What does it mean . . . to us?" Elizabeth forced herself to speak.

"It means we'll have to take the long way around. Someone's making it impossible for the Northwest Stage Company to maintain a schedule. That's between the two of them, but when they tear up the bridges it hurts everyone in the territory."

"Why would anyone want to do that?"

"Any number of reasons. Wells Fargo, Overland Express or some other line may want this route. The easiest way to get it is to run Northwest out of business."

"That's underhanded."

"That's business. I've got to get that saw blade to Nora Springs within the next seven days or Ferguson Lumber will not be able to honor a contract, and we may be in deep trouble."

"And I'm holding you back."

"No. Didn't Burley tell you? We're starting at dawn and stopping wherever we are when it's too dark to travel. Have you ever camped out?"

Elizabeth's heart stopped dead before it galloped so fast it made her breathless. She knew he was looking at her. She turned to meet his eyes and slowly shook her head.

"You'll not be able to say that this time tomorrow," he said with a chuckle. "But don't worry. You'll be snug and warm. We'll throw up a shelter of sorts."

A shelter of sorts? Elizabeth turned her face away in case disappointment and dread were mirrored there.

Chapter Seven

The day proved to be far worse than Elizabeth imagined it could be. By midafternoon they had crossed a deep gulley and the narrow trail slanted upward. She was in such misery she no longer cared if Sam thought her rude and unsociable. She turned on the side of her hip with her back to him, murmuring that she was tired, and pulled the blanket up to her chin. Tears filled her eyes, but she blinked them away in case they should bring sobs she could not hide. At times she wiped cold sweat from her forehead; at other times she was too warm, but the pain was continuous.

Late afternoon brought a cold wind. Sam had not spoken since she turned her back to him, and she was grateful. She tried not to indulge in self-pity, knowing it was a useless pastime. But occasionally a few if-only thoughts crowded her mind. If only Stephen had come for her she could have told him about this embarrassing predicament. If only his brother had been a kinder, gentler person. If only Sam didn't resent her, or rather resent the type of woman he thought she was.

Huddled beneath the blanket, Elizabeth gritted her teeth stubbornly and vowed that Sam Ferguson would not be delayed one hour, one minute, because of her.

Surely somewhere in these mountains there was a woman who would help her apply hot packs and poultices. There was no doubt in her mind now that what she had was a severe boil, or even a carbuncle, which was a cluster of boils. She remembered the doctor ordering hot packs for the boil she had beneath her arm when she was a child. Later it had been lanced with a sharp knife.

She prayed they would come to a homestead soon. If a woman was there, Elizabeth would offer to pay for her help and for lodging until Stephen could come for her. Holding on to this small ray of hope, Elizabeth surrendered to her misery and tried to endure the constant jolting of the buggy. She had a blurred impression of going up one long slope, descending another and splashing over the bed of a creek.

Sam was uneasy. For the hundredth time he glanced at the woman huddled on the seat. She had said she was tired. He didn't doubt that, but instinctively he knew it was something more that had put the bleak, strained look on her face. At noon she had nibbled on the cold fried pie they had brought from Haggerty's, standing up all the while. She had refused the coffee Burley offered, excused herself and gone to the buggy. While they prepared to move out again, she had leaned against the buggy, looking in the direction they had come.

Sam wondered if she was homesick already, or afraid of going to this faraway, unknown place even if Stephen was waiting for her. But if she was afraid, she had a funny way of showing it. In fact, she had stood up well to the two scavengers who had so unexpectedly showed up beside the buggy.

Sam had known what they were the minute he saw them. They were hangovers from the old-time mountain men who had lived off the land fifty years ago. He had seen the fat man before. He was mean, but low-caliber. Sam didn't expect any trouble from the pair. They weren't the type to go up against three armed men. Nevertheless, he had told Jim and Burley what he knew about the fat man. He didn't usually range this far south. He was supposed to have a woman somewhere in the Salish Mountains.

The seldom-used trail they were on led northwestward, skirting Flathead Mountain where the pines grew thick and tall. Sam had been this way several years ago on horseback, but Burley and Jim had been over this trail with a wagon. He left it up to them to choose a campsite for the night.

In the deepening dusk the freight wagon left the narrow track and pulled into the woods. Sam followed, watching the careful way Jim maneuvered the wagon so the branches of the trees merely brushed the canvas covering the load. They stopped in a small clearing well back from the trail. Elizabeth had not stirred, and Sam decided she was asleep. He would not disturb her until a shelter had been built for her.

Elizabeth was so steeped in misery that she was scarcely aware when they turned off the main trail. She was grateful when Sam left her on the buggy seat without a word and began unhitching the horse. She eased herself down to lie on the seat and rested her head on her folded arm. The soft seat pressed pleasantly against her aching body. She drifted into drowsiness, then into a light sleep. Awakened by Sam's hand on her shoulder, she looked at the shadow that was his face.

"Elizabeth?"

"I had to come, Stephen. Netta wanted me to—" The daze of fatigue and pain slowly cleared. This man wasn't Stephen. It was his brother, Sam.

"Are you all right?"

"Oh, yes. I'm sorry. I was . . . dreaming—"

"Supper is ready."

"All right."

"Which one of your bags do you need?"

"Ah . . . my nightdress is in my trunk."

"I'll get it. Do you want me to help you down?"

"No, thank you. I'm fine." The words came out into the cold night air automatically, as if someone else was speaking them.

Sam looked at her for a long moment before he went around to the luggage platform. Elizabeth backed out of the buggy quickly but carefully, not wanting him to see her fumbling effort. With her feet on solid ground and her body shivering in the cold night air, she reached for the blanket and wrapped it around herself. Across from the buggy she could see the outline of the wagon, and in between the glow of a camp fire with shadowy figures moving around it. She was cold and terribly thirsty, but she needed to relieve herself before she could seek the warmth of the campfire.

"Behind the buggy and to your right is a good place . . . to be alone for a while."

Elizabeth swallowed hard as she looked into Sam's brown eyes. His gaze was as direct and intent as if her look was new to him. He scrutinized her every feature with the practiced care of an artist who was painting a portrait. The chilled wind had whisked a froth of hair across his forehead, softening the lines of his face. For a reason she couldn't begin to fathom, this big, rough man's reference to something as personal as bodily functions seemed perfectly normal.

"I looked around to make sure it was safe," he said with a gentleness that made her feel she had known him for as long as she had known Stephen.

"Thank you."

She watched him carry her trunk toward the camp fire, then made her way into the darkness behind the buggy. Slowly and painfully she did what was necessary. Then she returned to the buggy, wishing she did not have to join the men at the camp fire but knowing she must.

A lantern sat on a shelf let down from the side of the wagon. When she approached the circle of light, she could see Burley beside the fire spooning something from a black pot onto plates. A short distance away, Jim was piling pine boughs beneath a canvas that had been stretched between two saplings. Her trunk sat on the ground beside it.

"Come 'n' get it," Burley called.

Sam came out of the darkness with an arm full of ferny pine boughs and tossed them beneath the canvas. While Jim spread them out, Sam dug into the back of the freight wagon and pulled out a stack of blankets.

"Here ya be, ma'am." Burley picked up one of the plates he had filled. " 'Tis the last of Haggerty's stew."

"Thank you." Elizabeth dropped the blanket onto her trunk and took the plate.

"Ya can sit right over here by the fire," Burley invited.

"I'll stand." She softened her words with a smile.

"Suit yoreself."

The last thing Elizabeth wanted to do was eat, but she didn't want to draw attention by not eating, so she ate.

Sam and Jim picked up their plates, moved to the edge of the circle of light and squatted on their heels.

Sam was somehow different in the mountains. She looked down on his dark head and wide shoulders, not seeing the cocky, devil-may-care scalawag, but an older, unpolished, but very capable version of Stephen.

She looked at the open-ended shelter Sam and the Indian had built for her. It crossed her mind that under different circumstances she might enjoy an adventure such as this. She had never been in the wilderness, never slept without a roof over her head. Her eyes passed slowly over Sam's face, then the Indian's stoic features and finally to the gray-bearded old man. It was strange, but she felt as safe here with Sam and his friends as if she was in her home in Saint Louis.

On the heels of that thought, the lonely howl of a wolf echoed from a distant mountain. Elizabeth's eyes went to Sam's. The spoon had stopped on its way to his mouth as he waited for her reaction. An answering howl came from farther away. She lowered her eyes to her plate and continued eating.

When she finished the stew, Elizabeth held her empty plate, not knowing what was expected of her. As he passed her, Sam reached for it.

"Feel better?"

"Yes, thank you."

Elizabeth went to the buggy for her small travel bag. While she was there, she drank from the canteen, then carried it with her to the camp fire. Sam was hanging a canvas over the open end of the shelter they had prepared for her.

"Would you like the lantern inside?" he asked.

"I won't need it. I'm awfully tired. If you'll excuse me—"

"You should be warm, but if not, yell and we'll dig out a buffalo robe." He moved her trunk into the shelter and held the canvas for her to enter.

"I'm sure I'll be fine. Good night. Good night, Mr. Owens, Mr. Two-Horses."

She heard the polite murmurs that came from behind her as she stooped to enter her makeshift bedroom. The boughs made a surprisingly soft bed, and the blankets were soft and new. On her knees she removed her coat and scarf, sank face down in the soft nest and pulled the warm blankets over her. *Alone at last.* How was she going to get through the night? She couldn't undress without turning over and sitting up. She couldn't even reach her feet to unlace her shoes.

Tears came. This time it was impossible to hold them back. The deluge wet the blanket beneath her cheek, but not a sound came from her trembling lips.

While Burley cleaned up after the meal, Sam checked on the horses and mules and filled the water barrel, carrying the water from a spring that trickled out of the rocky cliff. Jim disappeared as soon as he had finished eating. The Indian always found himself a place to rest away from the camp but close enough so that he could sleep with one eye closed and keep the other on the wagon. The three men had spent many nights together on the trail, and each knew what was expected of him.

When Sam finished his chores, he poured coffee into his cup and motioned to Burley. The old man followed him into the darkness beyond the buggy.

"Burley, I swear something's wrong with Miss Caldwell, but I can't put my finger on what it is."

"She et supper 'n' she's still thankin' ya all the time fer ever'thin'."

"That thank-you business has been drilled into her since she was knee-high to a grasshopper. She'd do that even if she was dying."

"She 'ppears a mite peaked. Did ya treat her nice to-day?"

"Yes, I treated her nice," Sam growled.

"I heard ya yellin'."

"She yelled at me, too."

"Stephen ain't goin' ta like it none at all when he hears how ya treated her back in Missoula."

"Forget about that!"

"*She* ain't goin' to forget it."

"Oh, go to bed. I should have known better than to mention it to you. You don't know any more about women than I do."

"True." Burley spoke in a tone that said a *but* was coming. "But I know 'bout Jessie. She'd not stand for ya pukin' around her."

"Yeah." Sam grinned. "She'd have taken a buggy whip to me."

"After ya get this woman to Stephen, you better give Jess another look see. Jess is yore sort."

"What do you mean, my sort?"

"Yore kind. Jess's life is here, same as yores."

"Are you matchmaking again? Why don't you tend to your own business, old man?"

"Dang bust it! You 'n' Jess *is* my business. I ain't wantin' to see her heart busted in two. Miss Prissy-tail Caldwell ain't yore kind."

"Why're you calling her that?"

"Why not? You've been doin' it."

"Well, what's she got to do with it anyway?"

"Nothin'. I'm goin' to bed."

"No, you're not! Not until you explain. Do you think I'd try to take my brother's woman?"

"No. I ain't saying that. I'm sayin' Jess's got her heart set on ya. It's the only dumb thin' she ever done. I'm goin' ta bed."

Sam let him go. Sometimes Burley got off on the wildest notions. Hell, Jessie was just a kid. He reckoned he loved her, but like a little sister. He had cleaned more than one man's clock for taking liberties with her. He supposed that in three or four years, if she hadn't found a man she wanted to marry, they might get together. By then she would have grown out of her tomboy ways and be ready to settle down, raise kids and take care of a man. By then the thought of going to bed with Jessie might not seem as . . . indecent as it did now.

Jessie was a child compared to Elizabeth. Although last night, with her hair down, Elizabeth had looked no older than Jessie. Sam cringed when he thought of the cruel words he had said to her about her age. A woman was touchy about her age, especially an unmarried woman. Hell, she was seven years younger than he was—and one of the spunkiest women he'd ever met, and that included Jessie.

Sam's mind flashed to when she had walked into the restaurant, and to her standing on the porch of the hotel, looking down her elegant nose at him while he was acting the fool. Something had happened to her since that time. Something that had partially taken the starch out of her but had not dimmed her pride, something she was determined to keep to herself.

Sam flopped over on his side. Hellfire! Why did he have to keep remembering her green eyes bright with wetness and that lone tear that had slid down her cheek?

* * *

The night finally ended. Elizabeth knew this because the birds were chirping in the trees overhead. She watched the light from the camp fire flicker on the canvas and heard the clang of the skillet and coffeepot being set on the fire grate. She had been warm in the nest of blankets, but it had been the longest, most painful night of her life. The pain in her buttock now extended down the back of her thigh and throbbed with every beat of her heart. She dreaded getting up, but more than that she dreaded the day ahead.

On her knees she tried to tidy her hair, but failing to do that, she draped the scarf over her head and wrapped the ends around her neck. With her warm breath fogging the cold, sharp air, she managed to get into her coat. Knowing she must, she lifted the corner of the canvas and stepped out into the still, dark morning.

"Mornin'." Burley was placing sliced meat in the skillet. "Cold, ain't it?"

"Yes, it is."

"Snowin' higher up, or goin' to."

When Elizabeth stooped to pull a blanket out so she could fold it, she let out a small grunt of pain. She caught her lower lip firmly between her teeth and began to fold the blanket just as Sam came out of the darkness.

"I'll put those on the buggy seat." He reached for the blanket. "On second thought, you'd better keep this one."

Sam flipped open the blanket and draped it around her. With the edges in his hands he held her captive while he looked into her face. The ravages of a sleepless night were evident in the dark smudges beneath her eyes, the hollow cheeks, the way she pressed her lips together to still the trembling. But most of all her misery was reflected in dull green eyes that looked into his and then away.

He scooped up the rest of the blankets and carried them to the buggy. He returned and, with a quick jerk on the ropes, freed the canvases, rolled them, stored them in the back of the wagon and came back for her trunk.

Elizabeth watched, helpless to stop the events that would soon force her into the buggy. How was she going to sit in it all day? How was she going to sit at all? As soon as Sam and Jim came to the fire to eat, she went to the place behind the buggy where she had gone the night before. She blessed the split drawers that allowed her to relieve her aching bladder without squatting too low. At that, her legs trembled with the effort it took to support her, and she clenched her teeth to keep from crying out.

When she straightened, she cautiously cupped her hand over the painful lump and felt heat even through the material of her drawers and petticoat. The size of the boil frightened her. Now fears of fever and blood poisoning entered her thoughts, and she did her best to push them aside. She had to have help. Blinking her eyes rapidly to rid them of tears, she went to the camp fire and accepted the fried meat and biscuit Burley offered.

The mules were hitched to the heavy wagon, the horse to the buggy and Sam's horse was tied behind. Elizabeth waited until Sam was deep in conversation with Jim and Burley before she went to the buggy. She climbed up to the seat, carefully eased herself onto her left hip and braced her shoulder against the side of the buggy. After several grunts of pain, she managed to get into a position that would, at least, be bearable, and covered herself with the blanket. Her back would be to Sam, but it couldn't be helped. She searched her mind for a plausible reason, but none came to mind before she saw the wagon pulling out and him striding toward the buggy.

He appeared to be immune to the cold. He wore the flannel shirt with the sleeves rolled to expose his muscular forearms, the well-worn vest and a round-brimmed, flat-topped hat. Elizabeth admitted that he was the most masculine man she had ever known. An aura of power surrounded him, as if he was not afraid of anything or anybody. He was dangerously handsome. Her acquaintances in Saint Louis would be in a tizzy to meet such a man. To her, his masculinity and attractiveness were the barriers that made it impossible to confide in him. Those and his resentment of her because she reminded him of his mother.

If Sam wondered why she sat with her back to him, he kept his thoughts to himself. He flapped the reins against the horse, and they slowly left the clearing. Once they were out from beneath the trees, Elizabeth could see the sky. It was going to be another cloudy, windy day.

"Mr. Ferguson," Elizabeth said, and glanced at him over her shoulder. "Are there any people living along this road?"

"There was a family here a few years ago. But people come and go out here. I don't know if they are still there."

Elizabeth closed her eyes. *Oh, please, God, let them still be there.* She kept her eyes open, searching each side of the trail for signs of habitation.

They jarred across a rocky creek bed and went up a steep incline that passed through timber so thick she could see no more than twenty feet back from the trail. The light from the sky was shut off, making the trail dark and gloomy. The roadbed was so cushioned with pine needles that they couldn't hear the horse's hooves. The quiet was awesome in the dark forest. There was not even a bird song to break the stillness.

Elizabeth welcomed the light when they came out onto a shelf that wound around and down a steep slope into a valley where the bushes grew thick. As the trail straightened, Elizabeth loosened her grip on the side of the buggy to pull the blanket closer around her. It had been hours since a word had passed between her and Sam. She was past caring if he thought her rude. The hip she was sitting on felt as if the bone was pushing through the flesh; the other hip felt as if it was on fire.

Sam was more puzzled than ever by Elizabeth's behavior. Once he had cleared his throat and had spoken her name. When she didn't answer, he had leaned over to see if she was sleeping. Her eyes were open and staring.

He was disturbed by Elizabeth's remoteness. The hardest part of the journey was still ahead. Was she losing her mind? The shout that broke into Sam's thoughts went right along with his thinking.

"Stop! Stop! Oh, please . . . stop!"

Sam pulled up on the reins. "Whoa, whoa!"

"Thank God!" Elizabeth threw off the blanket. "I see a house . . . and a wash pot and a clothesline."

Sam put his fingers to his lips and let out a shrill whistle. The freight wagon stopped. While he was winding the reins around the brake handle, Elizabeth climbed out of the buggy and hurried up the overgrown path to the house. Sam called for her to wait, but his call went unheeded.

Chapter Eight

Squatting low on the ground, the cabin was sturdily built of split logs and cobblestones. Weather and years had treated it cruelly, but recent repairs had been made— a new glass window had been installed, and the solid door was hung with black iron hinges, and a hinged iron hasp with a padlock was fastened to it. Smooth stones were laid flush with the ground before the door and a large one for a step.

Elizabeth knocked hard. "Hello! Hello!"

"Miss Caldwell! Good Lord! What in the world's gotten into you?" Sam said behind her.

"Hello!" She hit the door with her fist, making hardly any sound at all. "Lady, please . . . come to the door!"

"Why are you doing this?" Sam placed his hand on her shoulder in an attempt to turn her around. She resisted and slapped the door with the palms of her hands.

"Please, let her be here!"

"*Her!* What the hell?"

Elizabeth turned. Tears filled her eyes and streamed down her cheeks.

"I saw a . . . wash pot in the yard, and a . . . clothesline. A woman is here."

"There isn't anyone here. The door is locked." Sam's voice was low and patient, his eyes clouded with worry. *Had she lost her mind?* "Look at what's written here." He turned her to face the slab of white bark nailed to the wall beside the door. "It says, 'Gone to Helena. Back before snow I hope.' The people who live here have gone away."

"The woman didn't go," Elizabeth insisted, shaking her head. "She wouldn't have left the wash pot—"

"It's turned upside down so it won't fill with water, freeze and break."

"Nobody here." A whisper.

Sam had never heard two words uttered with more despair. Her face crumbled, her lips quivered, and her eyes, full of misery and defeat, looked into his. Suddenly the dam of her resistance broke; she buried her face in the crook of her arm, leaned against the door and burst into a storm of weeping. Fueled by disappointment and the misery of the past few days, the sobs gushed forth with a force impossible to hold back.

Sam was stunned. He couldn't equate this sobbing woman with the self-possessed one he had met in Missoula. He wanted to comfort her, but he didn't know what to do. He placed his hand on her heaving shoulder. She shrugged it off.

"Tell me what's wrong. I'll fix it if I can."

"You . . . can't—"

"I'd like to try." His hands were insistent on her shoulders.

She allowed him to turn her around, then came willingly into his arms. With her face against his flannel shirt, she continued to cry. He held her, stroking her back. The scarf had dropped from her head, and unruly black curls teased his chin. Over her head Sam saw Burley and Jim coming up the path to the house, puzzled looks on their faces. He waved them away and lowered his head to speak softly to the sobbing woman.

"You'll get cold standing here in the wind. Let's go back to the buggy."

"No. I...can't..."

Sam's mind spun crazily to his thought that perhaps she had lost her mind. "What do you mean, Elizabeth?"

"I can't r-ride...anymore."

"Why not? Are you sick?"

"I need a woman...to h-help me." The muffled words came from against his chest.

"There's no woman here. There isn't anyone here. Let's go back to the buggy."

"You don't understand. I can't...s-sit down!"

"Can't sit down?" Sam echoed stupidly, not really believing what he had heard.

"I've got a boil on...on m-my d-derriere." The dreaded words were out. Elizabeth turned her cheek to his chest and covered her face with her hands. Tears seeped between her fingers.

"Derriere? What is that?"

"M-my...b-bottom."

"Your sit-down place? Good Lord, woman! Why didn't you say something?"

She didn't answer, couldn't answer for the trembling that shook her. It started in her knees and worked upward. She would have collapsed if not for the arms holding her.

"Oh...I'm going to be s-sick—"

Sam turned her away from him just as she bent over. The contents of her stomach came gushing out. With his hands at her waist, he moved behind her to hold her. His thigh brushed against her.

"Oh . . . Please! Don't touch me—"

"I'm sorry! God, I'm sorry! Burley!" Sam shouted over his shoulder. "Bring a crowbar."

Elizabeth heaved and gagged. The spectacle she was making of herself made her sick to her soul, but there was nothing she could do but hang limply from Sam's arms.

"Ya ain't breakin' into this place?" Burley came up the path with Jim close behind him.

"That's exactly what we're doing. She's got to have a place to lie down."

"We can camp—"

"Pull the nails from the hasp. We'll put them back when we leave."

"Her pukin' serves ya right," Burley grumbled as he pulled the big nails from the door in such a way as not to bend them.

"Get the blankets, Jim. It'll be cold in there."

Elizabeth was shaking violently. Sam opened his vest and held her against him, trying to give her the warmth from his body. "You can lie down in a minute. Burley has just about got the door open." She was soft and trusting in his arms. An overwhelming feeling of tenderness filled Sam as he held her.

Elizabeth started to protest about delaying them, but Sam began to move with her, guiding her through the door and into the cabin.

"Lie down here on the bed." He spoke as if to a child. "The bed looks clean. Its even got a patchwork quilt on it. I'll cover you with the blankets while we get a fire going."

"I'm so ashamed! I'm . . . holding you back—"

"Don't worry about that. I'd help you get on the bed, but I'm afraid I'd hurt you."

"I can do it."

Elizabeth crawled onto the bed and lay face down, clenching her teeth to keep from moaning with pain. There was not a joint or a muscle in her body that didn't ache. The soft bed offered some relief for the aches, but none for the throbbing pain in her bottom. Not since she was a child had she been so helpless or forced into such a humiliating situation. The humiliation was almost as hard to endure as the pain.

Sam covered her with several layers of blankets and left her. Burley and Jim followed him outside.

"She can't sit down. She's got a boil on her bottom." Sam spoke almost as soon as he closed the door.

"Jehoshaphat!" Burley exclaimed. "No wonder she et standin' up. How bad is it?"

"She's feverish and sick. She thought there was a woman here when she saw the wash pot and the clothes-line. She was too proud to tell us."

Burley scratched his head. "What are ya goin' ta do?"

"Me? Don't you mean what are *we* going to do?"

"No. I don't mean *we*," Burley said gruffly. "Ya know more 'bout women's bottoms than me or Jim. Yore the hell-raisin' Ferguson, ain't ya?"

"Damn you, Burley. This is no time for you to go stubborn on me."

"What ya goin' ta do?"

"The only thing I can do. Put a poultice on it and let it run its course. Hell! What else can I do?"

"Snow comin'." Jim's matter-of-fact statement was thrown in casually.

"We got ta get that blade ta Joe," Burley retorted with terse impatience.

"You don't have to tell me that," Sam said irritably. "We'll have to know how bad the boil is before we decide if she can go on. If she can't, I'll have to stay with her and try to catch up. Take a look around and see what the homesteader left."

Sam opened the door and stepped into the cabin. Elizabeth had turned on her side. The green eyes came reluctantly to his, flickered with pain then with embarrassment.

"I t-thought you'd gone—"

Sam came to the side of the bed and knelt so she didn't have to look up. His face was only a few inches from hers when she looked into his eyes. They were a deeper brown than Stephen's, quick and brazen and tender all at once. He had just the suggestion of dark whiskers on his cheeks that, rather than making him look unkempt, emphasized his masculinity.

"You don't know the hell-raising side of the family very well if you think Sam Ferguson would go off and leave a pretty woman here all by herself." His teasing words were accompanied by a smile that dented his cheeks.

Elizabeth's large green eyes looked directly into his, stirring him in the most disturbing way. They transmitted a quietly confident knowledge that she knew his innermost thoughts and was aware that he was playing the fool again to cover his anxiety.

"I knew you'd not leave me by myself. I thought that you'd go on and Mr. Owens would stay with me."

"We've not decided yet what to do," he told her frankly. "If the boil is small and has already come to a head, we may be able to rig up a way for you to lie down in the buggy seat, and I'll lead the horse. We won't know until I see it." Her eyes were so raw with hurt and humiliation that he had to look away from them. "This is embarrassing for both of us, but it's got to be done and there's no one else to do it. Will you be able to arrange your clothing so that I can see the boil?"

After a moment of silence, she whispered, "I'll try."

His hand closed, warm and reassuring, over her arm. "Trust me, Elizabeth. You needn't be afraid of me. I just want to deliver you safely to Stephen."

"I'm not afraid of you. I know that you don't like me much, and I'm holding you back—"

"As for not liking you—I think I'm just beginning to know you. And I don't blame you for not liking or trusting me. I wasn't putting my best foot forward back there in Missoula."

"I'm sorry to be such a bother."

"Out here in the West people help each other. If someone is sick, the neighbors come in to help. No one considers it a bother because it may be their turn next to need help." He got to his feet and backed away. "I'll start a fire in the cook stove and in the fireplace. It's cold in here. When it warms up a bit, I'll be back."

Elizabeth watched him fill the cook stove with kindling from the wood box and light a sheet of paper torn from a catalog with a match he took from his pocket. He hadn't sneered at her or been angry, as she had feared he would be.

He knelt to kindle a fire in the fireplace, and Elizabeth noted the spinning wheel at the end of the fireplace and the wool carders on the mantel alongside a ball of yarn with several sizes of wooden knitting needles stuck through it.

This one-room cabin was someone's home, Elizabeth thought, although it was scarcely larger than her bedroom in Saint Louis. It was neat and arranged to take advantage of the heat from the fireplace and the cook stove, one being on each side of the room. A single bunk was attached to the wall opposite the cook stove. The small square table was covered with a cloth, and a lamp sat in the middle of it. A long work counter, covered in front with a cloth curtain, stretched from the back door to the wood box beside the cook stove. Two hide chairs, a bench and a bureau were the only other furnishings in the cabin besides the double bed Elizabeth lay on.

"Do you need me to help you get out of your coat?" Sam stood at the end of the bedstead.

"No, thank you."

"I'll be back in a little while."

Elizabeth watched him walk across the room and let himself out the door, closing it behind him. She wondered how she was going to endure the humiliation of exposing herself to Sam Ferguson. Tears of self-pity flooded her eyes. She had no choice in the matter, she told herself sternly. The problem was how to do it and hold on to as much dignity as possible.

Slowly and painfully she removed her coat and pulled up her skirt and petticoat so that she could unfasten the waistband on her drawers. Never had she imagined having to do what she was doing—taking off her drawers to show a strange man her bottom. It was so unreal that she felt as if she was in another place and another time. With tears streaming down her cheeks, she tucked up her petticoat to bare the painfully swollen boil. She pulled the blanket over her legs and arranged her skirt so that only the inflamed area was exposed. Having done what she could, she tugged the corner of another blanket over her throbbing flesh, buried her face in her arms and waited.

* * *

"Feller cut a good bit of wood fer winter." Burley commented after he spit out a stream of tobacco juice. "Got dry grass piled in the rafters of his shed."

Jim was carrying water to the team from the stream that ran along the edge of the woods. Sam noticed the homesteader had planned well. The lot where he kept his animals drained downhill, away from his water supply.

"That stream will freeze up soon. I wonder where he gets water then?"

"Hot springs is all over these parts. In the winter time ya can see them steamin'. Sam, I'm feelin' mighty bad about Miss Caldwell, but I'm thinkin' bout snow in Bitterroot 'n' Joe countin' on gettin' that blade in time ta stave off that hungry banker."

"I know it. I'm hoping that what she's got isn't as bad as she thinks it is, and we can rig up a way for her to travel. But if we can't, you and Jim will have to go on. She's been hurting something awful, or she'd never have broken down and told me."

"Womenfolk! Why in tarnation didn't she stay in town or at Haggerty's?"

"You know damn good and well she couldn't have stayed at Haggerty's without his wife being there. Maybe it wasn't bothering her much when we left Missoula."

"And maybe she was jist stubborn."

"I thought you liked her."

"She be all right as far as womenfolk go, I guess," Burley admitted grudgingly. "If'n ya ask me, they're all a parcel o' trouble."

"All but Jessie," Sam growled sarcastically. He turned and stomped away.

Somehow it didn't set easy with Sam to hear Burley criticize Elizabeth. Dammit! It wasn't her fault. She had held out as long as she could and hadn't let out a peep of a complaint. He remembered when Burley had a boil on his back. He had moaned and groaned and lapped up the attention Jessie and Amanda had so freely given him. He had lain about for a couple of weeks until Amanda caught on to his put-on and demanded that he take a bath. That had been the end of Burley's loafing around. Suddenly he was well enough to go back to work.

Sam rapped on the door before opening it slowly. "Is it all right if I come in?"

"Yes. Come in."

Sam hung his hat on the peg beside the door. The cabin had warmed up considerably. He shrugged out of his vest and hung it beside the hat. Knowing how embarrassing this was for her, and for him, he delayed going to the bed as long as possible. She lay on her stomach with her head in her arms. Sam didn't know what to do, so he knelt beside her and touched her arm.

"Elizabeth?"

She brought one of her arms down and pulled back a corner of blanket. Sam stood, bent over the bed and looked closely at the exposed flesh.

"God almighty!" he murmured.

The reddish-purple mound was the size an egg, with red streaks fanning out on the soft white flesh of her buttock. As far as he could tell the boil was a solid lump without a sign that it was coming to a head. How she had endured riding in the buggy he would never know. He reached for the corner of the blanket, pulled it over her and knelt beside the bed again.

"You'll have no relief until it's brought to a head and lanced." Sam's voice was low, reflecting the tension gripping his body. He pushed her hair from her cheek with gentle fingers. "Did you hear me, Elizabeth?"

Drawing a deep breath, she whispered, "Yes." Slowly her hand moved toward his, then her fingers circled his thumb and held it tightly.

Sam realized with a jolt that he could barely breathe. She had reached out to him with a silent cry for help. A spasm of longing flicked across his face—a bittersweet yearning to fill the emptiness of his life, to have someone of his very own to love, to care for, to depend upon him for happiness and contentment just as he would depend on that sweet someone.

"We'll stay here," he said, rushing his speech in order to bring his thoughts into focus. "Burley and Jim will go on to Nora Springs. In case of a big snow up on Bitterroot, they'd have a time getting through with that heavy wagon. My father needs that saw blade or he stands a chance of losing the mill."

"I'm sorry. Truly, I am. I didn't intend to cause trouble for you."

"Don't say anything more about being sorry. I know you didn't want it to happen. But it did, and we've got to make the best of it. I'll go talk to Burley and Jim." Sam stood, then knelt again. "Elizabeth, you'll be safe here with me. You can bet that Burley wouldn't leave if he thought otherwise. He's straight as a string about womenfolk."

"I'm grateful to you, Sam. It never entered my mind to be afraid of you. Eleanor's son would never harm me."

At that his gut twisted, and he rose and headed out of the cabin.

An hour later Sam stood in front of the homestead and watched the freight wagon pull away. The buggy was in the lean-to beside the shed; the horses were in the pole corral. Elizabeth's trunk and boxes, Sam's saddlebags, a small valise, a lantern and extra blankets were just inside the door. Burley had sorted out foodstuff from the supplies on the wagon, also making sure Sam had ammunition for his rifle and handgun. While Burley was doing this, Jim vanished into the forest. When he returned, he put a lump of pine resin in Sam's hand.

"Melt with a little bit o' lard. Put on boil. Cut when white shows." Without another word, the Indian had climbed upon the wagon seat and sent the whip over the backs of the mules.

Sam looked at the resin. He had planned to put a raw-potato poultice on the boil. Burley had insisted that he use tobacco and had begrudgingly left a plug. Instinct told Sam the Indian knew best.

A cold wind whistled around the corner of the house, causing Sam to peer at the sky, dark and heavy with an impending storm. It depended on the temperature whether it would be rain or snow by night. In case of a heavy snow, he wondered how a citified woman would fare on a mountain trail. Don't borrow trouble, he told himself. At least they had a roof over their heads and plenty of food and wood to burn to keep them from freezing. He blessed the homesteader who had left his ax leaning against the wall behind the cook stove.

It was gloomy inside the cabin with light coming only from the small glass window. Sam put extra wood on the fire for warmth and also for light, wanting to conserve the fuel in the lamp. He filled the reservoir beside the stove and put the teakettle on to heat. He emptied a can of peaches into a bowl, washed out the can, added a small lump of lard and the resin and set it on the stove to melt. Every so often he glanced at Elizabeth. Believing she was sleeping, he moved quietly, storing the foodstuff on the counter and putting his extra ammunition on the bureau well away from the fire.

When he had done all he could until the resin melted, he stood at the end of the bed and looked at the woman lying there. What if he couldn't bring the boil to a head? What if she got blood poisoning? If it was a man lying there, he wouldn't have a doubt in his mind about what to do. But with a woman like Elizabeth who was new to the hardships of this country, who would have gone to a doctor in Saint Louis, who now had only him to take care of her...

The toes of her shoes were sticking out from beneath the blanket. Sam carefully folded back the cover and began to unlace the soft black leather shoes with the slender heels that flared at the bottom. He pulled off one shoe and held her slim foot in his hand for a moment before he unlaced the other one, pulled it off and covered her feet.

"Thank you," she murmured.

"I thought you were asleep."

"I dozed for a minute. Are they gone?"

"About a half hour ago. It's past noon. Are you hungry?"

"No. No, thank you."

"All right, we can eat later."

"Sam. Is is bad?"

"I won't lie to you. It's big and has to be brought to a head so I can lance it."

"How long do you think it will take?" She turned her head to look at him with anxious eyes.

"I don't know. I've got pine resin melting on the stove to use as a poultice." She looked scared, so damn scared, and she was trying not to show it. "I'm going out to chop some wood. I don't want to use up the homesteader's supply."

"Will you be gone a long time?"

"I'll be where I can keep my eye on the door, and I'll rap on it before I come in. Do you want me to bring your trunk over here and open it?"

"Yes, please."

Sam pulled the trunk close to the bed and lifted the lid. A scent of flowers wafted up to him. The scent was hauntingly familiar and brought back painful memories of his mother, young and pretty and sweet-smelling. Then, as though he was looking at a painting, his mother's face appeared in his head—the mother who had kissed him good night, the mother who'd rocked him . . . the mother who'd left him.

Without a word, Sam put on his sheepskin vest, picked up the ax and went out the door.

Chapter Nine

Elizabeth got off the bed as soon as the door closed behind Sam, glad for the chance to get out of the clothes she had worn for a day and a half. Surprised and a little frightened because of her weakness, she held on to the head of the bed until her dizziness passed. Then she shed her clothes as quickly as her aching limbs would allow.

The flannel gown felt wonderfully warm and comfortable, especially after she covered it with the thick, soft robe. She folded her clothes and underwear and put them in the trunk. She yearned for warm water to wash her face and hands and for a drink of water to rinse her mouth, but she had more pressing needs. It had been hours since she had relieved herself. She felt beneath the bed for the chamber pot, pulled it out and used it, not knowing when she would get the chance to empty it.

How her life had changed in just a few short weeks. Until two nights ago, the only man who had ever seen her in her nightclothes was her father, and that had been years ago. It seemed incredible that she was in an isolated cabin, totally dependent on a man she had known for less than a week.

Sam rapped on the door, cutting off her thoughts. She had taken the pins out of her hair and was holding them in her mouth while she tied the heavy tresses at her nape with a ribbon.

"Come in."

She felt the cold draft on her bare feet when he opened the door. He went directly to the wall beside the cookstove and stacked the wood. The room seemed so much smaller with both of them standing.

"Before you get back into the bed, I'll spread one of our blankets on it. We have plenty." He spoke as if it was the most natural thing in the world to see her in her nightclothes with her hair hanging down her back.

"Mr. Ferguson? Is there a way I could clean my teeth and rinse my mouth?" She spoke to his back as he removed his vest and hung it on a peg beside the door.

"*Mr.* Ferguson." He turned and met her gaze with a chiding grin, although the tightness encasing his chest was destroying his breathing. "Are you going to call me that after you and Stephen are married?"

"I guess not."

"Come over here to the wash bench. Do you have something for your feet? There are splinters in this floor."

She stuck her feet in the slippers beside the bed and moved around to the heavy end posts that supported the frame. It seemed a mile to the wash bench. She turned her head, but Sam had seen the anguish in the green depths of her eyes.

"Are you all right?"

"Oh, yes," she said with forced lightness. "I'm just weak, and I forgot to get my toothbrush."

"Where is it?"

"You needn't bother."

"Where is it?"

"In a small ivory box in the tapestry valise."

Sam snapped open the valise, took out the box, then took her arm and held her firmly to his side. He was swamped by the most intense desire to take care of her. His response to her need of him was overpowering. He didn't try to analyze it or rationalize it. Instead he fought to stifle it. Feeling dangerously exposed, he left her at the bench and turned away, his hands curled into tight fists.

He spread one of the new blankets on the bed, then lit the lamp so he could see into the can of lard and resin.

"Do you have a clean cloth we could use to apply the poultice?" he asked.

"Yes, and towels, too."

"We'll need them."

"Why am I so weak all of a sudden?"

"You haven't eaten much for the past three days, and fever will make you weak."

"I don't know how to thank you for helping me, Sam."

"Then don't," he said curtly.

Sam's abrupt words washed over her like a bucket of cold water. With her head lowered so that she could watch each step she took, she went to the bed, determined not to ask any more of him than was absolutely necessary. Holding on to the bed with one hand, she rummaged in the trunk with the other and brought out a soft white tiered petticoat and several towels.

Sam watched her out of the corner of his eye as he stirred the resin. He wished he hadn't barked at her. But hell! He didn't want her thanks. He just wanted to understand why she aroused this fierce protectiveness in him. He should feel nothing but anger and contempt for her and her kind, but the feelings he was experiencing were far from that. His calm, rational mind told him that he was just feeling sorry for her. But Sam knew himself well enough to know that it was more than that. With that lone tear rolling down her cheek she had started getting under his skin. She struck a spark in him that had never before been touched.

Abruptly realizing that his thoughts were leading him toward treacherous ground, he attempted to eject her from his mind. He could not, no matter how strong the feeling he had for her, lose sight of two very important facts. She was a woman who was used to living in splendor, and she belonged to his brother.

Dammit to hell! Burley was right. She wasn't for him even if she didn't belong to Stephen. She'd not last out here any longer than Eleanor had. They were two of a kind!

"How large a cloth do you need?" She looked at Sam, her eyes tormented, her voice low.

"Not very big, but I'll need several."

"I have more if this isn't enough."

"It'll do."

He heard the creaking of the bed ropes when she crawled onto the bed. After a minute or so, he glanced at her to see that she was lying facedown and had covered herself with a blanket. Her face was buried in her arms. The swatch of thick dark curls lay on her back. He thought of how she had looked when she walked into the restaurant in Missoula, and he thought of how she looked now—pale, anxious and scared. There was a world of difference between that woman and this one.

Sam felt a pang of remorse for his sharp words and once again experienced feelings he dared not acknowledge. He swore silently, berating himself for being an unreasonable bastard. Hell! She'd had to swallow her pride, bare her bottom and accept help from a man she considered little more than a savage. This situation had to be a hell of a lot harder on her than it was on him. He picked up the white garment she had laid on the foot of the bed. It was soft and white and smelled like roses. He crushed it in his two hands, then took out his knife, made a slit in it and ripped off the bottom tier. Damn! The woman had punched a hole in his resistance, and it was becoming harder and harder to remain detached.

Elizabeth heard Sam ripping the petticoat and knew it wouldn't be long until he would be wanting to apply the poultice. The pain in her buttock was constant, unrelenting, but it would pass. The mortification of baring her bottom to this hostile man would be with her forever. While she arranged her gown and the blankets to cover every inch of her flesh except what he had to see, she wondered what she had done to deserve this humiliation, and what had caused the change in his attitude toward her.

"Here's the poultice. Do you want to see it?"

"No."

The muffled word was spoken as she hid her face in the bedding. She reached blindly behind her and moved the blanket as she had done earlier. The lump was larger than Sam remembered. A muscle twitched in his jaw as he saw it rearing up out of her white flesh. As gently as he could, he placed the resin-coated cloth over it, saw her flinch and cursed silently.

"Now we've got to put a hot, wet cloth over it, and a dry one to hold the heat in." His tone was low, and there was an impersonal quality to it. He was forced to move aside some of the covering, but he replaced it with the warm wet cloth and the towel. "That should take care of it for a while." He covered her with the blanket.

She had not moved or made a sound. Sam experienced a sudden flash of insight. This was an emotionally shattering experience for her as well as a painful one, even more than he had thought. He knelt beside her. This time she didn't reach out to him. She kept her face turned toward the wall.

"Did I hurt you?"

"You had to."

Sam could feel her withdrawing into herself, and suddenly it was important to him that she didn't shut him out. He stroked the hair from the side of her face with gentle fingertips. Willing her to look at him, he leaned forward and spoke in a low, urgent voice.

"Look at me, Elizabeth." He hadn't really expected her to, but she did. She turned her face toward him. Her green eyes were dry, but the soul-destroying look of utter despair he saw there caught him by surprise. "You're going to be all right."

"I know."

He tried to ignore the disturbing sensation her barely audible answer evoked in him.

"You need to eat something. How about a handful of raisins?" Not waiting for her to reply, he left her to return with a small bag. He pulled open the drawstring top and placed it on the bed. "Fresh from the store in Missoula. Raisins are a favorite of mine. Raisins and dried peaches and peanuts. We don't get many peanuts up here, but we have a lot of walnuts."

The only indication that she was listening to him was that her eyes clung to him almost desperately. Sam didn't think he could stand the tortured look in them any longer.

"Why don't you sleep for a while? I'll put some meat on to cook."

Moving around the cabin as quietly as possible, Sam found an iron pot turned upside down on a lower shelf.

It was clean and had been greased to prevent rust. He blessed the homesteader's wife. This humble home was as neat and as clean as Amanda's rooming house in Nora Springs. He cut the meat in small pieces and put it on to cook, then filled the coffeepot and set it on to boil.

Elizabeth lay as before, except her hand was on the bag of raisins. Sam went to the bed to tell her that he was going out to see about the horses. Her eyes were closed. He moved quietly away and blew out the lamp.

Sam led the horses to the stream to drink, then to the shed, where he gave each a scoop of the oats from the bag Burley had left. He wasn't as restless as he'd thought he would be. It was almost pleasant knowing that meat was cooking on the stove and that a quiet evening with nothing to do but tend Elizabeth awaited him.

As he emerged from the shed, Sam's eyes fell on the small garden plot on the downhill side of the cabin. A row of ferny growth told him that there were still carrots in the ground. Telling himself that he would make it right with the homesteader, he pulled six long orange carrots and shook them free of clinging soil. A spattering of large, plump raindrops fell, causing him to look at a sky that had become increasingly dark. A bank of iron-gray clouds hovered on the northern horizon. Sam hurriedly stacked the rest of the wood he had cut beside the cabin door, took an armload and went inside just as the rain, driven by a gusty wind, pelted down.

Sam lit the lamp, then scraped the carrots and put them in the pot with the meat. He had learned to cook the first year he and his father were alone. At first neighbors had helped him prepare meals for himself and Joe. Later, when he had gone to school in Missoula, he had a room in the home of a spinster schoolteacher. Miss Margery Theiss had been a big influence in his life. She not only helped him with his studies so that he finished school in record time, but she also taught him to cook, wash his clothes, develop personal grooming habits, and most of all she had taught him cleanliness. Five years ago she had retired and had written to Sam that she was going East to be with her sister. Sam had made the trip to Missoula to see her off on the train.

An hour passed during which Sam drank two cups of coffee and cleaned his gun. He sat at the table. The cabin was tight; not a drop of the rain pounding on the roof came inside. Knowing that he must, Sam took a warm, wet cloth to the bed. Elizabeth's face was turned to the wall. He lifted the blanket and quickly exchanged the cool cloth for the warm one and covered her again.

"You don't make much noise." She turned her face toward him, lifted her hand and brushed the dark curls from her face.

He knelt so she didn't have to look at his knees. "I took off my boots. I was bringing in a ton of dirt, and I didn't want to have to clean it up."

"Makes sense."

"You'd better be hungry. I've got a pot of meat on the stove, and if you don't help me eat it, I'll be eating it for days."

"It smells delicious."

"Well, that's a relief." He smiled, and it spread charm all over his face. "Did you sleep?"

"A little."

"Did the rain awaken you?"

"I suppose it was the rain. You were certainly quiet. Will Mr. Owens and Mr. Two-Horses be all right?"

"Those two old mountain rats are used to all kinds of weather and are prepared for it. This little sprinkle will not bother them at all."

"I bet they're relieved to be rid of me."

"Their loss is my gain." He smiled into her eyes and suddenly, sincerely meant what he'd said. He wanted to keep her talking. He wanted to move his hand to cover hers, but he didn't dare.

A quick smile tilted her lips and brought a light to her eyes. "You're full of nonsense, Samuel Ferguson."

"Better that than whiskey," he said, then groaned, not wanting to remind her of what had happened in Missoula.

But it did remind her, and her smile spread so wide that it creased the corners of her eyes. "That's true."

His hand moved without his being aware of it and covered hers. He gripped it tightly.

"Elizabeth, I've never done such a rotten thing before in my life. I want you to know that I'm sorry. Pa raised me to be respectful of women."

"Even prissy-tail, citified women?" she asked, still smiling.

"Even prissy-tail, citified women." His smile answered hers until hers faded and a serious expression appeared in her eyes.

"I'd like to be your friend, Sam. I didn't come out here to disrupt your life or bring painful memories."

"I know that. You came to marry Stephen." Something like a chill settled around Sam's heart. His hand left hers, and he stood. Changing the subject abruptly, he said, "You're going to have a time trying to eat lying on your face."

"I'd turn on my side, but the poultice will fall."

"Not if I banked something against your . . . whatever it was you called it."

"My derriere? It's French."

"I'm not much good at fancy words. Let's just call it your sit-down place, shall we?"

"All right. I feel like an intruder using the things in this home without the owners' permission."

"They won't mind. It's done out here all the time. They'll appreciate the cash I'll leave. Cash money is hard for a homesteader to come by."

"They have so little, yet they've made this small cabin into a home," she said wistfully. Holding the poultice in place, Elizabeth turned slowly onto her side. Sam reached behind her and placed a pillow against her backside. "Is that better?"

"Yes, thank you."

"We'll change the poultice after supper and again in the night."

Elizabeth watched him as he went silently across the floor to the cookstove, lifted the lid on an iron pot and poked the meat with a long fork. She had never known a man who cooked until she saw Burley cooking over the camp fire. Sam seemed to be doing it as if it was something he was used to doing. His gray-stockinged feet were large like the rest of him. Tight britches, slung low on his narrow hips, showed sinewy strength in his hips and thighs and left no doubt as to his male endowment.

Sam Ferguson was a ruggedly handsome man. Her eyes fastened on the bulge at the joining of his muscular thighs. Her cheeks grew hot. Mercy! Had she lost her mind, staring at him *there*? She looked away quickly, but her wayward eyes returned to him again and again. His face and neck were bronzed by the sun and weather. Thick brown hair grew low on the nape of his neck. Shoulders that had seemed broad in the buggy were even broader in the close confines of the cabin and were suited to his wide chest and slim waist, which carried not an extra ounce of surplus flesh.

Sam was nothing but a virile male, yet he was doing feminine things, cooking and tending her as if it came naturally to him. He was all muscle and masculine strength, gentle at times, hard at other times such as when he'd dealt with the fat man and his friend. He was a man well suited to this rough land.

The sight of him standing shirtless in the doorway of the room in Missoula flashed through Elizabeth's mind. The soft hair on his chest had been only slightly darker than the hair on his head, but not as dark as the hair on his upper lip. Was there a streak of vanity in him that caused him to keep the mustache so neatly trimmed? Or did he do it because the woman, Jessie, liked it? Another thought crowded unbidden into her mind. *What would it feel like to be kissed by a man like Sam?*

Elizabeth moistened lips that had gone suddenly dry. She felt like a schoolgirl who had become aware of the opposite sex for the first time. Surprised by her thoughts, she blamed them on curiosity. She had never been kissed on the lips the way it was done in some of the novels she had read. Stephen always gave her a peck on the cheek. One time it landed on the corner of her mouth. He had looked apologetic and hurried away.

Outside the rain continued to fall, but inside the cabin was warm and cozy. Elizabeth wondered about the two men and the freight wagon. She couldn't imagine, even without the painful boil, sleeping outside in such weather. When Sam brought a plate of food to her, she voiced her concern.

"Mr. Owens can't even build a fire in this weather. What will they do?"

"As soon as they were sure it was going to rain, they picked up wood and put it under the tarp. They'll have a fire and a hot meal tonight." Sam was surprised that she was concerned about them.

"Where will they sleep?"

"Under the wagon. They'll hang a canvas on the wind side, put an oilskin on the wet ground and their blankets on top of that."

"Is that sleet hitting the window?"

"It sounds like it. Temperature must have dropped. Would you like a cup of coffee?"

"No, thank you. I'd like a glass of water."

"Are you hot?"

"A little."

"That robe you're wearing looks as if it would keep you warm in a blizzard."

"It's made of angora wool."

"Hmm—goat or rabbit?"

"I don't know." She thought to tell him that her father had bought it for her in Scotland, but she didn't for fear he would think she was flaunting her wealth.

Sam ate at the table. He sat on the side facing her, and every so often Elizabeth looked up and found him watching her. She ate without appetite, forcing herself, knowing that she needed the strength and that it would be impolite not to eat the meal he had brought to her.

"It was very good," she said when he came to take her empty plate.

"Now *you're* full of nonsense, Miss Caldwell," he teased. "It was eatable, and that's all." He dumped the plates into a pan, sat and pulled on his boots. "I think I'll go out to see about the horses. If you should get up while I'm gone, leave off the poultice. I'll make another one when I come in." He put on his vest and pulled a poncho slicker out of his saddlebag. Without looking at her, he slipped it on over his head, put on his hat and went out the door.

Elizabeth knew Sam was making time for her to use the chamber pot, and she was grateful. Not stopping to think of the intimacy they shared, she threw back the covers and removed the poultice. Slowly, painfully she got off the bed, clenching her teeth against the searing pain. It was far worse when she was standing. She took off the heavy robe and tossed it on the trunk. She was hot and shaky and terribly tired of the steady, intense pain. Slowly and carefully she pulled the chamber pot from beneath the bed, used it and slid it out of sight.

Feeling as if her legs would no longer hold her, Elizabeth crawled onto the bed and lay facedown. Not until the pounding of her heart eased did she reach down and pull the blanket over her. She hurt all over—her buttocks, her thighs, her back. She closed her eyes tightly to hold back the tears of helplessness.

Chapter Ten

Sam sat in the hide-covered chair, his long legs stretched in front of him. He rested his head against the back of the chair, his eyes going from the toes of his stockinged feet to the dim form of the woman on the bed. This was the second night they had spent in the cabin. When morning came, Sam was sure he would have to lance the boil, and he wasn't looking forward to it. The resin poultices and the hot towels he had applied were finally bringing it to a head.

Elizabeth had lain with her eyes closed most of the day. He knew she was hurting badly, as she no longer reached to cover her exposed thighs when the blanket slipped down. The pain had robbed her of some of her modesty. Yet she had not complained. Since noon she had seemed to barely notice when he changed the hot, wet cloth.

Hearing a small sound, Sam listened intently. The wind had come up toward evening and was blowing hard. Burley and Jim should be in the Bitterroot Mountains by now and in a few more days should be in Nora Springs. He wondered what Stephen would think about his fiancée spending this time alone with him. Would he be outraged? Would he fear for his future bride's virtue?

Elizabeth was beautiful, gutsy, proud, intelligent: all the things Stephen had said she was. Sam's respect for her had doubled and redoubled since the morning they left Missoula. She was a woman of principles, not afraid to speak out for what she believed in. He thought about her riding in the buggy for two and a half days with the boil, enduring pain that would make some men weep.

Something had happened in Saint Louis that had frightened her into making this trip. He had never known a woman who had such rigid control, who kept all her emotions bottled up inside her. He wondered what she would be like if she ever let herself go and did what came naturally to her.

Sam heard the sound again, stood and walked silently to the side of the bed. All he could see in the light of the flickering fire was her shape beneath the blankets. A faint, muffled sound that could only be a sob reached him. He bent over her, touching her lightly on the back.

"Elizabeth? Are you all right?"

"Y-yes." The word came from deep in the soft pillow.

"But you're . . . crying."

When she didn't answer, he knelt beside the bed and stroked the hair from the side of her face. As she turned her face toward him, he felt the wetness of tears on her cheeks. Suddenly the need to comfort her was so great that he had to swallow the huge lump that clogged his throat.

"Ah...honey, don't! Don't cry...." Sam wasn't aware of the endearment. It was gut-wrenching to know that she was so miserable and that he couldn't do a thing to help her. Her hand found his and wiggled into it. Her fingers curled around his thumb. "Is it the pain that's making you cry?"

"Y-yes, and I'm so . . . l-lonely—"

"You're not alone, honey. I'm here. You need only to call me if you want something."

"I know, but—" Her voice broke on a sob.

"But what?" he murmured, his fingers slipping beneath her heavy dark hair to rub the nape of her neck.

"But . . . you don't want to be h-here," she choked.

"Have I said that?"

"N-no."

"Elizabeth, I want to be here. I want to help you any way I can."

"You've got . . . obligations, and I'm keeping you from them."

"Nothing that can't wait."

"But . . . I've been pushed off on you." She took a gulping breath, and when she spoke again, her voice was a tortured whisper. "Netta wanted to get rid of me, and now Stephen's stuck with me." She turned her face into the pillow, and sobs shook her shoulders. "He's too much of a gentleman . . . to . . . to go back on his word even if he doesn't want me."

"Ah . . . honey, Steve wants you. He was very concerned about you." Sam grasped her shoulders and pulled her into his arms. "A man would be crazy *not* to want you." He held her to him, stroking her soothingly, his cheek against her wet one. "Ssh . . . don't cry."

"Sam, hold me, p-please."

Her hand crept up to his shoulder, and her arm circled his neck. She clung to him almost frantically, her wet lashes, her wet cheeks and her soft, wet lips against his throat. Her trusting acceptance, coming into his arms with only the nightdress between them, was the most pleasurable thing that had happened to him.

Tightening his arms, he hauled in a ragged, shallow breath. An incredibly strong feeling flooded through him. He wanted nothing more than to hold her and relieve her despair. He couldn't move; he couldn't think. All he could do was savor the sensation of holding her, feeling the softness of her breasts against his chest. The palm of his hand moved searchingly over her back, feeling her ribs, her spine, her shoulder blades through the material of her gown. He wanted to touch every inch of this body that had suddenly become precious to him.

"Ssh . . . it's all right, love," he crooned. "You're not alone. This will be over soon, and we'll be on our way again."

Sam closed his eyes and brushed his lips across her brow. A tremor shook his powerful body as her face moved against his neck. It wasn't passion he was feeling; it was something deeper, stronger, something that filled that empty place in his heart. *I don't want to fall in love with you, Elizabeth Caldwell.* He nuzzled the line of her hair, his lips moving over her brow to sip the tears in her eyes. Her breath stopped. He waited for her to pull away, but she didn't.

"Have you k-kissed a lot of women?" He felt her lips move as the barely audible words were whispered against his neck.

"Not a lot, but a few."

"I'm j-just what you said. I'm a prissy old m-maid."

"No, you're not!" He moved his lips across her brow, wondering how he could have been so cruel to say that to her.

"It's true."

"I'm sorry I said that, honey."

"No one's ever kissed me or held me like this. No one's ever called me honey but my father, and that was a long time ago. I'm almost twenty-six years old, Sam, and no man has ever called me honey."

Drained and completely vulnerable, Elizabeth knew she was saying things to him in the dark that she could never say to him in the light of day, but once she started, she couldn't seem to stop. The words just tumbled out.

"Not even Stephen?"

"No. I don't think he ever wanted to kiss me like a lover. He always kissed me like a brother kisses a little sister."

"That isn't the way I want to kiss you! I want to kiss you like a man kisses a beautiful, desirable woman. I want it so much I can hardly stand it. But I won't . . . unless you want me to." Sam's heart sang and beat in a rhythm that barely allowed him to breathe.

"If we kiss like that, will you think that I'm . . . vulgar and loose?"

"How could I think that when you're the sweetest, bravest woman I've ever known?" he whispered brokenly.

"Then, kiss me, please."

Elizabeth tilted her face to his, refusing to question this irrational need for the kiss of this strange, tough, exciting man who was so intensely alive. His arms were a safe haven where nothing could harm her, where she would never be afraid or lonely. He felt so good, so strong. Even his breath on her face was strong, warm and sweet. Tears for all that she had missed in her life rolled from the corners of her eyes.

"'Lizabeth, honey, don't cry. It tears me up!"

He lightly brushed his lips across hers. That's all it was, a simple, light caress, but she felt a trembling in his strong arms. His lips remained on the corner of her mouth, his nose pressed to the soft, wet flesh of her cheek. He waited, wanting more but refusing to seize the sweetness of her mouth again until it was offered. Then his lips moved across hers in another fleeting kiss, as if they couldn't keep away.

"Don't tease ... me—" she whispered pleadingly.

"I'm not! Oh, I'm not! I'm afraid I'll scare you if I kiss you the way I want to."

"I want ... I want—"

His lips closed over hers, and his arms tightened. For long moments he simply savored the feel of her mouth— soft, wet, warm, sweet and so ... innocent. It melted against his. In spite of his hunger, he didn't demand greater intimacy.

"Honey, you're ... so sweet," he murmured, then carefully fitted his mouth over hers again.

For a time their lips clung and there was only their mingled breathing. Then he raised his lips, only to lower them again, rocking his mouth from side to side over hers. She sighed, and her hand moved to the back of his head to increase the pressure of the kiss. Her lips parted just a little, and the tip of his tongue moved slowly between them. When it was over, Sam moved his lips and buried them in the softness beneath her ear. His breath came in and out deeply.

"Thank you."

For what? he thought. He couldn't believe she had thanked him for kissing her.

"Did you like it?"

"Very much. Your mustache is so ... soft." She cupped her palm against his cheek. "May I touch it?" He lifted his head, covered her hand with his and moved it to his mouth. Holding her fingers to his lips, he kissed them before he released them. Her fingertips moved lightly over the silky hair above his lip, then over his cheekbone to his brows, then to the mustache. "Do you wear it all the time?"

"I have for a long time. Usually in the winter, during the cutting season, I grow a beard to protect my face from the cold. By spring I look like a grizzly bear."

"I'll knit a face stocking for you."

"I'll hold you to that."

"Does Jessie like it?"

"The mustache? I've never asked her."

"Are you going to marry her?"

"Did Burley talk to you about Jessie?"

"A little. He said you were suited to each other, or words to that effect."

"I suppose he's right, just like you and Stephen are suited to one another."

"Mr. Owens is fond of her. He thinks she's pretty."

"Yes, Jessie is pretty. Her hair is like a flaming sunset, and her eyes are bright blue. She laughs easily. I think every man in Nora Springs is half in love with her."

"How old is she?"

"I don't know. She must be eighteen or nineteen by now. Her father worked for us. He was killed one winter during the cutting season. Since then my pa and I have looked after her and her mother."

"Do you . . . love her?"

"I suppose I do. I've known her since she was just a little squirt."

"Like I've known Stephen."

"Yes, like you've known Stephen."

"Have you kissed her like this?"

"I've never kissed anyone like *this*."

"My life is half over, Sam," she said sadly, and pulled away so she could look at his face.

"What makes you say that?"

"Most women have a husband and children by the time they're my age."

"You will . . . soon." Then feeling a desperate need to change the subject, he said, "I should change the poultice. I have a fresh one ready." He eased her down on the bed, feeling a chill where her warm body had lain against his chest.

"I hope you won't have to light the lamp."

"I'll put a few sticks of kindling on the fire. That will give me enough light."

He worked quickly. After applying the resin poultice, he poured hot water from the teakettle over a towel and tested it against his face to be sure it wasn't too hot. Then he put it in place and covered her. She lay with her face buried in the pillow, her arms in a circle around her head.

"Are you going to bed?"

"I might as well if there's nothing more I can do for you. Do you want a drink of water?"

"No, thank you. The night is so long. I wondered if . . . if you'd lie down here by me so I can hold your hand. No one will know. It isn't as if we'd be doing anything wrong."

Once over the initial shock of her request, Sam said in a matter-of-fact tone, "Sure, I'll get my blanket."

He lay on the far edge of the bed and pulled his blanket over him. He turned on his side to face her and took her hand in his when she reached out to him. Holding her hand tightly in his, he lay staring at the shape of her in the darkness. Although there were more than two feet between them, he feared she could hear the pounding of his heart.

"Tell me about your life out here. Where did you go to school?" Her voice was a soft, intimate whisper.

"When I was twelve, Pa took me to Missoula to go to school and found a room for me in the home of a teacher.

I was there five years. I thought a lot of Miss Theiss, and I think she was fond of me.''

"Didn't you go home?"

"For a month in the summer, but I wanted to finish my schooling so I could get back up north and work with Pa. Miss Theiss was willing to give me extra lessons, and she saw to it that I worked hard. Pa and I started the lumber business my first year out of school. I handle the logging end. I like the quiet of the forest. Since Pa likes working with machinery, he runs the sawmill.''

Sam talked on, telling her about the logging camp and how the town of Nora Springs grew around the mill. He was careful to leave out any reference to his mother and the sadness he and his father felt after she left them. He stopped talking when he realized she had fallen asleep.

After a while the fire died down, and only glowing coals remained. Sam lay listening to the regular breathing of the woman beside him. He had to be sure she was sleeping soundly before he could take care of a chore he must do in the dark because it would be too humiliating to her if she should see him doing it.

Sam gradually loosened his thumb from the grip of her fingers and eased himself off the bed. He slipped on his boots, then went quietly to the side of the bed and pulled out the chamber pot. He carried it to the door and let himself out into the dark, crisp night.

A short time later he returned, slipped the chamber pot under the bed and banked the fire. For a long while he stood staring at the glowing coals. He felt exhilarated, frustrated and aroused when he thought of holding Elizabeth in his arms. Thinking about her soft breasts against his chest and her lips on his neck caused his stomach to knot with savage want.

His logic told him that he should be putting up barriers between him and this woman, instead of tearing them down. She was a city woman like the one who had broken his father's heart, *and* she was his brother's future wife.

Sam muttered a curse. It was too late. She had seeped into his soul. She had woven a spell, so gracefully, so innocently, and there was no escape. He started for the bunk on the opposite wall, then paused and looked toward the bed. *The night is so long. No one will know.* Her whispered words came back to haunt him. He pulled off his boots and shirt, and closed his mind to the pain he was inviting.

As quietly as possible, he lay on the bed beside her. When he reached for her hand, hers met it halfway and her fingers curled tightly around his thumb.

Elizabeth's eyes felt as if they were full of gravel when she opened them and looked around the room. It was day, according to the light coming through the small window and through the doorway. The door had been left partly open. She had lain in the same position for so long that the upper part of her body was protesting. The lower part was terribly aware of the pain that tormented her flesh.

Several times during the night she had awakened, aware that Sam was beside her on the bed. One time she thought she was alone and had reached blindly for him. He was there. In the light of day, what had happened between them seemed like a dream. Had it been a dream? No. She felt her lips. She had been kissed. She had asked him to kiss her.

"I'm not going to be embarrassed about it!" she muttered. "I'm not!" She had wanted the kiss, craved it, and she was entitled to it. At the time it had seemed a right thing to do. It hadn't hurt anyone. And now she had a memory to carry with her into a future that was likely to be loveless.

Sam pushed the door open farther and came in. He had the ax in his hands and was carefully wiping the blade on a cloth. Their eyes caught and held. He smiled.

"So you're awake. I thought you were going to sleep all day." He set the ax behind the stove and came to the bed. "We're going to lance that thing this morning, then you'll feel a lot better," he said confidently.

"When will you do it?"

"In a little while. I removed the poultice while you were sleeping. Do you want me to help you get up before I go outside?" He spoke so gently and with such a caring look in his dark eyes that she wanted to cry.

"No, thank you. I can manage."

"Take your time, but stay next to the bed. I don't want you trying to make it to the washstand and keeling over." His mouth smiled, his eyes teased. "I'd have to mop you up off the floor."

"I've got to wash. I can hardly stand myself."

"Later. After we finish with that thing on your sit-down place, I'll bring you a pan of warm water and you can wash and change your gown if you want to."

From the doorway Sam looked at her. Her hair was a black cloud of ringlets, her face almost as pale as the white pillow she lay on. She looked so slim, so fragile, but her eyes, staring into his through thick black lashes, were a startling emerald green, and they showed not a trace of regret or shame for what had happened between them. He dragged his gaze away from her, releasing them from the spell that bound them together, and went out the door.

After it closed behind him, he stood on the step and breathed deeply. He had expected her to be embarrassed, unable to look at him, maybe offering excuses for her "irrational behavior." But she wasn't at all ashamed of what had happened between them. He felt as if a tremendous burden had fallen from his shoulders.

Sam went to the shed and stooped to look once again at the footprint he had discovered that morning. It had been made by a down-at-the-heel boot sometime during the night. The rain the day before had left the ground soft but not muddy. Whoever it was had let the bar gate down and failed to put it back. Had someone intended to steal the horses or just let them out to draw Sam away from the cabin? It was an old trick. Sam's horse had been too smart to leave a place where he was given a measure of oats each day, and the mare had stayed with him.

Irritated with himself because he had been careless, Sam went to the front of the cabin and looked down the narrow, seldom-used track. Two freight wagons had passed the cabin yesterday. Sam had talked to both drivers. One had met Burley and Jim on the upper trail and had told them the bridge at Bitterroot would be fixed by the time they got there. The other freighter was heading north. He had said the bridge above Haggerty's was being repaired and that the freighters waiting to cross had pitched in to help.

It worried Sam that someone was sneaking around near the cabin. If the man was on the up-and-up, he would have come to the cabin and asked for a meal or permission to sleep in the shed. Sam didn't want to leave Elizabeth alone, or he would have saddled up and scouted the area for more signs. The best thing to do, he decided, was to get back on the main road. He decided that they would go tomorrow or the next day. Elizabeth could lie on the buggy seat. He would ride his horse and lead the mare pulling the buggy. Once they reached the stage road, they could stay at the stage stations and wait with the freighters for the bridges to be repaired.

He sat on the step, took a small whetstone from his pocket, spit on it and began sliding the blade of his knife over it. The thought of cutting into Elizabeth's flesh was so repulsive to him that he refused to think about it.

After Sam went out, Elizabeth threw back the blanket and moved backward off the bed. She stood for a moment before she reached under the bed for the chamber pot, moving it carefully. When she removed the lid, she was surprised to see that it was empty. She straightened and covered her face with her hands. *Sam had emptied it while she slept.* Merciful heaven! She had shared an intimacy with this man during the past few days that she hadn't shared with anyone before. *Sam. Samuel.* Just thinking his name caused crazy things to happen to her heartbeat.

Her hair brushed and tied with a ribbon, Elizabeth lay on her side watching the door. When Sam rapped, she called out and he opened the door. He didn't look at her immediately, but went to rummage in their supplies. Then he looked at her, really looked at her, and she at him.

A part of her wanted him to cross the few feet that separated them and lift her in his arms. Then logic prevailed. It would be insanity to fall in love with Sam Ferguson. They had nothing in common. She had a lot in common with Stephen. They were used to the same life, and they were fond of each other. Then, she asked herself, why couldn't she see Stephen's face clearly in her mind when all she had to do was close her eyes and she could see Sam's? Maybe it was because he was such a raw, sexual, masculine man, and she was attracted to the forbidden. Or maybe it was because she was totally dependent on him. The thought was immediately rejected.

Gratitude had nothing to do with the feelings she had for him. There was more, much more, to Sam than his raw good looks. He was as much Eleanor's son as Stephen was. His exterior was rougher. He had been terribly hurt when the mother he adored left him, and he used his hell-raising image to cover the deep and lasting hurt.

"I'm not going to drink it—" Sam was speaking and holding up a bottle of whiskey "—but maybe you should. If you're drunk enough you'll not feel the pain."

Chapter Eleven

Elizabeth wondered at Sam's silence as he tore strips of cloth from her petticoat and sterilized his knife in the pan of water boiling on the cook stove. She had no dread of what he was going to do. The pain had been with her for days, and this was the means of getting rid of it. She turned on her stomach and arranged her gown and the blankets to preserve as much modesty as possible.

When Sam came to her, his mouth was stretched in a smile, but there was little humor in the expression.

"Ready for the big operation?"

His words were light, but she could see the agony in his eyes, could feel it as if it were her own. She wanted to put her arms around him and tell him that it was all right, that she understood his reluctance to perform the distasteful task. She reached out her hand, and his fingers tightened over hers.

"I'm ready. And, Sam, don't worry about hurting me."

He released her fingers to loop a dark curl over her ear before he bent and placed a light kiss on her cheek.

"I'll be as quick as I can," he promised, his voice huskier than usual.

"I know."

Elizabeth circled her head with her arms and buried her face in the pillow. When Sam folded back the blanket, she felt the cool air on her hot flesh. She gathered herself for the pain. It came suddenly and sooner than she expected. It was so sharp that she gasped and bit into the pillow, bracing herself for more pain. Sam's fingers touched her, squeezed gently, moved and touched again. Then he was swabbing with a whiskey-soaked cloth. She turned to see the side of his face. His jaw was clenched, and the vein in his temple was throbbing.

"It's over, honey! It's over! Now all I have to do is clean up. It'll not hurt so much now."

He splashed more whiskey on the cloth and continued to dab. She could feel the sharp bite of the whiskey, but the sting was nothing compared to what she had suffered. He made a quick trip to the fireplace and tossed the cloth he had used into the fire. The relief was evident on his face and in his eyes when he looked at her.

"That wasn't so bad, was it?"

"It happened so fast, I didn't have time to dread it."

"I'm a damn good surgeon! I just might give up logging and practice medicine. Is there something else you want cut, Miss Caldwell? I'm at your service."

"You've let your success go to your head, Doctor."

"That I have." His relieved smile showed white teeth against the bronze of his face.

"What now?"

"I'm wondering how in the hell we're going to keep a bandage on that part of you. You should get up and move around a little. We've got to get all the matter cleaned out before that cut I made heals over."

"Where did you practice medicine, Doctor?"

"Ferguson logging camp, five miles north of Nora Springs, in Montana Territory, ma'am."

"Then you haven't heard about the new glue tape they use for holding bandages in place?"

"No! Do you have some?"

"No." Laughter danced in her eyes when he lifted his to the ceiling in a gesture of exaggerated frustration. "But leave the bandage to me. I'll rig up something if I'm given a little privacy."

"We can arrange that." He showed her the stack of cloths he had folded into pads. "Dampen one of these with the whiskey. The whiskey will help keep down infection."

"Oh, my! You do know a lot about medicine."

"Of course, I know about medicine. And I'll have none of your sass, woman. Treat me with a little more respect or I'll not fix your breakfast when I come back."

After he left, Elizabeth lay for a long time with a smile on her lips. Never in her life had she indulged in such nonsensical banter with a man. Sam was charmingly witty when he wanted to be, and she had responded with whatever came to mind without a thought of decorum.

She got off the bed and stood for a moment, surprised that most of the pain was gone. Plenty was left, but it wasn't the agonizing pain of before. When her head stopped feeling fuzzy, she pawed in her trunk and found a pair of tight-fitting knit drawers that she wore in the wintertime. She searched in her valise until she found a small box that contained safety pins and selected two. Then, holding the pad in place with one hand she pulled the drawers over her hips with the other.

By the time Elizabeth had pinned the pad in place she was worn out. Hanging on to the side of the bed, she waited until her breathing slowed, then reached for her robe. She was not going to spend the day in bed even if she had to stand up all day. She wanted to wash, dress and make herself tidy. She refused to admit that she wanted to look nice for Sam.

Elizabeth was brushing her hair, her arm feeling as if the brush weighed fifty pounds, when Sam knocked on the door.

"Come in," she called, and turned her back, conscious of her appearance now that she was on her feet. No one except her maid had ever seen her in such disarray.

"How are you feeling?"

Elizabeth heard him cross to the stove and open the door to the firebox.

"Much better, thank you. But I'm weak from lying in bed."

"And you haven't eaten enough to keep a bird alive." He came up behind her and reached for the hairbrush. "Hold on to the bedpost. I'll do that."

"I can do it."

"I'm the doctor. Remember?" He started at her forehead and brushed all the way down to the end of her hair, which hung several inches below her waist. She held the bedpost with both hands and tilted her head back. After several long swipes with the brush, she sighed with pure pleasure. "Feel good?" His voice was like a caress, low and intimate.

"Oh, yes. It feels heavenly."

"You have beautiful hair."

"It's too thick, too curly—"

"I don't think so."

"I hated it while I was growing up," she rushed to say. "One of my mother's friends had a little girl with beautiful blond hair. When she got mad at me she'd tell me my hair looked like a horse's tail with cockleburs in it. I wanted to scratch her eyes out."

"Why didn't you?" His laughter was husky and deep.

Elizabeth glanced at him over her shoulder. He had lifted a handful of her hair and was staring at it with the hungry look of a small boy looking into a jar of peppermint sticks. She dragged her eyes to her hands and stared at them while she pondered his expression.

After what seemed to Elizabeth a very long time, he began to brush again. She loved the scrape of the bristles against her temple. When he placed his hand on her shoulder to steady her, her fluttering heart felt as if it would jump right out of her breast.

"You're very good at brushing a lady's hair," she said when she felt she could keep her voice light. "You must have had a lot of practice."

"I've never brushed a lady's hair except my..." His words faded as memories of standing behind his mother's chair, brushing her lustrous, honey-colored hair, flashed into his mind. *Ah, Sammy, that feels so good! That's my boy. Come sit on Mama's lap....*

The brushing stopped. She turned to look at him. His expression told her a battle was raging inside him. His brows had drawn together, and he was looking at her as if she was his enemy.

Abruptly, he tossed the hairbrush on the bed. "That's all I have time for. I've things to do." Quick strides took him to the door.

Once outside, Sam went toward the shed and the pole corral. He leaned his arms on the top rail and looked toward the mountains, where the clouds hovered threateningly. The wind that struck his face had a bite to it, but he didn't notice. He swore, using words he had not thought of for a long while. When he exhausted that vocabulary, he hit the rail with his clenched fist.

He loved her! He had lost his heart, suddenly and irrevocably!

The realization had been there all the time, but he had to acknowledge it. He was totally, recklessly in love with his brother's intended bride—a woman who was as much like Eleanor as two peas in a pod.

The awful part of it was that it was not the kind of love he'd known once or twice when he was younger, the randy kind of love centered in his groin and disappearing once he got the woman into bed. This love had crept up on him and sunk deeply into his heart and mind. It was the cherishing kind of love that made him want to be with her every minute of the day and night, both mentally and physically. He wanted to hold her in his arms, plant his children in her warm, fertile body, keep her by his side forever.

He swore again. He should have known it was happening. He had not been able to think of anything else since he had met her.

Closing his eyes, he could see her as vividly as if she were standing in front of him. Her eyes were a bright, clear, emerald green when she was smiling, stormy green when she was angry, glassy green when filled with tears... Shifting uneasily, he tried to shut out the images, but they refused to go from his mind.

He knew that a woman like Elizabeth had no place in his life. They were as different as night and day, rain and sunshine, silk and steel. When they reached Nora Springs, they would say goodbye. Stephen would take her to Saint Louis, where they would pick up the threads of their lives. Sam would stay in Montana, logging in the winter, working at the mill in the summer. Would he forget her when she was gone? Would she be only a pleasant memory?

On his way to the cabin he realized it would not be any easier for him to forget Elizabeth than it had been for his father to forget Eleanor. He had not understood the extent of his father's grief at the time, but he did now. He didn't want to feel the pain, but it was inevitable.

Elizabeth washed her body the best she could without stripping completely. It was wonderful to be clean again and rid of the throbbing ache and accompanying worry that had plagued her. The soreness that lingered was irritating, but not painful.

After dusting herself with powder, she put on fresh underclothes and an ash-gray cotton dress with a white V neck collar. The sleeves were long, the bodice fit the curves of her breasts perfectly, and the skirt was full. The comfort of being without a corset was spoiling her. She dismissed the thought with a shrug, a puckered frown, then a sigh. When she reached Nora Springs, she would once again be forced into the mold of propriety. Stephen would expect it.

She searched in her trunk for something warm and pulled out a frothy three-cornered shawl the color of her eyes. Flinging it across her shoulders, she tied the ends in a knot just below the neckline of her dress.

Moving around seemed to strengthen her. She paced the small room, then rested on the bed when she began to feel shaky. Her empty stomach drew attention to itself. A handful of raisins staved off the hunger pangs for a while. She pondered whether or not she should attempt to prepare a meal and decided to wait for Sam. It seemed to her he had stayed away for an unusually long time.

When he rapped on the door, her heart picked up a beat. She smoothed her skirt with the palms of her hands and adjusted the shawl to frame the collar of her dress.

He entered, hung his hat on the peg and added a few sticks of wood to the coals on the grate. He seemed totally unaware of her. As her eyes traveled over the lean, powerful length of him, he suddenly turned to face her. He was scowling. His eyes were hard, his mouth firm. He looked at her as if seeing her for the first time. She swallowed, trying to think of something to say.

"With your hair pinned back like that you look like an old maid—or a peeled onion."

The attack was so sudden that she blinked at the shock of it. She could feel the color draining from her face and caught herself just in time to prevent her teeth from biting into her lower lip. An invisible protective shield slid suddenly into place, a shield developed to deal with Netta. She couldn't give him the satisfaction of seeing how much his cruel words had hurt.

"I'm sorry if my looks displease you." Her voice was calm, even. She hardly recognized it.

"Take it down and throw away those damn hairpins. While you're with me you'll look like a woman should—soft, pleasant to look at, and not like a skinned rabbit. When you're with Stephen you can fix yourself any damn way you please."

He strode to the stove, banged a big spider skillet on the iron top and began slicing strips from a slab of bacon.

Elizabeth turned to the window and blinked rapidly to stave off the tears she felt stealing into her eyes. Why had he turned on her so suddenly? What had she done to earn such contempt? She lifted her hands to remove the pins, wondering why she was obeying him, why she wanted to please him. With her hair hanging down her back, she massaged her temples with her fingertips for a moment before she went to her trunk, put the brass hairpins in a small box and pulled out a length of white ribbon. She slid it beneath her hair at the nape of her neck and tied it loosely. When she turned, her features were carefully arranged to show no expression. She didn't speak until she was sure there would be no quiver in her voice.

"May I help?"

"No, you may not. You don't know the first thing about how to cook on a stove like this."

"I may surprise you."

"It would surprise me if you didn't burn yourself."

"I'm not helpless—"

"Stop jawing, Elizabeth, and sit down."

Her tongue stuck to the roof of her mouth for a moment before she could answer. "Y-you know I can't."

She went to the window to look out, seeing nothing but watery trees and gray sky. Couldn't their unspoken truce have lasted just a little longer? Regret and humiliation fought for control of her thoughts. For a terrible moment she could do no more than stand and stare through the small glass pane.

Sam came up behind her. She didn't know he was there until he cupped her shoulders with his hands.

"I'm sorry, 'Lizabeth. I didn't mean to hurt you. I'm just a bear at times." He made a disgusted sound.

"It's all right." A lie. "You didn't hurt me." Another lie.

Her words and the forced lightness of her voice cut him deeply. "Then look at me." He tried to turn her to face him, and she resisted the pressure.

"Please don't. Even an old m-maid has her pride."

"Oh, Lord!" He lowered his face to her shoulder and rested it there against her neck. His hands moved up and down her forearms, lightly stroking. When he tried to turn her again, her body was unresisting. He tilted her face to his. He had dreaded seeing tears, but what he saw hurt him even more. Her eyes were wide and . . . empty. "Don't look at me like that," he whispered urgently. She shivered, and he realized how tightly she was holding on to her emotions.

"I'm sorry."

"And don't ever say you're sorry to me again!" The words exploded from him; his hands clasped her shoulders in a tight, unrelenting grip. "Hear me?"

"Yes. I'm not deaf."

He stared into her calm face, his eyes caressing every feature before looking into hers.

"'Lizabeth! Oh, God! What am I going to do?" His voice cracked and his features twisted in agonized despair. Breath hissed from between clenched teeth as he stared into her face.

The hands on her arms slid slowly over her back and crossed. He pulled her against him, locking her to him with gentle strength. Elizabeth closed her eyes against the impact of her body against his. This was insanity. She should move away while there was still time. Then, quite unexpectedly, there was no more time. The palms of her hands were against his chest, feeling the strong beat of his heart. She could feel his breath stirring the curls at her temple. She could smell the masculine odor of his body. She was tired. Tired of being strong, tired of being alone. It felt so good to be able to rest against him—just for a moment. She struggled to keep from blurting that she never wanted to leave this safe haven.

He bent his head. His lips moved lightly across her temple and into her hair. They stood that way for a long time. When he finally spoke, it was in a whisper against her ear.

"You're a beautiful woman, Elizabeth. Beautiful and sweet and proud and spirited. You're all the things a man wants in the woman he plans to spend his life with."

"Sam—"

"Don't say anything, honey. Let me say these things while I can. I'll never be rich. I'll never be anything but what I am—a woodsman. I spend a good part of the year in the forest among men, cussing and fighting and getting drunk on Sunday. I love this country and wouldn't trade places with Stephen for all the money in the world. I'm what you said, a hell raiser. What you need is a gentleman." He moved his hand under her hair and curved it around her neck. His hard fingers stroked behind her ear.

"Yes," she agreed in a dreary, low voice. "I need someone, but no one needs me."

"That's where you're wrong, honey," he said, then went on determinedly. "I'll never forget this time with you." He clasped her head tightly in his two hands, burying his fingers in her hair. He tilted her face and looked into green pools, wet and shiny. His heart thumped with the pain of lost dreams. "We've got to leave just as soon as you can travel. I've got to get you to Nora Springs—to Stephen."

"You're anxious to get back to Jessie?"

"Yes," he said slowly, his eyes moving hungrily over her face then away. "I'm anxious to get back to Jessie."

The climate inside the cabin was as bleak as the weather outside. The sky had darkened to a smoky gray that had the look of late evening instead of midday. The noon meal was eaten in almost total silence. Afterward, Sam insisted that she lie down and rest. He went out and cut wood until he had more than replenished the homesteaders' supply. Then, taking a pair of buckskin breeches from his pack, he went to the shed.

Time crawled for Elizabeth. When she could stand the inside of the cabin no longer, she put on her coat, covered her head with a shawl and went out. It was the first time she had been outside the cabin since they arrived. She walked toward the almost overgrown track, turned and scrutinized the squat and comfortable-looking cabin. A plume of smoke came from the chimney, drifted upward and was lost. With all her heart she envied the woman who lived there, envied her preparing the meals for her man, washing his clothes in the black pot, sitting with him beside the fire in the evenings, sharing with him what had occurred during the day.

When she and Stephen were married, they would live in New York at least part of the time. She would entertain the wives of his business associates—women like her stepmother, who scratched and clawed for social recognition. At the top of their list of priorities was the need to be seen with someone more socially prominent than they. The highlights of their lives were invitations to gatherings of the rich.

Those people did not even know what life was about. *This* was life—carving something out of a new land for the generations that followed. What in the world had caused Eleanor to give up all this for the shallow life of ease in Saint Louis?

Elizabeth began to fantasize about morning glories planted beside the door, a rope swing hanging from the limb of an oak tree for the children, a garden that included tomatoes and green beans that she would can in glass jars for winter meals, Sam coming home after a day's work to grab her up in his arms, whirl her around and tell her he'd missed her.

Why was she thinking these foolish thoughts, dreaming these foolish dreams? They were not for her. Sam would do these things with Jessie by his side. Tomorrow they would leave this cabin in the mountains. She looked at it for a long time, imprinting it in her memory for future dreams.

Elizabeth went into the cabin, her mood as dreary as the day. She changed the bandage on the boil, hurrying before Sam returned. In light of what had passed between them, she wondered how she could have bared her backside to him. She washed, then prowled through the supplies. There were flour, lard and dried apricots. Unable to stand another idle minute, she rolled up the sleeves of her dress, tied the remainder of one of her petticoats around her waist and went to work.

An hour later, when Sam came in the door carrying something over his arm, he stopped in open-mouthed astonishment.

"What in the hell are you doing?"

Elizabeth, flushed from the heat of the stove, glanced at him briefly then looked at the skillet. "Making pies," she said matter-of-factly as she lifted one out of the pan and onto a dish, adding it to the ones lying on a cloth on the table. "I'm making enough to last for several days. They keep well if cooled first and wrapped in a cloth."

"I didn't know society women knew how to cook."

She ignored the slight disdain in his voice, added another pie to the hot grease and moved it around with a fork to make room for another.

"This one does. I was taught at boarding school so I could supervise a cook when I had a home of my own. Later, I was taught by our cook, Mary Lincoln—"

"Mary Lincoln?"

"Yes, Mary Lincoln. Her mother loved people who were involved in the war. She named one of her boys Abraham Lincoln and another Ulysses S. Grant and insisted he be called by his full name. Anyway, Mary Lincoln taught me to make pies. I spent a lot of time in her kitchen." Elizabeth didn't add that it was a good place to avoid her stepmother, who seldom went to the kitchen. The butler conveyed Netta's orders to Mary Lincoln.

"You do surprise me, Miss Caldwell. What else do you cook?"

"Curried rice, lobster bisque, chocolate mousse, marble cake with cherry frosting—"

"I shouldn't have asked," he said dryly.

"—fried chicken, cream gravy, buttermilk biscuits, pot roast with onions and cabbage rolls, apple cobbler—"

"Well, I'll be damned!"

She glanced at him, smiled at the pleased look on his face and flipped the pies over without as much as a single splash.

"What's that? What have you done to your britches?"

"I'm trying to make something for you to sit on. I've stuffed the legs with straw. I'll tie the top and the bottom—"

"You're making a ring! That's a wonderful idea. How did you ever think of it?"

Her praise washed over him like a cool breeze on a hot summer day. He hid his feelings behind mock arrogance.

"I'm no dummy! Miss Theiss told me so—once."

"Only once? I think I'd like your Miss Theiss. She didn't want you getting a swelled head."

"I figured you'd want to sit down sometime during the next few days."

"You figured right. Now, as soon as I finish these pies, I'm going to mash the beans you cooked yesterday, make them into patties and fry them in the skillet. I already have a pan of corn bread in the oven."

Chapter Twelve

Whether she liked it or not, she was in love with Samuel Ferguson.

The thought was not a sudden discovery, but rather a quiet inevitability, seeming to be something she had known all along. She was in love for the first time, and there was no possibility of a future for her and this man who had been propelled into her life and had turned it upside down. Their lives lay on different paths. Those paths had only converged briefly.

Sam cleaned up after the meal. He insisted. She eyed him as he swiftly and efficiently washed and greased the iron skillet and set it on the back of the stove. With the lamplight casting shadows over his lean features, she saw the strength of his jaw, the curves of his cheekbones, the flash of white teeth when he smiled at her, as he was doing now.

"Don't wrap up all those pies. I get another one for cleaning up."

"You had two already." Her eyes shone at him.

"I could have eaten them all."

"That's why I'm getting them out of your sight."

Why had she not noticed the velvet warmth in his voice? It eased down her spine and spread warmth all the way to her toes. Her heart threatened to stop, as if the sudden rush of happiness was more than she could bear. His nearness caused the tension that had lurked in her stomach all evening to tighten. A flush came to her cheeks. She bowed her head, grateful for the loose curls that covered her face.

She wanted to touch him, slide her hands over his shoulders and feel his strength. She wanted the magic of being held in the haven of his arms as he had held her the night before. She wanted to relive that time, return to that heaven she'd had for only a moment.

"You're awfully quiet. Are you all right?"

His hand on her shoulder and his words brought her to the present with a jarring thud. What a fool she was, sitting here daydreaming. She prayed that he didn't know that his touch caused her heart to race in undignified delight, or that it awakened anew her wild hopes and dreams. The warmth of his touch lingered after he took his hand away.

"I'm fine, thank you. Just a little tired."

"You did a lot today. How's your...sit-down place?"

"Better." Watching him, she had almost forgotten it.

"Good. We'll leave in the morning. It'll take us a full day to get back onto the main road and to Underwood's Station. Are you up to it?"

"Yes. I can drive the buggy."

"Not the first day. I'll ride my horse and lead the gray. That way you can lie on the seat and rest."

"We'll have pie to eat on the way."

At first all she had wanted to do was to get to Nora Springs and Stephen. Now she wished the journey would last forever. Leaving here would be heartbreaking. This was the last evening she would spend alone with him. Her eyes skimmed over the room—his hat on the peg, his rifle in the corner, her trunk beside the bed—imprinting the scene firmly on her mind. It had to last forever.

"I'd like to clean the cabin—leave it as we found it," Elizabeth said.

"We will."

"And leave payment for using it."

"It isn't expected."

"But I want to."

"I'll take care of it." He lifted his gun belt from the peg, strapped it around his waist and settled the gun against his thigh. "I'd better see about the horses." He put on his vest. "I want to see the pad you take off the boil."

"Why?"

"So I can tell if it's draining."

"I mean why wear the gun to go see about the horses?"

"Habit. A man gets used to wearing a gun in this country. He puts it on before he puts on his hat."

Elizabeth nodded, accepting the explanation. His eyes caught hers and held them for a timeless moment with a strange intensity. She wasn't sure what she saw in their velvet depths before he slipped out the door, but it wasn't happiness.

Elizabeth shook the thought from her mind and slipped off her dress. The boil was not nearly as sore as before. She blindly probed the area with her fingertips, then washed it with a whiskey-soaked cloth and pinned a clean pad in her knit drawers. In her nightdress and robe, she packed her clothes, leaving out the heavy shirt, blouse and coat she'd been wearing when they came to the cabin. How long had they been here? How could a person's life change so drastically in such a short time?

Standing beside her trunk filled with clothes far more valuable than this cabin and the land surrounding it, she looked at the stark walls, the sparse furnishings, and took a deep, shuddering breath. Happiness was not possessions. Happiness was living rabbit poor if there were no other way, with someone she loved and who loved her.

Deep in her heart Elizabeth knew that what she felt for Sam was real and that it would be with her forever. It was more than sexual infatuation, although it was that, too. She liked the way he had accepted the responsibility for her even though he didn't want to. She liked his sense of fairness when he told her that he was a woodsman, would always be a woodsman, and that she would not fit into his life. She liked his sense of humor and his innate kindness. What she didn't like was the resentment or hatred he felt toward his mother. Knowing how sweet and loving Eleanor had been, Elizabeth couldn't believe that Eleanor had left Sam without good cause. She remembered Eleanor telling her that true love was when a person loved someone despite their faults, not because they had none. Eleanor had loved Joe Ferguson until her dying day, Elizabeth was sure of it.

Elizabeth suddenly wanted to leave a gift for the woman whose home would always hold such cherished memories, memories of Sam holding her, kissing her, calling her honey. She wanted the gift to be something pretty and frivolous. She untied her hat box and took out the gray felt hat with the pink silk rose dangling on the brim. Her gift should be something she liked herself, and this hat had always been her favorite.

She was removing the long hat pin, thinking to replace it with a different pin, when the door opened.

"Sam, I'm going—" Aghast, she stood stark still.

"Howdy."

She was in such a state of shock that she didn't realize who the man was at first. Then it dawned on her that it was the fat man who had talked to her a few days ago. On horseback he had seemed taller. On the ground he looked like a fat toad. His short arms made parentheses around the curved sides of his body. His eyes, made smaller by his fat cheeks, darted around as he waddled into the room, leaving the door ajar.

"Get out! You've no right to come in here."

"Button yore lip, sister." He held up his rifle. "This gives me all the leave I be needin'."

Fear knifed through her. Her stomach rolled, and bile rose in her throat.

"Sam..." It was a whimpering sound. Then, "Sam!" Her scream filled the room and echoed into the night. She darted for the doorway. The fat man's bulk filled it before she could reach it.

"Back off, missy!"

"What have you done to him?" Her voice was shrill with near hysteria.

"Nothin' yet. Ya behave yoreself or he'll get his head blowed off. Hear?" His eyes darted around the room and rested on the trunk. He wet his thin lips. "Yore a city woman, ain't ya?"

She could do no more than nod.

"Where'd ya come from, anyways?"

"Saint L-Louis."

"Where's that?"

"In Missouri."

The fat man lifted his head and sniffed. "Ya been cookin' up a batch o' grub. Fix me a bit."

Elizabeth stood as if she was nailed to the floor. "Where's Sam?"

"I'm thinkin' ya ain't hearin' me, sister. I'm wantin' ta eat some fixin's."

Elizabeth tossed the hat on the bed and slipped the hat pin in the pocket of her robe. The fat man reached out and grabbed her arm as she was trying to go around him.

"Get your filthy hands off me!" She tried to jerk her arm away and struck out at him with her other hand. He growled menacingly but let her go. She hurried to the other side of the table to put distance between them.

"I'm thinkin' ya don't know who's got the upper hand here, sister. I'll do more'n put my hands on ya 'fore we're done." He made an obscene movement with his hips that left no doubt about his intentions.

Elizabeth's face flamed then turned white. Her heart pounded as if it was trying to escape her body. Something had happened to Sam or he would be here. The door had been left open, so the fat man must be confident that Sam wouldn't come rushing in. Her stomach churned. She felt herself go cold. The next second she was burning hot. In a daze of fear, her hands trembling, she unwrapped the fried pies and set them on the table.

"Pie! Hell! It's a spell since I had me some pie." A dirty hand snatched one off the table and crammed it in his mouth. He chewed with his mouth open. It was sickening to see the food in his open mouth and the gluttonous look on his face. While he was eating, he watched her like a snake might watch a small frog.

"Take the pie and go!"

"I'm takin' ya with me when I go. I'm thinkin' ta make ya my woman."

"No!" she croaked. A fresh flush of fear raced through her body. She screamed, "Sam! S-Sam!"

At that instant Sam was shoved into the room. His holster was empty, and his hands were clasped behind his head. His eyes sought Elizabeth then moved quickly to the fat man, who was still shoving pie in his mouth. The man with the leather patch over his eye prodded Sam in the back with the barrel of his gun, urging him farther into the room.

"What's she hollerin' fer, Vernon? Ya ain't done nothin', have ya?"

Elizabeth dashed around the table toward Sam. The fat man dropped the pie and grabbed her arm with a greasy hand.

"No, ya don't."

"Let go of her!" Sam's angry shout filled the room. "Hurt her and I'll hunt you down like a mad dog and kill you!"

"Talks big, don't he?" The one-eyed man jabbed Sam with the gun barrel. "He's thinkin' he's gettin' off free 'n' clear, Vernon. Want me ta shoot him now?"

"Ya don't shoot till I tell ya. Hear? We got thinkin' ta do." Vernon's fat jowls quivered. "Stay back!" he commanded, and turned his rifle on Elizabeth when Sam took a step toward her. "Stay back or I shoot her purty face off."

Sam obediently froze. "Take what you want and get out!"

"Why, thanky." The one-eyed man leered at Elizabeth. "Ain't that good o' him, Vernon? I'll jist take this woman, seein' as how he's givin' thin's away. She be the sweetest-smellin' woman I ever smelt. 'Sides, I ain't never had me a highfalutin woman. Is they different from a regular woman, Vernon?"

Vernon ignored his companion, puckered his lips and spit toward the fireplace. His beady eyes danced over the room but returned to Sam.

"What ya doin' here, anyways?"

"Maybe we live here." Sam's eyes darted to Elizabeth and back.

"Hog waller! I know who lives here, and they ain't got no fancy buggy. This ain't a place a tony woman like her'd settle for."

"You don't know diddly squat," Sam said contemptuously. "You don't have the brains of a pissant or you'd know that every law man in the country will be on your tail if you harm her."

"Why's that, Mister Know-it-all? Why'd they know it was us what done it?" Vernon spat again.

"Because if we don't show up tomorrow my men will come looking for a fat bastard and a one-eyed son of a bitch. We took your measure when we met you on the trail. You're nothing but a couple of no-good scavengers."

"He's lying, Vernon. Want me ta shoot him in the leg?"

Elizabeth's heart dropped like a rock, and fear had a cold hand at her throat.

"Not yet." The fat man edged toward the trunk. "What ya got in there, sister?"

"C-clothes." Elizabeth's voice shook. Her eyes sought Sam's and found fleeting comfort in the calmness she saw there. His eyes held hers. He was trying to tell her not to get rattled, to stay calm, to wait.

"That ain't all ya got. Open it." The fat man wiped his mouth on his sleeve.

"We can take the whole kit and caboodle, can't we, Vernon? We can load it in the buggy." The one-eyed man's good eye was like a bottomless pit of evil.

"We ain't takin' that buggy, ya dunderhead! Everybody what's seen it knows it's her'n. It'd be like puttin' our head in a noose. I swear, Ollie, ya ain't got no sense at all.''

"I ain't likin' ya talkin' to me like that, Vernon. I do too have sense. Plenty a sense. You 'n' me is partners in this. Ya said we was.''

"I ain't sayin' no different. I'm sayin' we got to use our heads. Open the trunk, sister.'' Vernon pushed Elizabeth toward the trunk with the end of his rifle. Her terror-filled eyes sought Sam.

"Open it, honey,'' he said calmly. "Give the scums what they want so they'll get out. They're smelling up the place.''

"Ya sure talk big fer a man on the down side of a gun. I jist might shoot that thin' off 'tween yore legs afore I go, *then* shoot ya in the head.'' Ollie emphasized the words with pokes of the gun in Sam's ribs.

The words seeped into Elizabeth's mind as dread spread over her like a chill. Then sweat broke out on her forehead, gushed cold and clammy in her armpits. Dizzily, she reached out and steadied herself against the bedpost.

"Open the trunk.''

Elizabeth heard the order as if it was directed to someone else. *They were going to kill Sam!* What were their plans for her? If they killed Sam it wouldn't matter. The smelly, low-life bastards! This was too much! She'd not stand for it. They were not going to hurt him. He was worth a million of their kind. She was sure he'd not give up without a fight even if the odds were against him. He was staying calm, waiting his chance. If she could only give him one—

"Girly, I ain't askin' ya again.''

"What? What?'' Elizabeth looked dazed. She put her hand to her head as if she was going to faint.

"I ast ya to open that fancy trunk. A tony woman like ya is ain't travelin' stone broke."

"You want my money? Oh, for goodness sake! All this over money."

Beady eyes flicked with interest. "Have ya got money, sister?"

"A little."

"How much?"

"Not much," she said in a small, scared voice.

"Gol darn it! Don't ya be stallin' or I'll give Ollie the go-ahead to shoot yore man. How much?" Vernon's voice was shrill with impatience.

"Only about six or seven hundred. It's in a secret place." Her voice dropped to a weak whisper. "You won't find it unless I show you."

"D-dollars?" Vernon almost choked on the word.

"What's that? What's that she said, Vernon?" Ollie moved around Sam until the gun barrel was pressed beneath Sam's upraised arm. The face with the patch over the eye swiveled from Sam to the fat man. "Move," he snarled at Sam. "Move closer, so I can see. What'd she say?" he demanded again.

"Said she had money in a secret place," Vernon yelled angrily. "Now hush yore mouth!"

"Tell her to get it, or . . . or I'll blow his head off!"

"Oh . . ."

"Shut up, Ollie. Yore scarin' her. Get the money, missy. We ain't goin' to hurt ya none. We just be takin' it 'n' leavin' ya 'n' yore man be." Vernon spoke in an oily, placating tone.

"You'll not hurt . . . h-him if I s-show you?" Elizabeth asked in a thin little-girl voice.

"I'd promise on a Bible if'n I had one. I ain't ne'er killed nobody in all my born days. Ollie gets to runnin' off at the mouth, but he don't mean no harm."

Elizabeth let out what she hoped would pass as a sob of relief. She lifted the lid of the trunk, removed the tray, set it on her hatbox, looked straight into Sam's eyes and blinked rapidly.

The fat man grabbed her arm. "Get the money, gal."

"It's ... down there." She put one hand to her head as if she was going to faint; she put the other hand in her pocket.

"Where?"

"In the corner under the ... c-corsets is a little panel. Just slide it back." She moved to the side of the trunk.

A smile splitting his fat face, his eyes bright with greed, Vernon bent over the trunk and grabbed a fistful of clothing and threw it out. He held the rifle in one hand as he searched the bottom of the trunk with the other.

Elizabeth waited, the head of the hat pin snug against her palm. When the fat man chortled on finding the panel, she drove the pin into his bottom with all her strength. He screeched and reared into Sam, shoving Sam back a second before Ollie's gun discharged. The roar was thunderous. It reverberated through the room. The fat man fell screaming to the floor. Sam's arm sent Ollie flying across the room where he crashed against the solid plank door.

Elizabeth's fear turned to relief when she saw Sam on his feet. Within seconds it turned into anger and blossomed into full-grown rage. She grabbed the rifle Vernon had dropped and swung it at his head as he lay writhing on the floor. He screamed and tried to cover his head with his arms.

"You nasty, vile, stinking piece of horse dung! How dare you do this?" She whacked him sharply on the head with the rifle barrel. "Stupid, ignorant lout! I'd horse-whip you if I could." She hit him on the back with the rifle stock.

"Honey! Stop! It's over." Sam took the rifle from her hands and pulled her to him.

"Dirty swine! Fat pig! I'll k-kill him," she gasped.

"You've done enough to him."

"No! I want to shoot him!"

"You've given him something to remember. He'll not sit down for a while, and old One-eye here shot him in the leg when he stumbled against me. Besides that, he's going to have a hell of a headache from the pounding you gave him. Are you all right?"

"I'm all right. Just mad. Did they hurt you?" She moved her hands over his upper arms to his cheeks.

"No. I'm all right, thanks to you. Good Lord, sweet-heart, you're a regular buzz saw once you get going."

She looked around him. Ollie, out cold, was slumped against the door, his nose spouting blood.

"They're m-mean, rotten! They were going to shoot you, weren't they? I was so scared!" Her arms tightened around him. She pressed her face into the curve of his neck.

"I was scared for you, sweetheart. That bastard said the fat man would cut you if I didn't give up my gun. Lord! I'd have given him my head to keep you safe." They were both trembling, each scared for the other.

A loud wail came from the fat man on the floor. Sam glanced at him, then held Elizabeth away so he could look into her face.

"Are you sure you're all right? Really all right?" He gazed at her upturned face with a loving look in his eyes that went all the way to her soul.

"Yes." She shivered as what had occurred began to sink into her senses. Sam could have been killed! She could have lost him. Just to know he was not on earth, even if not with her, was more than she could bear. Gooseflesh rose on her arms. Her mouth was suddenly dry. She pressed the tip of her tongue to her lips to moisten them.

Sam bent his head and kissed her forehead as if she was as fragile as a dandelion puff. Then he walked her backward until she was against the wall beside the bed. She made no protest. He stroked her cheek with his fingertips and gave her a soft, sweet peck on the lips.

"Stay out of the way, honey, while I get this trash out of here."

She nodded and watched him with bright, anxious eyes. The bond between them had been made stronger. She knew it. He knew it. They had faced death together, fought together. His smile made her heart race with happiness, his voice melted away her fears, his arms were her haven. Whatever she needed, he seemed to supply it magically.

Sam tossed the rifle and the handgun on the bed. He jerked his own gun from the belt of the man slumped against the door and shoved it into his holster. The fat man was moaning and trying to reach his buttock, where about an inch of the hat pin was visible. Sam put his foot in the small of the man's back and jerked the pin out.

Vernon bellowed with pain.

"You drove this thing to the bone, 'Lizabeth." He held up the five-inch pin and tossed a glance at her white face. Her eyes were as large and as green as new oak leaves in the spring. Sam was astounded at what she had done. A strong surge of pride was reflected in his brown eyes.

The toad of man groaned again. Sam poked him in the ribs with the toe of his boot.

"You're lucky this hat pin didn't break. I think you should keep it as a reminder not to bother *tony* women." The grin he threw at Elizabeth was beautiful. Sam slipped the knife from the fat man's scabbard, slit his britches up the side and looked at the gunshot wound. "You're not hurt much. The shot went through the fleshy part of your thigh. Hell! You've got so much blubber on you it spattered fat all over the floor. I'll tie a rag around it. That's all the help you'll get here."

"I'm hurt! I'm bleedin'," Vernon moaned as Sam tied the cloth.

"I hope so. I hope you bleed all the way to Missoula. Now, get on your feet."

"I can't—"

"You will or I'll roll you out the door."

"Oh, God! Oh, Holy Mother! I'm hurt bad—"

"You'll hurt worse if I shoot you in the other leg."

The fat man grasped the end of the bed and pulled himself up. He stood, swaying. "Oh . . . my head," he whimpered.

Sam watched cold-eyed. "You're alive, but you won't be for long if you don't get the hell out. It goes against the grain to let you walk out of here, but if I ever see you again, if you even look at anything that's mine, I swear to God, I'll kill you." Sam was seething. "You'd better tell that to that one-eyed bastard friend of yours, too."

Ollie was on his hands and knees, shaking his head. Sam reached him in two strides, lifted him by the scruff of the neck with one hand, opened the door with the

other and flung him outside. Then he was beside the fat
man, shoving him toward the door.

"Our guns—"

"Hell! What guns? You don't have any guns, you filthy bush-bottomed clabberhead."

"We got ta have guns!" Vernon's voice rose hysteri-
cally. "There's bears 'n' cats—"

"You'd make a good meal for a cat. Now get the hell
out of here before I change my mind." An expression of
fury was on Sam's face. He put the sole of his foot
against the fat man's rear and shoved him out the doorway.

"Oh . . . Oh, sweet Jesus, help me—"

"Hush your blubbering. Bar the door, honey," he said
over his shoulder.

Elizabeth could hear Sam cursing and the two men
begging. Sam was using words she'd never heard even
from the dockworkers along the river. She moved around
the bloody spots on the floor and hurried to the door.

"Sam," she called. "Where are you going?"

"I'll see these two on their way, honey. Bar the door
and don't open it for anyone but me."

Elizabeth didn't want to leave Sam out there in the
dark with those two vile men. But she closed the door,
leaned her forehead against it and pondered for a second about taking the rifle and going out to help him. No.
She knew him well enough to know that he would resent
that. He had told her to stay inside. She would stay. Her
"man," as the fat man had called him, knew better how
to cope with those two bastards than she did.

Chapter Thirteen

The voices outside the cabin faded away. Elizabeth stood with her back to the door, her arms wrapped around herself, and listened to the silence. She locked her knees in an attempt to strengthen legs that were weak and trembling. The minutes passed without sound until a low rumble of thunder broke the stillness. Centuries seemed to pass before she was able to draw an easy breath. When she did, she looked around the cabin as if seeing it for the first time. It seemed a strange and unfamiliar place with the ugly spots of blood on the floor.

She would not tolerate them here in this sacred place! She ladled water into the wash pan, poured it onto the soiled floor and began to sweep the mess away with a straw broom she found behind the wood box. Most of the water went into the cracks between the boards; the rest she swept out the door, which she opened a fraction. When she was finished, she built up the fire in the cook stove and set the coffeepot on to boil.

The wind came up and moaned over the rooftop while she tidied the cabin. Gusts came down the chimney and set sparks dancing in the fireplace. Rumbles of thunder came nearer. She went to the window to peer into the darkness. Flashes of lightning lit the sky with eye-searing brilliance. Thunder roared in its wake. In the brief silence that followed she heard a sharp crack that could have been a shot from a gun. Fear grabbed at her throat with icy hands. She closed her eyes tightly and prayed.

"Oh, God! Bring him back! Please bring him back! I'll never ask for another thing."

To stave off her feverish imaginings, she reminded herself of how perfectly adapted Sam was to this wild country. She forced herself to believe that he knew how to take care of himself. He had acted quickly and put two armed men out of commission. Didn't that prove his ability? Oh, Lord! He had to be all right. He had to come back with that hell-raising grin on his face or . . .

Outside, the wind slammed against the side of the cabin. Inside, Elizabeth huddled beside the window and tried to think of absolutely nothing. She didn't want to think about Sam, out there in the gathering storm with men who would kill him if they could. She didn't want to think of anything at all. She just wanted to hang on to her control.

The coffee boiled up and out the spout, and sizzling drops landed on the hot stove. She grasped the handle of the pot with a cloth and pulled it to a cooler spot. The pounding on the door startled her, and she almost burned herself. The pounding came again before she could let go of the pot.

"Hey! Open up. It's me."

Her heart leaped. She sped to the door and lifted the bar. Sam came in with a gust of wind that flattened her robe against her legs. He pushed the door shut and dropped the bar.

"Storm coming," he said calmly as if they had not faced death an hour ago. His eyes skimmed over the room quickly before they settled on her face.

She looked into his eyes and the world danced, then faded away, leaving only the two of them. She held her hands to keep them from reaching for him, while her eyes could find nothing else to do but stare into his. Even her feet moved her closer to him.

"I heard a s-shot." Her tongue felt thick and awkward.

"Just a little send-off. I didn't think about it scaring you."

"They're gone?"

"Yeah, they're gone. Lord, Lizabeth, I'm sorry I let it happen. I thought the one-eyed man was by himself until he told me Vernon was in here with you. Then there was nothing to do but play it by ear. I knew you were up to something when you put on that helpless act."

"Are you all right?"

"Yes. You?"

The intense silence that followed seemed to press the breath out of her and drain all coherent thought from her mind as love for him flared in her heart. She felt his need, his desire pulling her. She felt the hunger in her heart echoing the hunger in his. Silently she went into his arms without a single doubt that he wanted her there, without a single doubt that that was where she belonged.

His arms welcomed her, drawing her closer. He pressed his cold face against the side of hers. Her breath left her in a half sob. All that mattered was that he was safe, holding her as she was holding him. They stood with their arms wrapped around each other for a long while.

Then sparks as alive as those in the fireplace flew through her veins, igniting an intense longing in her heart to know that every inch of him was all right. Her hands crept over him—his upper arms, his shoulders broad enough to shield her from any storm. Her hands moved over his chest to his back and up to his face, touching, touching. When assured, she turned her head to seek his lips with her own.

With a savage sound, Sam pressed her so close to him that their hearts seemed to be beating as one. Her mouth was soft, giving welcome to his, trying in every way to let him know how very precious he was to her. Elizabeth's heart was pounding so hard that it frightened her. She spoke his name with such an imploring inflection that he raised his head to look at her.

"Sam! Oh, Sam!"

"Ah . . . sweet—"

His open mouth moved to hers as if it would be too painful to stay away. Gently, he barely touched her lips. They exchanged breaths until he felt her yearning body strain against him and her parted lips reach for his. They kissed as if they were starved for each other. He was her universe, her protector, her comfort, her love.

"Liz . . . sweetheart. I died a thousand times thinking what would happen to you if they killed me."

"Ssh . . . it's over. Let's don't think about it." She dropped kisses around the curving lines of his mouth, loving the feel of his mustache against her face. His breath quickened; his arms tightened.

"Honey, sweetheart, we shouldn't be doing this."

"I know. But—"

The word ended with an indrawn breath as Sam's tongue delved into the corner of her mouth. She shivered, enjoying the gentle, exciting caress.

"You know I want you." His voice trembled with raw emotion that sent a shiver down her spine. He spoke with his lips pressed against hers. "Don't you?"

"Yes."

She couldn't deny the rigid evidence swelling fiercely between his legs, for it was pressed tightly to her belly. Her unschooled body moved against it and met its masculine, urgent thrust with one of her own. Mindless of what she was doing to him, she stood on her tiptoes in an attempt to cuddle him between her thighs. He moaned against her mouth.

Suddenly it wasn't enough just to hold her. He needed to feel more of her, needed to let his hands and his heart and that most vulnerable part of his body feast upon her tenderness. He loosened her robe, opened it. His hands moved over the sides of her breasts and spread wide over her back, pulled her so close that her breasts were flattened against his hammering heart. Her breath quickened and her mouth clung to his, opening so he could drink more fully of the passion burning between them.

The fire in him was building hotter and hotter, and with each moment it was harder to control.

Sam lifted his head and looked into the jeweled green eyes. She was as innocent as a child when it came to sex. The knowledge gave Sam a deep and unexpected pleasure. He smiled into her eyes and nuzzled her mouth, licking her tender, swollen lips.

"Do you like that, little sweetheart?" he asked in a soft whisper, feeling her answer in the quivering breath she drew. His fingers smoothed the hair from her ears. She looked as hungry for his love as he was for hers.

"Yes. Oh, yes." The words were a soft sigh against his mouth. "It's wonder—"

The word was cut off by the flick of his tongue caressing the soft inner surface of her lips.

"Oh, honey, I like it, too!" He covered her mouth with fierce, hungry kisses, random and violent, different from the gentle kisses he had given her before.

Clasped tightly to his chest, she could feel her heart hammering against his.

"I want you so much," he whispered against her lips.

"I want you, too...."

Breathing raggedly, his face flushed with passion, he pulled away from her, took her hands, drew them from his neck and brought them to her sides.

"If we don't stop now, I won't be able to." His voice was unsteady.

Coming out of her daze, she felt as if her heart as well as her body was exposed and quickly lowered her eyes. She wrapped her robe around her and tied the belt.

"You must think...that I'm—"

"Hush!" He picked up her hand and held it to his chest. She felt the thud of his strong heartbeat. "You do that to me."

His words sent a shower of joy through her. She closed her eyes for an instant and shivered with pleasure.

"I'm a normal man with normal urges, and you're a beautiful woman. We just got carried away." He dropped her hand and turned away.

Her heart reeled with an inexplicable disappointment. Dear God! She loved him so much, and that gave him this awesome power to hurt her. Keeping her voice carefully in check, she said, "I'm sorry."

Shaking his head, he said something, but thunder drowned out his words. He went to the stove for coffee. She put the straw ring on the chair and sat, because she didn't know if her legs would hold her another minute.

"Coffee?"

"No, thank you. I made it for you."

Sam brought his cup to the table and sat. It took all her courage to face him as if her love wasn't tearing her apart.

It was a physical effort for Sam to look into those luminous green eyes and keep his hands from reaching for her.

"Tell me about Stephen."

It was the last thing she had expected him to say. Stephen. Her mind refused to accept thoughts of Stephen. It was as if he was a stranger intruding in her dreamworld. A long shudder shook her, and a chill passed over her skin. Embarrassment rosied her pale face.

Sam flinched at the pain he saw in her eyes. His hand reached out and covered hers. "What we did was no more your fault than mine."

Always sensible and straightforward, she nodded in agreement, even though pain jabbed at her heart. She squeezed his hand, wishing she could ease the pain of guilt that must surely lie in his heart, too.

The light from the lamp on the table began to flicker. It drew their attention, and their hands pulled apart.

"We're about out of oil. I can get the lantern out of the buggy."

"Don't bother on my account. I think I'll go to bed."

"It was a gutsy thing you did tonight." He smiled, spreading that irresistible charm across his face. "You were great. No woman I know could have done better."

"Not even Jessie?"

"Not even Jessie."

"That's gratifying to know." Her eyes met his briefly. Then she got to her feet and went to the bed.

The smile faded from his face as he became aware of the hopelessness he had seen in her eyes and heard in her voice.

"I'll put on my slicker and go out for a while."

"There's no need for that. Do you think they'll come back?"

"No. We've got their guns. They'll find a place to hole up and nurse their wounds. They're low-caliber crooks."

"Well, thank you for what you did."

The words hung in the air between them. He watched her take off her robe and get into the bed. She turned her face to the wall and pulled the blankets up to her ears.

Sam sat at the table with his hands around the coffee cup and pondered her words. *Thank you for what you did.* So cold, so formal. There'd been a huskiness in her voice when she'd said them. Dear Lord! He didn't want it to be this way, but what else could he do?

The lamp flickered and went out. Sam sat and listened to the rain on the roof. Through the shadowy darkness he could see Elizabeth, curled up on the bed. He shut his eyes, willing the image of her face, her large sad eyes, out of his mind. God, how it had hurt to push her away. The knowledge that he could have carried her to the bed and made her his ate at him. She had been as eager for him as he was for her. But had he carried her to the bed and taken her, it would have been total commitment, and how could he have faced Stephen when they got to Nora Springs?

The wind died down and the rain settled into a light drizzle, then stopped. Sam let the fire go out. He told himself to go to bed and try to get some sleep. He thought of Vernon and the one-eyed man. The bastards! He didn't care if they died in the rain and the cold. He had given them their lives. It was more than they had planned for him and Elizabeth.

A small sound came from the bed, breaking the silence and sending a shard of pain through his heart. What dreams were haunting her? Was it Vernon and his friend, or was it guilt for what had happened between them? He was at her side even as the thoughts crossed his mind.

"Elizabeth," he whispered, and sat on the edge of the bed. "'Lizabeth, honey. Are you dreaming?" He touched her face with tender strokes and felt her tears. "You're crying! Is it your...sit-down place?"

"No. It's my...my heart."

"Your heart? Ah...honey..." It was a sigh, a prayer.

He rubbed her back, trying to ease her tension. It also satisfied his need to touch her.

"I'll get up, Sam. It wasn't fair of me not to tell you about Stephen."

"Don't get up. It's cold in here. You can tell me to-morrow."

She reached for his hand and, holding it in both of hers, brought it to her lips, then held it beneath her chin.

"I keep wondering what I've done that fate would play these cruel tricks on me." For her, the words just came out. It was like talking to herself.

"What cruel tricks?"

"Making me...wanton, lustful, forgetful of my promise to Stephen. I've been acting like a common w-whore...wanting you to kiss me."

"How many whores have you known?"

"One."

"That's what I thought. Whores don't want kisses. They want money."

"Mary Lincoln's daughter, Becky, was one. She gave her favors to every man she met, colored, that is. She wouldn't have anything to do with white men. But she'd make them sing to her before she'd do it—even if they couldn't sing very well."

"Did she tell you that?" Sam wanted to chuckle, but most of all he wanted to keep her talking.

"Becky and I played together when we were little. I learned a lot of things from Becky. She liked to tell me about the things she did because it shocked me."

"It doesn't sound to me like Becky was a whore. A whore gets paid."

"Mary Lincoln finally made her marry George Brown. Becky didn't care—he sang and played the banjo."

"What's this got to do with you?"

"I remind myself of Becky. I wanted you to l-love me." Her voice cracked. "I s-still do."

Sam leaned over and buried his face in the curve of her neck. "Lord, honey—"

"It's wrong even to want to, isn't it?"

"For us it is," he said regretfully. "If we were free to love each other, it wouldn't be wrong or lustful or wanton. It would be natural and beautiful. I would . . . love you all night long."

"I shouldn't have put the burden on you to call a halt to our madness." She lifted a hand to stroke his head, not even wondering how she could be saying these things to him. "I'm sorry. Oh, Sam, Sam . . ." She murmured his name as her lips glided over his straight brows, short, thick eyelashes, cheeks rough with stubble. The thought that this was as much as she would ever have of him was a stab of agony in her heart.

"Let me lie down here beside you." His urgent whisper came from lips pressed to her neck. "I won't do anything but hold you. I swear it."

Her answer was to move over, make room for him and fold back the blanket that covered her. He unbuckled his gun belt and let it slide to the floor, slipped off his boots and pulled his shirt off over his head. He lay down and drew the blankets over them. Then, turning on his side to face her, he reached for her and pulled her into his arms.

Their groans of pleasure mingled as her soft body came against his. She placed her palm against his chest and snuggled her face in the curve of his neck. The happiness she felt made her a little crazy. *I love you.* The words echoed in her heart and mind. She thought that surely he could hear them. She turned her lips to his skin, knowing that she shouldn't, but needing to, for later, when all she would have would be sweet memories. She felt him tremble violently.

"'Lizabeth—Oh, love, please don't. It's agony to be with you like this and not do more. I should never have lain down by you." He moved to take his arm from beneath her head.

"Don't go!" Her plea came whispering out of the darkness and echoed back to her like a lost wail. She clung tightly to him.

"You don't know what it does to me. It's agony not to kiss your sweet mouth, hold your breast in my hand, feel you surrounding me." As he spoke, he turned on his back and drew her head to his shoulder. Her breasts, pressed to the side of his chest, were like a hot brand.

"Sam?" Her fingertips raked across the soft fur on his chest. She had felt his throbbing hardness through his britches and her nightgown as she lay against him. "If it hurts you so badly, I'll move away." She began to inch away.

His arm tightened, drawing her closer to his side. "It hurts like hell, but it would hurt more if you moved away. Just lie still, honey. Go to sleep."

"I couldn't."

"Try."

"What are you thinking?"

"I'm . . . pretending." The words were wrenched from him. The arm beneath her head moved slightly, and his fingers fondled the hair over her ear. He drew in a long, shaky breath and stroked the hair at her temples.

"Pretending what?"

"Don't ask me, beauty. Don't ask me," he said wearily.

"I don't want to cause you pain."

"Then talk to me. Tell me about Stephen."

"All right." She moved her hand on his chest and felt his heart thudding beneath it. The rest of him was still, with a peculiar, silent waiting. "We played together as children."

"Did Becky teach him the facts of life, too?"

"No! He had gone away to school by then. My grandfather and his grandfather were business partners, and had been since before the war. The families were close, and I think they wanted my widowed father and your mother to marry, but it didn't happen."

"Why didn't Eleanor divorce Pa and marry your father? She had the money."

"I don't think it even occurred to her."

"Bull!" The word was wreathed with contempt.

"Stephen went off to school when he was twelve," Elizabeth went on quickly, wanting to get off the explosive topic of Sam's mother. "Two years later I went away to school, and Stephen and I saw each other only during the summers. After he finished school, he worked in the New York office of the shipping company. He would come home for a month or two, then go back. We have always been friends."

"It would seem to me that you should be more than *friends* if you're going to marry him," Sam said harshly, and grabbed the hand on his chest to hold it still.

Elizabeth was quiet for a while. She could feel the emotions roiling in him. Anger. Resentment. Frustration. Whatever they were, they were tearing him apart.

"Well . . . let's hear the rest of it," Sam said.

"Two years ago my father died. He was very ill for more than six months. When Stephen came home for the summer, they spent a lot of time together. Father was worried about what would happen to me when he was gone. He'd married Netta when I was fourteen, thinking to give me a mother. It was a mistake. He came to realize it a few years after they married. Netta had no intentions of mothering a girl my age."

"Why didn't he take off and leave her? That seems to be what *tony* people do when they make a mistake in marriage."

Elizabeth knew the bitter words referred to his mother, and she hurt for him, but she made no comment.

"Father asked Stephen to look out for me. We both knew that the family wanted us to marry, so Stephen asked me."

"Why didn't you marry him right away?"

"I couldn't leave Father. He died soon after, and we had a year of mourning. And then . . . Aunt Eleanor's health began to decline. I didn't want to leave her, either." His hand stopped stroking her hair when she mentioned his mother. "As soon as Father died, Netta began putting pressure on me to marry."

"Didn't Stephen want to?"

"She wanted me to break my promise to Stephen and marry Judge Thorpe. He's twice my age and has a daughter in her teens who is bedridden. He's very wealthy and influential. Netta craves social power, and being stepmother-in-law to the judge would put her in the top echelon of society."

"Why doesn't she marry him herself?"

"He doesn't want her. He wants...me. If she can't have him, it's the next best thing."

"I can't blame him for that," he murmured wearily.

"Stephen came home when his mother died. We decided we'd be married right away to keep Netta from scheming with Judge Thorpe. Mr. McClellan, Stephen's grandfather, thought it a good idea, too. He didn't want his relationship with the judge strained in any way, because they do business together."

"Greed rears its ugly head."

"That's one way to look at it. By then Stephen had found out you and his father were alive. He was so excited and could hardly wait to come to see you. I wanted him to come—it meant so much to him. I didn't think Netta would go as far as to start arranging a ball where I was expected to act as hostess for Judge Thorpe. I was being drawn into their net."

"So you packed up and ran. I'm surprised you didn't stay and fight." The condemnation in his voice cut her to the quick.

"I was tired, and I guess frightened I'd get caught in Netta's trap. After talking it over with Stephen's grandfather, I decided to come out to Stephen. Mr. McClellan is afraid Stephen won't come back."

"There's not much chance of that." There was a hardness in Sam's voice that softened when he added, "It's a different kind of life out here. I can see where it wouldn't suit him."

Elizabeth could feel the ache that lay deep in his heart. His resentment of a mother he had adored and who had abandoned him in childhood was eating at him. It would be there forever unless a way could be found to bring him peace. She was mystified as to why Eleanor had left

Montana, mystified as to why Eleanor would tell Stephen his father and brother were dead. Eleanor had been one of the sweetest, kindest people Elizabeth had ever known. Eleanor had suffered, too. Sorrow had turned her hair gray and lined her face at an early age.

"Sam?" She hesitated after saying his name. "Sam, let me tell you about...your mother and what she was like."

"I know what she was like. She was a spoiled, pampered bitch!" The words were spit out harshly.

"She wasn't!"

"She fled to a life of ease, leaving the man who had worked his fingers to the bone for her, keeping from him the pleasure of seeing his son, his *seed*, grow into manhood." He drew a deep, ragged breath. "I'm glad I wasn't the one she took with her. Pa and I got along just fine without her. She and her kind don't have the guts for real living. At the first little hardship, they tuck in their tails and run."

"You're wrong about her—"

"What's it to you? I'll thank you not to meddle in matters that don't concern you." His voice vibrated with hurt and anger.

The harshness of his words cut her to the heart. They brought a knot to her throat and incipient moisture to her eyelids. She had expected resentment, but not rage.

Physically they were still close, but there was a spiritual distance between them that was a mile wide. He had retreated from her, putting her firmly in the place of an outsider. She wanted to weep.

After he threw off the blanket and left the bed, she gave in to the urge.

Chapter Fourteen

It was a cold, damp morning.

Elizabeth had spent a restless, sleepless night and was awake when Sam placed his hand on her shoulder to awaken her. He immediately went to the shed to tend the animals. He hitched the mare to the buggy and saddled his horse, then brought them to the front of the cabin.

After a quick meal, Elizabeth sat at the table to write a note to the owners of the cabin, telling them of her appreciation. She placed the gray hat with the pink silk rose in the middle of the bed and the note beside it. She wanted to leave money, too, but feared she would step on Sam's masculine pride, because he had said he would take care of it.

Sam was a polite escort and nothing more. She was hurt and confused by the swift change in his attitude toward her. He treated her as if they had just met, as if he had never held her in his arms, called her honey and sweetheart and kissed her. It was as though what had happened between them had meant nothing to him at all. The only conversation he offered was what was necessary to their departure. The warm rapport they had shared was gone.

Sam poured water on the ashes in the stove and in the fireplace. Elizabeth swept the floor one last time and looked around to see that everything was in place. She didn't want to linger for fear that she would show some sentiment for this place that had already been filed away in her bank of things to remember. She put on her coat and scarf, picked up her travel bag and the package of food for their noon meal and went to the buggy. She didn't notice the gawdy top with the red fringe as she climbed in and settled herself on the straw ring.

Sam hammered the nails into the hasp Burley had removed the day they arrived. Elizabeth listened and said a silent goodbye to the little cabin that had sheltered her when she had needed shelter so desperately.

"Are you comfortable?" Sam placed the hammer on the floor of the buggy alongside the weapons he had taken from Vernon and his one-eyed companion. He had put on a heavy coat and turned the collar up to shield his neck from the wind.

"Yes, thank you. The ring helps a lot."

"It's going to be cold. You'd better cover yourself with one of the blankets."

"I will if I need it."

"It could be snowing in the mountains." He avoided eye contact with her and pulled on a pair of leather gloves.

"I can drive—"

"No need for that now. Maybe later." He mounted his horse and moved out ahead of the mare, who seemed content to follow on the lead Sam had attached to her halter.

Elizabeth glanced back. The cabin seemed so small, forlorn, even terribly shabby. She could almost doubt her memory of what had taken place there. She turned away, her eyes seeking the man riding ahead. Could that polite but distant stranger be the same Sam Ferguson who had held her in his arms last night, who had trembled when she'd raked her fingers across his naked chest, who had been as hungry for her kisses as she had been for his? How long would it take her to forget him? With a growing dread she heard the voice of her heart answer insistently—until the end of eternity.

They were riding into the cold wind. Sam looked over his shoulder and saw Elizabeth pull the blanket over her lap and hug it to her chest. Curls that had escaped the shawl on her head framed her white face. Dark shadows outlined her brilliant green eyes. She was as weary from the sleepless night as he was. She had been through an experience that would have caused most women to go into hysterics. Although she'd been scared half to death, she had stood up as well or better than a woman who had lived with danger all her life.

Sam had no time to dwell on the thought. His horse's ears began to twitch, and Sam reached for his rifle. He let it drop in the scabbard when a deer darted from the brush ahead and raced for cover amid the thick growth of sumac that lined the opposite side of the trail. Sam was glad he'd brought Old Buck. He was spooky. His sire had been a wild mountain mustang, and self-preservation was bred in him. Old Buck could hear every sound and could see and hear better than a man. If there was a living thing nearby, the horse would know it.

Trusting the horse to pick his way, Sam searched every foot of the landscape with the eyes of an experienced woodsman. He would not be taken by surprise again. They came to the crest of a hill, and from where he sat, Sam could see over a broad stretch of country. Nothing moved as they followed the trail into a meadow that lay at the foot of the rugged mountains. He allowed himself another look at Elizabeth. His eyes collided with hers. At that distance he couldn't see the expression in them, but their impact was just as powerful as ever. She stared at him for a long, intense moment before she looked away.

Of all the women in the world, why did he have to fall in love with her? Just looking at her made his pulse quicken! She was like a china figurine he'd seen dancing on top of a music box, but there was nothing hard and rigid about her. She used her cool reserve to hide the fact that she was a frightened, lonely woman. There had never been a woman so beautiful, feminine and soft. She was sensual and exciting, loving and giving. When they were wrapped in each other's arms, he knew that she was as eager for their mating as he was. Yet he had never known a woman who was so totally wrong for him. Born to wealth and luxury, she would come to hate this country and him for keeping her here.

Elizabeth! What was she thinking? How could she know the effort it took not to make love to her? Had it happened, she would not have married Stephen—she'd have been Sam's forever. A woman like Elizabeth would not give her maidenhead to one man and marry another. But what would Sam have? He would have a brother who despised him and a woman who despised his kind of life—and later him. It would be history repeating itself. Hell! He would put her out of his mind, his heart, his life. When they reached Nora Springs, he would turn her over to Stephen and head for the logging camp.

They stopped at midmorning to let the horses rest and drink from a stream that came out of the mountains. Elizabeth got stiffly out of the buggy, taking the blanket with her to wrap around her. Her cheeks were red from the cold; her warm breath steamed.

"Is it this cold in Nora Springs?" she asked.

"Not this time of year. Nora Springs is in a valley. It's cold in the mountains even in the summertime." Sam pulled his horse away from the icy stream. "That's enough, boy. That water is cold."

Hugging the blanket around her, Elizabeth walked back and forth to get the blood circulating in her legs. Her bottom was healing. It was still sore but not as painful as before.

"Do you think you could drive for a short while? I'd like to ride ahead and look around."

"Of course."

"I'll not be far away." He waited beside the buggy while she climbed in and arranged the blanket over her lap. He reached out and tucked it more snugly around her legs. "She's lazy," he said gruffly. "You'll have to slap her back with the reins every so often to keep her going."

Sam mounted Old Buck and rode beside her for a moment before he moved ahead. Soon he was around a bend in the trail and out of sight. It surprised Elizabeth that she wasn't afraid. The guns lay at her feet. She was sure she'd be able to use them if she had to. How fast one could adapt to one's surroundings, she mused.

Her reverie turned to Sam and the way he had looked at her last night when he returned to the cabin after taking the men away. His gaze had told of a longing in him perhaps secret even from himself. He was lonely and hurting. Oh, Eleanor, how could you have hurt him so?

Nothing in Elizabeth's life had prepared her for loving a man, especially a one-of-a-kind man like Sam Ferguson. During her lifetime she had seen little of love between a man and a woman. Her stepmother had certainly not been in love with her father. And she couldn't remember that any of her friends spoke of undying love for the men in their lives. They spoke of the man's assets and his standing in the community. Most of them married to escape from the control of parents and have a home of their own.

She was alone in this vast country without another human in sight, and it was pleasant to daydream of a life with a man like Sam to love, to build a home around, to bear his children. *His wife would be a queen.* But it wasn't for her. All she would have of him were her memories.

She gazed at the trail ahead, but what she saw was a vision clear and powerful—Sam's intense brown eyes and the strong lines of his face. She recalled his mouth when he smiled and the way it rocked across hers in a seeking caress. The taste of his lips was in her mouth, and the feel of his silky mustache caressed her cheek. His hands, the only male hands to touch her breasts, cupped and caressed them.

Elizabeth shuddered helplessly. It was too late for her. Sam would never forgive her for being like the mother he despised. He wanted a woman like his Jessie, who was waiting for him in Nora Springs. In her mind she groped for a solution and found only one. It was not too late for Stephen. She would not let him toss away his chance for love and happiness because of her. She loved his brother, and she could not possibly marry him now. When they reached Nora Springs, she would talk to him, make him understand, without involving Sam in any way, that she loved another. She would free Stephen to seek love with a woman who would truly love him. Then what would she do? Why in the world was love so gut-wrenchingly painful?

She was jarred from her reverie when she saw Sam coming toward her in a gallop. As he motioned for her to stop, she pulled up on the reins.

"A party of Indians are riding this way," he announced casually. "I want to make sure the guns are covered." He flipped a blanket over the weapons on the buggy floor and tucked it snuggly around them. "Just keep going." He stepped back into the saddle.

"Are they... wild?"

"Not any wilder than Vernon and Ollie," he said dryly, but she thought she caught a glimpse of laughter in his dark eyes before he turned them away. He reached over and slapped the mare on the rump to get her started again and rode along beside her. His calm, steady manner was all that kept Elizabeth's terror at bay.

As they topped a crest, she saw five Indians riding single file on spotted ponies coming toward them. These were the first Indians she had seen beside the ones who loitered around the train stations of the towns she'd passed through on her way west. Stories of Indian atrocities sprang into her mind. She ran her tongue over dry lips at thoughts of scalps and burnings and flaming arrows.

"Crow," Sam said in a low voice as the Indians moved to the side of the trail. "Stop and stay here." Sam lifted his hand in greeting and rode ahead.

Elizabeth couldn't hear what was being said. The Indians sat their ponies stone still and stared at her and the buggy. They wore unadorned doeskin britches, tunic type shirts and seemed to be immune to the cold. Glistening black hair hung straight to their shoulders, framing stoical bronze features.

One of them said something to Sam. He answered with a gesture of his hand toward the buggy. What did they want to know about her? Then to Elizabeth's utter astonishment the Indians began to laugh. They laughed uproariously, pointed at her and nodded their heads in approval. She felt hurt and angry that Sam would permit them to ridicule her. She was even more angry when Sam turned his horse and came toward her with a huge smile on his face. The Indians yipped and raced their ponies around the buggy. The mare became excited, and it was all Elizabeth could do to hold her. One of the Indians rode up close to the buggy, bent his head so he could see beneath the top, and gazed at her.

"Why are they laughing at me?" she demanded angrily.

"Smile," Sam said. "They just want to look at you."

"Why?"

"I'll tell you later. Keep the blanket tucked around you."

Sam took his knife and slashed a length of the fringe from the buggy top. He gave it to one of the Indians. The brave whooped, and holding one end high over his head raced his pony so that the length flowed out behind. The others gathered around Sam, jabbering excitedly while he stripped the fringe from the buggy, giving each a share. They ran their ponies up and down the trail, yipping and yelling and stirring up a dust cloud.

"They're showing off for you," Sam said.

"They needn't bother." Elizabeth took a deep breath and wished that her lips would not quiver so noticeably. "Can we go on?"

"Not yet. Keep smiling."

Elizabeth kept her smile in place, letting no trace of the anxiety that had settled in her heart affect her smile or her voice when she asked, "What will they do?"

"They'll not hurt you."

As suddenly as if it had been rehearsed, the Indians came to line up in front of the buggy. The first one tied the strip with the fringe attached around his forehead; the others followed. Elizabeth smiled, thinking how ridiculous they looked with the red balls dangling over their eyebrows. The Indians took her smiles as approval and smiled back at her. A puzzled expression replaced Elizabeth's smile when one of the Indians took a blue feather from inside his tunic and placed it on the seat beside her.

"Smile and thank him," Sam said softly from the other side of the buggy.

"Thank you very much. It's a beautiful...feather."

The next brave rode up and handed her three brass buttons strung on a leather string.

"Thank you. I'm delighted to have...the ah... buttons."

She was then presented with a string of colored beads. "They are lovely," Elizabeth exclaimed. "Thank you."

A quirt made of three thin strips of leather bound with hide was placed on the seat, and the rider sped away before she could thank him. Then to Elizabeth's open-mouthed amazement, the last man took off his moccasins and handed them to her.

"Oh, but...I can't...take—"

"Yes, you can. Take them and thank him," Sam murmured quickly.

"His feet are...bare."

"Take them! Exclaim over them. He's trying to outdo his friends."

Elizabeth reached for the moccasins and hugged them close to her breast. She smiled broadly into the face of the pleased young brave.

"Thank you very much. It's sweet of you to give me your...shoes. I shall treasure them always. Thank you."

The young man raised his hand in farewell, gigged his pony with his bare heels and raced away. The others followed. Elizabeth sat still for a moment, then stuck her head out the side to see if it was safe to drop the gift. She saw nothing but a cloud of dust. She let out a long sigh of relief.

"Move over. I'll drive for a while." Sam tied his horse behind the buggy and climbed in beside her.

"What will I do with those . . . shoes?"

"Moccasins. One thing you'll not do is throw them away where that brave or any of the other Crow will find them." Sam put the mare into motion and they moved on up the track.

"Why did he give them to me?"

"You'll notice that the value of the gifts kept increasing. Each brave tried to out-do the other. First it was a feather; then the buttons, the beads and the quirt. The Crow use the quirt in combat. It's a valuable possession. If the young brave wanted to outdo the one who gave you the quirt, he had to give his shirt, his britches or his moccasins. He chose to give you the moccasins."

"Thank God he didn't choose to give me his britches!" Elizabeth looked at Sam and burst out laughing. He grinned back at her, his eyes drinking in the sight of her smiling mouth, her bright, laughing eyes.

"You came through fine, Liz. Just fine."

His praise was like a warm healing balm.

"Why did you give them the ball fringe, and why in the world would they want it?"

"They thought the buggy the most beautiful thing they had ever seen. They gazed at it in awe."

"So did I when I first saw it." This brought forth another burst of giggles.

"You thought I'd picked out this rig to embarrass you, didn't you?"

"Of course. What prissy-tail woman from Saint Louis wants to ride in a circus buggy?" she asked teasingly.

"I didn't choose it. I was as surprised to see it as you were. I told Jim Two-Horses to get a buggy with good springs and a top. This was all he could find on short notice." Sam looked at her and grinned. "It's awful, isn't it?" The warm light in his eyes was so beautiful that she couldn't look away.

"Awful is a mild word for it. It's atrocious! But you enjoyed it, didn't you?" She tilted her chin, and her eyes gleamed at him. "Sam Ferguson, you were a genuine horse's patoot that morning."

"Uh-huh. And I had a hell of a headache."

"That's no excuse. You'll get no sympathy from me after what you did." She was looking at him again in that alluring way, a smile curving her lips, laughter in her eyes.

"Lord, honey! I've apologized!" The endearment slipped out without his realizing it. "I'm trying to forget it, but I'm afraid that if I live to be a million, I'll not forget *that*!"

"I'm glad! Terribly glad, because I'll not forget it either," she stated flatly, and looked straight ahead, thinking that she would never forget for a different reason. "You still haven't told me what you told the Indians."

"Oh, that! Well . . . I told them I had given you the buggy as a special gift, that you were a special woman."

"That was sweet of you, Sam, but there's more. What did you tell them that made such an impression on them that they would give me gifts?"

"I told them that you were . . . pregnant."

"You...told them that I was...?" She shot him a look that questioned his sanity.

"...going to have my son any time and I was trying to get you to Nora Springs so my son would be born in my lodge."

She bristled instantly. "Sam! You liar!"

"They were really impressed when I said you were so big we were sure there would be two sons." His dark eyes sparkled with laughter. "Then I worried that you'd drop the blanket and stand up." The look he gave her was the old devilish look, both sweet and mischievous.

She couldn't resist asking, "Why would you tell a story like that?"

"The Crow are especially protective of their women, and they love their children very much. We're in their territory. You can never tell when we might need their help."

"Sam Ferguson! If you aren't the limit. Do you think they would have hurt us otherwise?"

"They might have tried to steal something."

Time passed swiftly. He told her the Crow Indians were an enemy of the Sioux, and if Custer had taken the advice of his Crow scouts, he would not have been wiped out at the Little Bighorn. Elizabeth listened with rapt attention. She was unaware that they had reached a summit and stopped until Sam said, "Hungry?"

"I hadn't even thought about it."

Sam tied the mare's lead rope to a branch. Elizabeth climbed down from the buggy and turned her back to the cold wind.

"You can go off if you want to. There's no one around."

"How do you know?" She desperately wanted to hold on to the friendly companionship that had existed between them during the past hours.

"Look at Old Buck's ears."

"Old Buck?"

"My horse. His ears will twitch if there's a rabbit within five hundred yards."

"Heavens! I'm not scared of rabbits! How does he feel about a man, a bear or a wildcat?"

"Don't worry, Liz. Take your hatpin and you'll be safe." He threw the teasing words over his shoulder.

Elizabeth went behind the bushes, her head spinning with dizzy waves of happiness.

When she returned, it was to see Sam coming from across the trail with a bucket of water for the mare. He held the canteen out to her. She took off the top and drank deeply of the sweet, cold water and gave the canteen back to him. Sam drank, his gaze locked with hers.

When he went to get a bucket of water for his horse, she opened up the food pack and laid out the fried pies, the bean patties and squares of last night's cornbread. They ate standing up at the side of the buggy away from the wind, and Sam told her about the trail ahead.

"We're about five miles from the main road. There's a particularly hard stretch between here and there. It's rocky and goes almost straight up. It may be that we'll walk up that incline. I wouldn't want you to be in the buggy if the mare should slip and it rolled backward."

"Will we reach the stage station tonight?"

"We'll get there if we can make it up that incline without breaking a wheel. When we reach the station, you may not have a room to yourself. The women usually stay in one room and the men in another."

"That's all right. I'll be fine."

The expression in his eyes as they roamed her face was softer somehow. "You won't be put out?"

"Put out? Heavens, Sam. I can adapt to my surroundings. It isn't as if I'll be sleeping in a communal room forever."

Sam was silent and thoughtful while he devoured two pies.

"I'm glad you poked Vernon with the hatpin. If nothing more than for eating my pie."

"I'll make you some more...." Instant regret for making a promise she would never keep caused her to turn away from him and wrap the beancakes and cornbread in the cloth should the misery be reflected in her face. "We have enough food for tomorrow noon if you'll be satisfied with two beancakes, two squares of cornbread and one pie."

"We'd better be going. Are you sure you don't mind driving?"

"No, I don't mind at all." She loosened her shawl to retie the ribbon at the nape of her neck. The wind blew strands of her hair against her cheeks. She turned, facing the wind. The cloud of dark curls fanned out behind her.

"Let me help." Sam took the ribbon from her hand, gathered the mass at her nape and tied it. "There. That should keep your neck warm."

For an instant before he lifted the shawl to her head she thought she felt his warm breath on her neck, his nose in her hair. Surely she was mistaken, she thought, when he came to tuck the blanket over her lap and about her legs without as much as glancing at her face.

Chapter Fifteen

We have two choices. We can cut up a steep incline to the main road and make the stage station by night, or we can continue on this lower, longer trail to by-pass the bridge and camp out."

"You mean camp out every night until we reach Nora Springs?"

"Every night. There isn't another way to get on the upper road that I know of."

They had stopped behind a thick stand of cedars that shielded them from the north wind. The sky was gray directly overhead but slightly blue in the north. It had become increasingly colder as the day wore on.

"I thought you had already decided we would go up the incline to the upper road."

"I had, but I've been thinking that I'd better take a look at it first. There may have been a landslide since I saw it last. It may be impossible to get the buggy up there. Will you be afraid if I leave you here for a while?"

"I'll be all right."

"That isn't what I asked you. Will you be afraid?"

"Maybe a little," she said honestly. "But I have a gun if something jumps out at me from the bushes."

"Can you shoot it?"

"Of course, I can...if I have to." She dug into her travel bag and brought out a small derringer.

"Good Lord! That thing wouldn't stop a jackrabbit."

"I hadn't planned on shooting a jackrabbit."

"Put it away." Sam stepped from the saddle and uncovered the pistol he'd taken from the one-eyed man. He checked the load and placed it on the seat beside her. "If you need me, fire the gun and I'll come."

"Do you think I'll need you?"

"No. I wouldn't leave you here alone if I did." He handed her the canteen and watched her while she drank. "This will give the mare a chance to rest—she'll need it if she has to pull the buggy up that slope."

Elizabeth held out the canteen, wiped her mouth on the back of her hand and let her thirsty eyes drink of him.

"I'll be here. Waiting." *I'd wait for you forever in this cold, lonely place if I thought there was a chance you'd come to me.*

His coffee-brown eyes were watching her so intently that a tingling started in her stomach and spread upward. Had she said aloud what had been in her mind? The skin on her face and neck felt as if it were being pierced by a thousand tiny needles. He pulled off his glove and touched her cheek lightly with the back of his hand. Unknowingly, she leaned into it to increase the pressure.

They stared at each other.

Her cheeks were rosy from the cold wind but warm to his touch. Small white teeth nibbled the inside of her lower lip. Her eyes...Good Lord, her eyes were driving him out of his mind! Gazing at him through the thick brush of sooty lashes, they were the wistful eyes of a child that yearned for some unobtainable something. Sam's throat was suddenly tight.

"I'll be back as soon as I can."

"How long will you be gone?"

"A half hour or so."

Elizabeth watched him step into the saddle. Their eyes caught and held for an instant, then he was riding up a narrow path and out of sight. She heard the sound of his horse's hooves striking rock, and then they faded. She was alone. Her eyes stayed on the empty path for a long time. Silence. Not even a bird song broke the stillness.

She wound the reins around the handle of the brake, threw off the warm blankets and climbed down out of the buggy. On the upward side of the trail was a stand of cedars. On the downward side a landscape of scattered pines, some cedar, and shrubs of which she knew nothing spread out before her. She had not realized that they were up so high. Not a thing stirred in all the vast area except for the gray clouds rolling overhead.

As she squatted beside the buggy to relieve her aching bladder, the wind struck her warm bottom with icy fingers. When she finished and adjusted her clothing, she walked briskly up and down alongside the buggy to limber her legs. It was then that she noticed the smell of pines and cedars.

This was Sam's country, his land. It was a strong, beautiful, challenging land. Elizabeth inhaled deeply. There was something about the mountain air, fresh, clear, like cold water in a dry throat, that made one want to inhale deeply.

Samuel . . . Sam. It was strange how the solid name fit the exciting man. She thought of all the great men she had read about who were named Samuel. Samuel Johnson, the English author. Samuel Adams, a hero of the War for Independence. Samuel Morse, inventor of the electric telegraph. *Her* Sam was just as great in his own way. He and his father had helped build this new land for future generations. Life had not been kind to *her* Sam during his younger years and perhaps that accounted for the hell-raiser side of him. If only she could tell him that she had enough love in her heart to make up for what he had missed.

Back in the buggy she snuggled in the nest of warm blankets and waited, wishing she had the small pocket watch she sometimes wore on a chain around her neck. Sam had said a half hour or so. Surely that much time had passed. Her mind wandered. She was strangely comfortable with her decision not to marry Stephen. She didn't know what she would do beyond that point, but she was sure of one thing; she would never return to Saint Louis. Stephen would understand and help her find a place to live.

It seemed to her that Sam had been gone for hours when she saw him coming back down the path on foot carrying his rifle. His long legs quickly covered the distance between them. He had turned down the collar on his coat and pushed his hat back. Breathing easily, he came up to the buggy before he spoke.

"I left my horse at the top," he said, but his eyes were asking if she was all right.

She saw the concern there and nodded. The bonding between them was becoming tighter and tighter. "What do you want me to do?"

"You'll have to walk. But before we start, I want to distribute the load in the buggy. I'll put your trunk up here on the floor, that is if it will fit on its side, and the other things on the seat."

"I'll help you."

She threw aside the blanket. Before she could turn to get out of the buggy, his hands had gripped her waist and he was lifting her down. Her heartbeat doubled its rhythm. She steadied herself with her hands on his shoulders and looked into his face. Time for her stood still. *Hold me,* she begged silently. He did. For a perfect moment that was over all too quickly he held her against him before his arms dropped and he turned away.

They worked together. He instructed; she obeyed without question. When the load was arranged to his satisfaction, he attached the lead rope to the mare's halter.

"It will be rough going, but if we take it slowly, we'll make it. Ready?"

"Ready." She smiled at him. "Lead on."

"No. You go ahead. I don't want you behind the buggy in case it should break away."

Elizabeth stepped out quickly, walking up the path that narrowed and became rocky as they left the stand of trees. She looked ahead at the steep incline and for a second doubted Sam's wisdom in attempting to take the buggy up over it. On either side of the upward path huge boulders jutted out. Only clumps of bushes dotted the hillside. As she progressed upward, small stones beneath her feet rolled and cascaded down the slope with each step.

"Slow down," Sam called. "You'll wear yourself out before you get halfway up."

She paused and looked back. The path she had come up was steeper than she'd realized. Sam was holding on to the mare's halter, calming her. The horse didn't like the stones rolling beneath her hooves and was putting each foot down carefully. The buggy rocked precariously as one wheel climbed over a large stone. The higher they climbed, the larger the stones seemed to be.

Conscious of the man behind her, Elizabeth was determined not to show any weakness. She moved steadily. Once she attempted to look back while still moving. Her foot slipped, and she went down hard on her knees. The sharp stones cut into her flesh, but even so she quickly got to her feet.

"Are you all right?" Sam called anxiously.

"I'm fine. It didn't hurt at all," she answered, watching now where she put each foot. Tears stung her eyes. It did hurt. "Damn!" she muttered aloud. Dear Lord! What was happening to her? She never used to even think swear words and here she was saying them.

They continued to climb, every step an effort for Elizabeth. Sam was taking it slowly, letting the buggy wheels ease over the large stones.

"There's a flat place just beyond that red boulder up there. We'll stop and rest a minute."

Elizabeth didn't answer. She was laboring to breathe and concentrating on putting one foot ahead of the other. Every so often she grasped a boulder with her gloved hand to help her along. Behind her she could hear Sam talking to the mare, urging her on up the grade. By the time Elizabeth reached the red rock jutting out from the hillside, her chest hurt and a moist film covered her face. She moved around to where Sam couldn't see her and leaned against the cold stone, breathing heavily, hoping to get back her wind before he reached her.

The mare's sides were heaving when she pulled the buggy up over the rim to the flat area. Sam patted the side of her face and talked to her.

"You did good, girl. We'll rest here awhile before we ask more of you." He dropped the lead rope to the ground and placed a couple of stones behind the buggy wheels. He checked the wheels over for cracks and inspected the shaft and harness before he took out the canteen and came to Elizabeth.

"Everything's all right so far."

"I didn't realize it would be so hard on the horse."

"She's doing all right. How're you doing?"

"Fine."

"Did you hurt yourself back there?"

"Not much. I just wasn't looking where I was putting my feet. You don't seem to be winded at all."

"Well, I am, a little." He held out the canteen.

"Did you ride up the first time?" She drank while waiting for him to answer.

"Part of the way." While he drank, his eyes stayed on her face. "It'll be cold on top. Do you have something I could use to wipe sweat off the mare? I'd use a blanket, but we may have to use them later, and I doubt you'd want to wrap up in dirty blanket."

"I'll have something in my trunk."

Sam capped the canteen, tossed it in the buggy and came to stand beside her. He leaned one shoulder against the boulder and looked intently at her profile. The hair at her temples was wet, and her face was flushed.

"Pretty hard going for a city woman, huh?"

She turned to look at him. He flashed her a smile, and she knew he was laughing at her. She was so tired that she was almost light-headed. She was hot but didn't dare take off her shawl and let the cold wind hit her damp head. Her knees felt as if holes had been bored into them straight through the bone. She looked into his grinning face and mocking brown eyes. Her temper flared out of control.

"You're hateful to say that! I'm not a mountain goat," she spit out.

"I'll agree to that." His low laugh only increased her anger.

"I've not done so badly—for a *city* woman! I've gotten this far without any help from you. You've not had to prod me or push me, have you? You haven't heard me complaining, have you? I'll even push the damn buggy if need be."

He gave a low whistle. "Hey... I didn't mean—"

Elizabeth's temper was so out of control that he could have been singing Yankee Doodle or reciting the Lord's Prayer and she would not have known the difference.

"You've been putting me down, Mr. Hell-Raiser Ferguson, since the morning we left Missoula, and I'm tired of it! I'm here to tell you that *this* prissy-tailed *city* woman has as much *guts* and stamina as your *sainted* Jessie has and is a whole lot smarter, because I see you as the cad that you are."

She turned her back to him, refusing to allow him the satisfaction of seeing her eyes tear and her lips tremble. Despite her inner turmoil, she was terribly conscious of him. She had tried her best. Evidently it was not enough. His ridicule hurt, angered and humiliated her.

"Honey, I didn't mean—" His hand on her shoulder tried to turn her. The action only angered her more.

"And don't call me something you don't mean! It's... it's deceitful, condescending and... demeaning! I'm immune to your flattery, Mr. Ferguson."

"How do you know I don't mean it?" His voice was low and rumbled close to her ear.

"Because... you say it as if you can't even remember my name."

"Hmm... by the way, what is your name?"

She whirled. "Samuel Ferguson, you make me so damn mad I could spit nails!"

He lifted his brows. "We might as well go if you're not going to at least try to be pleasant company."

"It will be my pleasure to put as much distance between us as possible."

"Then get going, Miss Prissy-tail city woman. If I come to within a yard of you, I'm going to poke you in your beautiful behind."

"If you so much as touch me, you'll be sorry. You and your damn buggy can roll back down the hill straight into hell as far as I'm concerned. You think you're so damn smart, but you're damn dumb! *Dumb as a stump*," she shouted over her shoulder.

"Now, now, now, Lizzy honey!"

"Don't Lizzy honey me, you…damn hell raiser, you!"

"Shame on you. Nice tony ladies shouldn't swear."

"Bull," she yelled defiantly. Then, "Damn it to hell! Damn it to hell! Damn it to hell!"

"Stop that!" he shouted. "I'll wash your mouth out with soap."

"You'll have to catch me first."

With angry tears blurring her vision, Elizabeth tackled the incline with a purpose—and that was to reach the top and watch him struggle with the mare and buggy. She climbed with fierce determination, concentrating on one step at a time and oftentimes leaning over to go on all fours, unmindful that her skirt was hiked, showing him an expanse of her legs and thighs. What difference did it make? He'd already seen more of her than anyone else except for old Aunt Marthy, her childhood nurse.

Watching her, Sam chuckled. He hadn't intended to make her angry, but as long as she was, he hoped she'd stay that way until she reached the top. It was giving her the extra energy she needed. Lord, what a wonderful, crazy, exciting woman! She would drive a man wild, but having her would be worth it. When they reached the top, he was going to bury his hands in her hair and kiss her sweet mouth until she was breathless.

He turned his attention to the mare, coaxed her up and over a high ledge. She stood quivering while he went behind the buggy and lifted its wheels over a large stone.

When he looked ahead again, Elizabeth was climbing over the rocks on all fours. Her skirt was hiked so high that he could see her drawers. What a sight! Miss Prissytail Caldwell scrambling over the rocks like a billygoat. The laughter he suppressed almost choked him.

Elizabeth reached the top. For a minute the cold wind felt good on her face. She drew great gulps of air into her tortured lungs. While her heartbeat slowed, she looked down the slope and felt satisfaction at what she had done. Now, just let Sam accuse her of being a weakling and she would laugh in his face.

She watched him and the mare labor to get the buggy up the last dozen yards. Dark shale shifted beneath the mare's hooves and Sam's boots. The buggy wheels jarred up and over stones as they made their way up the craggy hillside. Elizabeth forgot how weary she was and how angry she had been. She sent silent messages of encouragement to the horse and the man. Just a little farther. Come on, come on . . .

The last few yards were tortuous. Then the mare dragged the buggy onto the road and stood with her head down, her sides heaving, her coat covered with sweat. Elizabeth reached into the buggy for her valise and pulled out a long flannel nightgown and the only other thing she could find, a small towel.

"It'll be ruined. It might not come clean again," Sam said when she handed him the gown.

"That's all right. She's earned it."

Elizabeth wiped the mare's face and neck with the towel. Sam worked on the rest of her.

"It was mean of us to ask that of you," Elizabeth crooned. The mare's ears flopped as if in agreement. "You're a good girl and you deserve an extra treat to-night."

"It's a good thing Jim didn't get a pretty, dainty mare, or we'd never have made it."

"Pay no attention to him, pretty girl," she said to the mare. "He's insinuating that you're not pretty, and you are. He only sees what's on the outside."

When Sam finished wiping the horse, he tied the trunk and valises on the platform behind the buggy to make room for Elizabeth.

"If she stands there much longer, she'll stiffen up. Let's go. But first—"

He spun Elizabeth around, cupped her face with his hands, then moved his spread fingers beneath the shawl to comb through her hair. With his thumbs locked beneath her jaw, he tilted her head and put his mouth to the sweet, soft one that was driving him crazy. His lips pressed recklessly hard, giving hers no choice but to part. She clutched at his coat as she felt his tongue flick the corner of her mouth, slide between her lips and move across her teeth.

Lord, help me! She's so sweet, and it's been so long since I kissed her.

The pressure of his kiss forced Elizabeth's head back even though he cradled it between his hands. His lips moved hungrily, furiously over hers before he broke away and looked into her face. Their eyes locked; green eyes looked into brown unwaveringly. Ragged breaths hissed through wet, throbbing lips.

"Why...did you do that?" she gasped.

"That was for . . . swearing."

"That was punishment?" The question tumbled out of her heart through her lips.

"No," he muttered huskily. "That was wonderful." He lifted her into the buggy and wrapped her in the blankets.

Sam mounted his horse and picked up the lead rope. They moved down the road. Elizabeth sat in a daze, looking at the broad back of the man riding ahead. What had inspired the intimate kiss? Her heart thumped at the question that played over and over in her mind. Punishment for swearing was a feeble excuse. He had kissed her because he wanted to kiss her, and she had kissed him for the same reason.

Elizabeth ran the tip of her tongue over her kiss-bruised lips, searching for a taste of his. He was so blatantly male that when he touched her, she lost her anger and her need overcame her common sense. It wasn't fair. It wasn't fair that a man have such power over a woman that she would sell her soul for a few glorious hours in his arms.

As light faded from the sky, the air became increasingly colder. Sam kept doggedly on. The road was rutted in places but smoother than the trail they had been using. Elizabeth found herself dozing, then sat up straight, refusing to be overcome by weariness. She would not be caught sleeping. It would be a sure sign that she was not as strong or as durable as his infallible Jessie.

It was twilight when they approached Underwood's Station. Elizabeth saw a two-story ranch house. The lower part was stone, the upper hewn logs. It was a sturdy-looking structure with outbuildings and a network of pole corrals surrounding it. Light shone from glass windows in the front. A half a dozen heavy freight wagons were parked to block the wind, and several men loafed around a small fire.

When they passed the first wagon, Elizabeth realized how fragile the buggy appeared in comparison to the wagon. The huge wheels on the freight wagon were almost as high as the top of the buggy, and the covered load rose above the wagon's six-foot sideboards. Their arrival was an event. The men at the fire stood and gawked. Sam answered their greetings but ignored their remarks about the buggy. He didn't stop until he reached the station door.

Elizabeth threw off the blankets, climbed out of the buggy and waited for him to tie the horses to the hitching rail. Without a word he took her arm and escorted her inside. The large square common room was well lighted and filled with cigarette smoke, and it smelled of whiskey and beer. Three of the four tables in the room were occupied by men playing cards. Conversation stopped when Elizabeth and Sam walked in, and she pulled the shawl off her head. A man with bushy black hair on his face but none on his head came from behind the counter. He wiped his hands on the white apron tied around his middle.

"Howdy, Sam. Where'd you come from? Travelers has been scarce as hen's teeth since the bridges were knocked out."

"Hello, Roy. Have you heard who's behind it?"

"There ain't no doubt it's that new outfit, the Utah Stage Company, trying to keep Northwest from filling the contract. They've hired some good-for-nothin' drifters to do their dirty work. It's been hard on everyone who uses this road. The teamsters will string them up if they catch them."

While the man was talking to Sam, his eyes were darting between Sam and Elizabeth. He was plainly curious.

"How about the bridge up ahead?"

"Workin' on it. Shoring it up. Not strong enough yet for freight wagons."

"How about a buggy?"

"I heard they took a wagon across. How's Joe doin'? And Jessie? She was here a few weeks back, visitin' the woman."

"They're fine, far as I know. I've been away for a while. Do you have a room for the lady, Roy?"

"We're full up with freighters, but we'll find something. Come on back and we'll talk to the woman."

Mrs. Underwood was plump and pretty and considerably younger than her husband. Delighted to see Sam, she asked immediately about Jessie. After Sam gave her the same answer he had given her husband, she launched into details of the fine time they'd had when Jessie came to visit. She was polite but reserved when Sam introduced her to Elizabeth without any explanation as to why they were traveling together. Elizabeth was sure Mrs. Underwood was making comparisons between her and Jessie, whom everyone seemed to hold in such high esteem. Her dislike for the unknown woman built rapidly.

Mrs. Underwood took Elizabeth to a room not much larger than a closet. It had a narrow, neatly made bed and a stand for a pitcher and bowl and that was all. Several dresses for a small girl hung on pegs on the wall.

"I'll fix something for you to eat," Mrs. Underwood said, and left her.

After washing, Elizabeth returned to the kitchen and ate alone at the end of a long table. The eggs, potatoes and hot bread she was served were delicious. Again the innkeeper's wife was polite but offered no conversation.

Elizabeth caught the woman glancing at her from time to time but was too tired to make the effort to be friendly.

Within ten minutes after she returned to her room, she was in the bed and asleep.

Sam lingered in the barroom, talking with Roy Underwood and watching the men play cards. Two men at the far table looked familiar, and he finally realized they were the two who had tried to pick a fight with Jim Two-Horses at Haggerty's. Tonight they were sober. They'd had only one drink each in the hour Sam had been observing them.

"What do you know about the two in the corner nursing their drinks, Roy?"

"Not much. They've been here a few days. Pay their way, so I can't kick on it."

"Know their names?"

"They say their names are Pete Matson and Fred Davis. The one with the red kerchief is Pete. He's the mouthy one."

"Are they freighting?"

"Naw. They came in with only a couple saddle horses and a bedroll. Said something about goin' on up to Canada."

"They'll never make it hanging around here." Sam finished his drink. "I'll turn in. I want to get an early start. Is there a crew up by the bridge?"

"They've got a camp up there. One of the men said they're out cutting timber to use for shoring up. The freighters are gettin' heated up over this."

"Burley and Jim took the lower road. They should be in Nora Springs by now."

"The wagons out front got caught between here and Haggerty's. There ain't no way they could get on the lower trail. It'll snow any time now, and they're worrying about it up on Bitterroot.''

"So am I. That's why I'm crossing that bridge in the morning. If it'll hold a wagon, it'll hold a buggy.''

"In a hurry to get home, huh?''

"Yeah. I could be logging now.''

"Sam, who...ah...is the lady?''

"Elizabeth Caldwell from Saint Louis. I'm escorting her to Nora Springs. Well, good night.''

Sam was sure Roy was going to ask more about Elizabeth but thought better of it. Sam didn't see any reason to satisfy his curiosity.

Sam's departure did not go unnoticed. The two men in the corner had been watching him as closely as he had been watching them.

"That son of a bitch almost broke my neck at Haggerty's. I knowed him soon as he rode in with that woman in the buggy. Ain't no mistakin' that buggy,'' Pete said.

"They took out from Haggerty's with that Injun and old man. Where do ya reckon they went?''

"How in hell do I know?'' Pete glared at his friend. "They was takin' the lower trail, Haggerty said. There ain't no way up from that lower trail with a buggy less'n ya got wings on it. How'n hell did he get here?''

"Stay clear of him.''

"Don't be tellin' me what to do. I'm takin' him down a notch for what he done.''

"He ain't a man to be messin' with.''

"No? I reckon he's got to cross that bridge less'n he's stayin' here.''

"You dunderhead! Mess this up tryin' to get even with that feller and I'll shoot you so full of holes you'll look like a screen door."

"I ain't messin' nothin' up. The crew is off cuttin' lodgepole, ain't they? They is wantin' ta make that bridge strong enough to hold the stage, ain't they?"

"Yeah."

"Underwood told that son of a bitch a wagon crossed. He'll be takin' that buggy 'cross in the mornin'."

"Pete! I swear I'll—"

"Wait. Hold yore horses and listen—"

"We ain't gettin' paid ta settle yore grudges."

"If'n ya'll jist listen, I'll tell ya how we can do both and nobody'll be the wiser. They'll think the bridge warn't strong enough ta hold em."

"I told ya that Ferguson ain't to be messed with."

"He bleeds like any other feller."

"What do you have in mind?"

"It'll be as easy as fallin' off a log."

Pete put his head close to his friend's and began to talk earnestly.

Chapter Sixteen

Elizabeth."

Her name was a soft whisper wooing her from the depths of sleep. She awakened with Sam's hand on her shoulder. She knew instantly that it was his voice, his hand, and reached to cover it with hers.

"Are you awake?" he whispered.

"Yes."

"Dress and come out to the kitchen. You can eat while I load the buggy."

"It was an awfully short night."

"It's cold, so put on your warmest clothes." He struck a match, lit the lamp looked at her. Unruly dark curls framed her face. Her soft pink lips parted as she squinted her eyes against the light. "Open your eyes so I'll know you're awake."

"Mmm. I'm awake." Sleepy green eyes looked at him. A grin split her lips.

"Hurry up so we can get going," he said almost gruffly. Then he went out the door.

Shivering with cold, she used the chamber pot, then dressed, and packed her night things in her valise. Hoping for warm water to wash with, she hurried to the kitchen.

Mrs. Underwood, her forearms covered with flour, was kneading bread at one end of the table. She glanced up, her eyes rudely assessing Elizabeth's blue pinstripe wool skirt and the matching jacket she wore over a white high-necked blouse.

"Good morning. It's cold this morning." Elizabeth hung her coat with the Hudson Bay seal collar on a peg and went to the washstand.

The murmur that came from the woman was scarcely more than a grunt. So much for trying to be friendly, Elizabeth thought, and ladled water into a washdish. She carried the teakettle from the stove and poured in enough hot water to take off the chill. She washed her face and hands, then dried them on the towel that hung at the end of the wash bench.

"Help yourself to meat and mush." The woman spoke almost grudgingly, and Elizabeth's hackles rose.

"Thank you, I will."

Elizabeth served herself mush from the kettle on the stove and sweetened it with honey from the crock on the table. She poured coffee into a heavy cup and weakened it with milk. Then she seated herself at the far end of the table and silently began to spoon the mush into her mouth. It was hot and surprisingly good.

"Do you have relatives in Nora Springs?" the woman asked suddenly.

The question caught Elizabeth by surprise. She wondered why Sam hadn't explained who she was and why she was traveling with him. She didn't see any reason to satisfy the woman's curiosity, so she said, "No."

"Are you going to stay long?"

"I haven't decided for sure, but if I like it, I may stay there permanently."

"What will you do? The only work for a single woman in Nora Springs is in the laundry or keeping house for a widower with kids."

"Is that right? Well, don't worry about me, Mrs. Underwood. I plan to buy the bank."

She looked up to see the woman's mouth fall open and a blank look settle over her face. Elizabeth smiled around the spoon in her mouth.

"I've known Jessie for a long time," Mrs. Underwood said then. Elizabeth waited and wondered what that had to do with what she was going to do when she reached Nora Springs. When Elizabeth made no comment, Mrs. Underwood went determinedly on as if there had been no pause. "She and Sam stop here when they go to Missoula."

"Really? How nice." *Do they share a room?* She wished she had the nerve to ask, just to see the woman's jaw drop again.

"It gets awfully cold up there in the winter. The church women have quilting bees, and the church has a box social once in a while. Other than that there isn't much to do. They're snowed in up there for weeks at a time."

"That sounds delightful to me," Elizabeth exclaimed happily. "I'd get a chance to catch up on my reading." She smiled although she would have dearly loved to throw the bowl, mush and all, into Mrs. Underwood's bread dough.

"We'll go as soon as you've finished," Sam said from the doorway.

"I'm ready now."

"Sam, be sure to tell Jessie I said hello and to hurry back for another visit. You and Jessie stop for a few days when you go to Missoula in the spring. We always have such a good time while you're here.'' The short, plump woman pounded the dough as if she was trying to kill it.

"I'll tell her."

Elizabeth tied a scarf over her head and put on her coat. She smiled sweetly at the other woman.

"Thank you so much for the warm hospitality, Mrs. Underwood. Goodbye."

"Goodbye."

Elizabeth followed Sam through the darkened barroom and into the cold gray morning. He helped her into the buggy and wrapped the blankets around her.

"I don't think Hazel caught the sarcasm in your voice, but I did. What was that about?"

"She was about as warm as a frozen pond. She treated me as if I was a bear about to grab a choice morsel from her dear friend Jessie."

"She and Jessie have been friends for a long time."

"I'm terribly happy for both of them."

"What does she think you're trying to take from Jessie?"

"You."

"Me?"

"You. She and Mr. Owens both took pains to let me know that you are Jessie's property. Somehow everyone has the stupid idea that I'm a threat to their precious Jessie."

"Listen, lady. I'm nobody's *property*."

"Well, don't tell me about it. I'm not interested."

"Yes you are." His face wore a grin that she didn't trust. "You damn well are interested or my name's not Sam Ferguson." His grin broadened so that she could see the flash of his white teeth.

"Then, hello, *George Smith*," she snapped waspishly. Still grinning, he mounted his horse.

They left the station, moved past the freight wagons and went onto the road. There was no sound except for the thud of the horses' hooves and the whistle of the wind as it whipped the tops of the evergreens. Warm breath fogged the crisp morning air.

Sam looked back. All he could see was the white blur of Elizabeth's face framed in the fur collar of her coat. *She was jealous of Jessie!* That had to mean she had special feelings for *him.* She had responded to his kisses, but that could have been because she was love-starved. This was different. She resented Hazel pairing him with Jessie. The warm glow of that discovery lasted until Sam was forced to turn his mind to other matters.

He wished he'd made sure that Pete Matson and Fred Davis were still in their blankets in the room where the men slept. Something about the two men bothered him. Saddle tramps usually didn't hang around stage stations paying for bed and board. If they had money, they would rather spend it on whiskey than a place to sleep. There had to be a reason these two were being cautious.

Daylight brought the promise of another cloudy day. Sam heard a stream of honkers heading south. He peered up, and could barely see the V formation of a hundred or more birds. Their long necks were stretched in flight as they followed their leader to a feeding ground.

"You can't be fooled, can you?" he asked aloud. "You know when it's time to get out before the snow."

Sam loved the sights and the sounds made by the beautiful Canadian honkers. He loved the changing seasons—spring with the deer and antelope roaming the mountain meadows; summer with its clear flowing streams; fall with a panorama of color; winter with the country white and still. The sound of an ax biting into the trunk of a pine could be heard for half a mile.

As much as he loved the woman riding behind, Sam knew his life was here. He would never forget her, just as his father could not forget his mother, but time healed, and in the distant future Sam might find a woman who would give him some measure of contentment.

They came to the bridge an hour after daylight. Sam had not remembered it being that close to Underwood's Station. He stopped, tied his horse and the mare to a downfall beside the road and came back to the buggy.

"I'm going to walk out on the bridge."

"Can I come with you?"

"I guess so, but only as far as the edge."

The span, some fifty feet across and twenty feet above a cut made by a fast-moving mountain stream, was shored up with lodgepole pine. The sideless roadway, made of thick, rough plank, sagged in places, giving it a wavy look. The fierce wind rippled the loose boards, causing a rumbling sound. It also ripped at Sam and Elizabeth as they stood at the edge of the bridge, jarring them with sudden gusts that caused Sam to put his arm around Elizabeth, to hold her at his side.

"There isn't much water down there," Elizabeth said from the shelter of his arm, her voice almost lost in the wind.

"In the spring, when the snow thaws, it'll be bank to bank." He held her. "I'm going to walk across. You'd better go back to the buggy."

"Be . . . careful." She clutched his arm with her gloved hand before he pulled away from her. He anchored his hat firmly on his head and turned his collar up to shield his face from the wind.

Elizabeth didn't take her eyes off him or draw a deep breath as he crossed the bridge. The wind buffeted him so that he had to plant his feet wide apart to keep his balance. It seemed to take forever for him to reach the other side, but when he did, he paused, looked at her and waved his hand. He came back across the bridge holding the brim of his hat with one hand, the collar of his coat with the other.

"It seems to be pretty solid, but that damn wind is awful. I'll take my horse across and come back for the buggy. We'll have to take off the top or the wind will get under it and lift it right off the bridge, taking the mare with it."

"What do you want me to do?"

"Stay here. I'll take my horse over, then the buggy, then I'll come back for you. I figure if the bridge will hold the buggy and the mare, it should hold you." He grinned his devilish grin and bumped her chin with his gloved fist.

Elizabeth looked up to meet his smiling gaze. She had seen those eyes in so many moods; they had laughed, teased, grown fierce with anger. Now they were filled with warmth as the smile she adored claimed his face.

"Oh . . . you—"

Sam had to coax Old Buck to leave solid ground and take the first few steps on the bridge. The sound of his hooves on the planking scared him, and he balked. Finally, tossing his head and rolling his eyes, he allowed Sam to lead him onto the windswept span. Elizabeth watched with her heart in her throat until they reached the other side. Sam tied the horse securely to a tree branch and made the trip back. He went to the buggy and began removing the bolts that held the top in place.

"We could have given the whole top to the Indians if we'd known about this," Elizabeth said.

"I was wishing we had as we were coming up that slope. It would have made it easier on the mare."

As Sam unscrewed the last bolt, the wind helped him lift the top to the side of the road. He turned the top upside down and left it.

"The buggy doesn't look so bad now." Elizabeth stood back, tilted her head and laughed. "I'm almost fond of it. It's become a second home."

Sam checked the load, making sure the blankets in the seat were weighted down so they wouldn't blow out.

"You came up that slope, girl," he said to the mare. "The bridge shouldn't give you any trouble at all."

"Sam—"

"Don't worry. I'll be back for you." He motioned to the side of the road. "Why don't you stay down there in the gully out of the wind."

The mare was even more frightened than Old Buck had been. When she had all four feet on the bridge plank, she tried to rear. Only Sam's weight on the halter, holding her head down, prevented it. He talked to her, coaxed her, and finally she calmed enough to follow him.

It was torture for Elizabeth to watch Sam cross the bridge. She moved into the gully as he had told her to. Unable to help herself, she cast quick glances up, keeping track of his progress. She couldn't bear to watch, yet she had to know what was happening.

To keep her mind occupied, she glanced up and down the gorge. Among the rocks and trees a flash of color caught her eye. She squatted so that she could see beneath the bridge. What she saw was incredible, unbelievable. Two men, one with a red kerchief tied around his neck, were working furiously with a two-man saw, cutting through the timbers that supported the far end of the bridge. As she watched, they sawed through one pole and hurried to another!

"Sam! Sam!" she screamed as she scrambled out of the gully. Without a thought of danger to herself, she ran onto the bridge. "Sam!" Her wail was lost in the wind that pushed her perilously close to the edge, threatening to sweep her off the platform. Elizabeth stiffened her body, throwing her weight forward, and staggered on. "Hurry!" she sobbed. "Please, please hurry!"

It took all Elizabeth's strength just to stay on the bridge, and she made little progress forward. The wind billowed her skirt and swept the scarf from her head. Her hair flowed out behind her. She was halfway across the span when she felt the bridge shudder beneath her feet and saw the back of the buggy tilt. One side of the bridge sank, causing the plank behind her to pop loose and slide into the river. Crazed with fear, she got down on her hands and knees, hiked her skirt up around her waist and began to crawl across the tilted span.

It seemed an eternity before she heard a shout. She was too frightened to look up for fear Sam and the buggy had plunged to the rocks below. Sobbing his name, she crawled as fast as she could. Then he was there, pulling her to her feet, forcing her to run with him over the slanting planks, stumbling over those that had come loose and were flopping in the wind. They reached the end. A gap of several feet separated them from the bank, but Sam didn't slow the pace or hesitate.

"Jump!" he shouted.

She did. They landed on solid ground and took several staggering steps before they could stop. Elizabeth turned and flung her arms around his neck. Sam crushed her to him, lifting her off her feet and swinging her around. He held her in a vise-like grip, buried his face in her neck. Low moaning sounds came from his throat.

"Oh, sweetheart! Oh, my precious love!" The words broke from him in a sob when he was finally able to speak. "You silly, wonderful, precious woman! I love you! I love you so much!" Then he was kissing her eyes, her nose, her lips. "Oh, Lord, I died a million times! Are you all right?" He didn't wait for her to answer. "I thought I'd lost you. Oh, sweetheart! I thought I'd lost you!"

She clutched him with fierce desperation. "I thought...I thought...you'd not make it across in time."

"Dear God! My heart stopped when I saw you out there!"

"I had to come...to tell you to h-hurry."

"I felt the bridge go." His lips moved over her cheek. "I looked back and saw you. My heart almost stopped...I had to get to you...I ran...Somehow the mare got the buggy to the bank. Oh, love..." Words tumbled from his mouth in snatches, words whispered against her ear.

"The men were sawing the posts...so you'd fall—"

"Sweetheart! Thank God, you're safe! I didn't realize you were so precious to me." Hungrily his eyes slid over her face. He kissed her hard on the mouth. Then he raised his face and looked into her eyes. "What did you say?"

"Two men were under the bridge. They had a saw, one on each end. They were sawing through the posts. I wanted you to hurry—I was scared you'd not make it across in time!"

"They were cutting the shoring on this side? Where it sank?"

"I could see them from the other side. They sawed through one post and ran to another."

He swore viciously and put her from him. "Lead the mare away from here and stay with her. Can you do that?"

"Yes. What will you do?"

"Do as I say, sweetheart." He ran to his horse and grabbed his rifle from the scabbard. "Stay away from the bridge," he cautioned, and went into the bushes that grew along the roadway.

Sam dug his heels into the hillside and slid to a ledge above the water. He moved, hunched over, until he reached a pile of partly burned and split poles left by the building crew. He crouched. He could see where the support posts had been cut. One side of the bridge angled almost straight down. The boards creaked as the bridge swayed in the wind. The end of the bridge would break loose at any time, pulling the rest of the bridge with it. Thankfully he was on the windward side.

For what seemed a long while Sam saw nothing. Then he caught a movement on the bank upriver. As he watched, he saw it again. A moment later two men emerged leading horses. One had something red tied around his neck. Without hesitating, Sam got to his feet, lifted the rifle to his shoulder and took careful aim. The bullet struck one man in the leg, right where Sam wanted it to go. Before the echo of the shot died, Sam pumped another shell in the chamber and fired again. The bullet struck the other man high up on the thigh. Both men fell to the ground. The frightened horses took off, splashing across the river.

"Don't touch those guns, or I'll blow your heads off," Sam shouted as one of the men clawed at the holster on his thigh.

Minutes ticked by. When the men didn't move, Sam went toward them, edging his way along the rocks. He had needed those minutes to control the fury that raged within him. The bastards had come within an inch of killing Elizabeth. Had they finished their mission a minute sooner, she would have fallen into that rocky gorge. As he approached, one of the men was thoroughly cursing the other.

"Damn you for a stupid son of a bitch. You bone-headed idiot! I should never have hitched up with a brainless fool! We're through!"

"You sure as hell are," Sam snarled. "I should belly shoot both of you for what you've done. Toss your guns in the river and be damn quick and damn careful doing it. I'd just as soon save the marshal the trouble of taking you to jail, that is if you live that long."

"Don't . . . shoot," Pete begged.

Both men, keeping their eyes on Sam, tossed their weapons into the stream.

"You're the ones that's caused the trouble for the stage line. The bridge crew and the teamsters will give you a welcome when you get back to Underwood's. Get going up that bank unless you think getting shot is better than what's waiting for you."

"We can't! I . . . can't walk . . ." Pete whined.

"Then crawl. I don't give a damn how you do it. I'll give you to the count of three to get started or I shoot you in the other leg. One—"

Fred staggered to his feet. "Get up or lay there and get shot, damn you! I'm not carin'. Ya had to get your own back and ya ruined everythin'!"

"Two—"

Moaning with pain, Pete got to his feet. Both men climbed slowly up the bank, leaving a trail of blood on the rocks and boulders. They had almost reached the top when three men came from the road.

''We heard the shots. The lady told us what happened.''

''You're the bridge crew?''

''Part of it. The rest is bringin' in the poles we cut this mornin'.''

''You'll need plenty, thanks to these bastards, who sawed through your shoring and almost dumped us in the gorge.''

''We didn't do nothin'. It was two other fellers. We was chasin' 'em,'' Pete blabbered.

Sam ignored him. ''You'll find a two-man saw around here someplace,'' he said. ''Get on up to the road.'' He poked Pete in the back with his rifle. ''The lady will know if you're the ones she saw cutting through the piling while I was on the bridge.''

''We ort to string 'em up,'' a bearded crewman growled.

''I suspect they're being paid to keep the bridges out of commission. How's the one up north?''

''All right, far as I know.''

Elizabeth was waiting at the edge of the road when they reached it. Her worried eyes sought Sam's. She hurried to him and slipped her hand into the crook of his arm.

''I heard the shots!''

''These two felt the bullets. I should have aimed higher and they'd have felt nothing at all.'' Sam looked into her anxious face. ''Are you all right?''

''Uh-huh. You?''

''Yeah. Honey, are these the two you saw cutting the timbers under the bridge?''

Elizabeth faced the men. Neither of them could look her in the eye.

''They're the ones. That red neckerchief is what I saw first. Then I bent down and saw what they were doing.''

She placed both hands on Sam's arm as if to reassure herself he was all right. "They were hurrying to cut the posts so that you and the buggy would fall in the river. You are despicable creatures," she fumed at the men with her pert chin high in the air. "You are the dregs of humanity, unfit to live among decent people, and you should be locked up."

"And you should be—"

"Don't say it," Sam said softly.

"They are the ones who were trying to kill Sam," Elizabeth said to the men of the bridge crew. "I will go to court and identify them if that is what it takes to convict them."

Suppressing a grin, Sam looked each crewman in the eye. "Is that enough for you?"

"More'n enough," one answered.

"Then they're yours." Sam walked to his horse and shoved his rifle in the scabbard.

"We'll hold them for the marshal. That is if we don't decide to turn them over to the teamsters at Underwood's for a hangin'." The big black-bearded crewman winked at Sam.

"If they give you any trouble, tie them together and throw them in the river."

"Now, wait a—" Pete sputtered.

"Shut up!" the black-bearded man snarled, then motioned to one of the crewmen. "Tie them up. If they give you any lip, bust them in the mouth." When it was done, he turned to Sam. "What's your name, mister?"

"Sam Ferguson."

"The Sam Ferguson from up around Nora Springs?"

"The same."

"Well, what do you know! I thought your face was familiar. Reckon when I saw it you'd let it grow over with whiskers. It'd be a pleasure to shake the hand of the best all-round lumberjack in the Territory."

"Grossly exaggerated." Sam extended his hand.

"Ain't no such. One time I saw you shimmy up a lodgepole pine and top it before a man could gather a mouthful o' spit."

Sam grinned. "That was when I was young. I'm getting too old for such shenanigans."

"I might come up to Nora Springs someday and hit you up for a job."

"Do that." Sam turned to Elizabeth and led her to the buggy. "We'll be on our way."

"The stage company will be obliged to you for catchin' these two. They've given us a heap of trouble."

"They've given all of us a heap of trouble, especially those freighters back at Underwood's. I wouldn't want to be in their boots when you take them back there."

"We'll see to it they're turned over to the law."

Sam tied his horse to the back of the buggy, climbed in beside Elizabeth and tucked the blankets around her. He lifted his hand to the crew and flicked the horse on the back with the reins.

Chapter Seventeen

Rested, the mare stepped out briskly without much encouragement.

Elizabeth buried her chin in the fur collar of her coat to shield her face from the wind. *They had almost been killed.* The horror of it was still with her, but it was too new for her to think about.

"The mare seems eager to go," Elizabeth said after a silence of several miles.

"She doesn't have to work as hard without the buggy top to hold the wind."

"I hadn't thought of that."

After letting the mare trot for a while, Sam slowed her to a fast walk.

"This buggy will make a good sleigh. I'll remove the wheels and fit it with runners when I get home."

"Do you have a house in Nora Springs?"

"Not a house. I have land, a barn and sheds. The house burned a few years ago. It was just a shack anyway. I was going to tear it down. I've some good lumber aging to build a house when I get around to it."

She wanted to ask if the house was for Jessie. Instead she said, "I've never ridden in a sleigh."

"No? Don't you have snow in Saint Louis?"

"Yes, but seldom so much that a buggy wouldn't do."

"Didn't you have a sled when you were a kid?"

"Young ladies didn't slide down the hill on their bellies and roll in the snow." She laughed nervously. "I used to watch out the window with envy at Becky playing with the stable boy and think it would be fun not to worry about getting wet and dirty and not care what the neighbors would think."

Sam made no comment, and they rode in silence. It seemed strange to Elizabeth to be riding in the buggy without the top. Strange, but nice. She felt more attuned to her surroundings—she smelled the tall pines that lined the road, heard the crisp leaves drifting with the wind, watched the gray clouds rolling overhead. She was acutely aware of the man beside her, and she knew he had mentally distanced himself from her since they left the bridge. She glanced at him. He appeared to be deep in thought.

Perhaps she had imagined that he had said he loved her. And if he had, he was likely sorry about it now and was probably wondering if she had taken his words seriously.

Elizabeth was so engrossed in her thoughts that she did not notice that a few snowflakes had begun to fall. She wished she could move closer to Sam, tuck her shoulder behind his and snuggle against his side.

"How many stations between here and Nora Springs?" It was suddenly very important for her to know how much time she had with him.

"One station, but there are several homesteads where the stage stops for fresh horses."

"Then we'll be in Nora Springs two days from now."

"If all goes well. Are you tired of traveling?"

"I'd be lying if I said I wasn't. I'd like a bath and a chance to wash some clothes. But—"

"But?"

"I'm not anxious to get there," she said in a rush.

Emptiness flowed through her at the thought of not being with him, of seeing him with Jessie, of knowing she and Stephen would be leaving, never to see him again.

Sam's head swiveled slowly. She was looking straight ahead. He couldn't see her face, but he knew she would never make the statement she had just made without giving it serious thought.

"Aren't you eager to see Stephen?"

"Oh, yes. I'm eager to see Stephen. He's a wonderful man."

"I wouldn't know about that. I don't know him very well."

"I do. I know him very well, and he'll understand when I tell him that I want to break our engagement."

"You...want to...what? You're not going to...to marry him?" Sam had never stuttered in his life, but the words just refused to come out.

"No. It wouldn't be fair to him. He's a good, sweet person, and he deserves a wife who would love him to distraction. If I free him, he'll meet her someday and be grateful to me."

"And you...don't love him...like that?"

"I love him like the dear brother I never had. He's been my best friend, my protector, the buffer that stood between me and my stepmother. Now I realize that isn't enough. My heart doesn't pound at the thought of kissing Stephen or spending the rest of my life with him. I'm sure he feels the same about me. Stephen is honorbound to marry me, and I mean to release him."

"How come you didn't realize all this before you left Saint Louis?" Sam demanded almost gruffly.

"Somewhere along the way I forgot the talk I had with your . . . a dear friend who told me about love between a man and a woman. My friends were getting married. I was reaching the age of spinsterhood and feeling depressed, thinking that I'd never find a man to love me for myself alone."

"Are you saying that no one came to call? I can't believe that."

"No. I had plenty of callers. Most of them saw me as a connection to one of Saint Louis's most respected families, and my inheritance was an added incentive."

"Didn't any of them appeal to you?"

"Not a one."

After a long and profound silence, Sam asked, "What were these words of wisdom you've suddenly remembered that have caused you to change your mind about marrying Stephen?"

"My friend told me that love is the strongest emotion in the world. She said that the love between a man and a woman can be even stronger than the love a mother has for her child, that I would know it when I met the right man, and that I should never settle for less. She believed that there was a certain man for every woman, and when she found him, she would give him her heart and soul regardless of any differences between them."

Sam thought about what she said. He knew for certain that he was in love with this woman—completely, utterly, ridiculously in love for the first time in his life. It was as if God had taken his rib and made this woman just for him. Looking at her made his heart stop, then race wildly as it did when she explained her feelings for his brother.

A chill wind caused him to hunch his shoulders and grit his teeth. Even if by some miracle Elizabeth loved him and married him, he would live each day with the fear that she would leave him without warning, just as Eleanor had left his father. To live with that fear each day would be worse than not having her at all.

Large flakes of snow were falling. The mare had slowed to a fast walk. Sam sat hunched over, his forearms resting on his thighs. Elizabeth felt strangely relieved now that she had made her intentions known.

"I'm sorry for the trouble I've been, Sam. I firmly intended to marry Stephen when I left Saint Louis."

"What will you do?" Sam asked without turning his head.

"I don't know. Stephen will help me. Money is not a problem."

"I didn't think it was," he said dryly, making her wish she hadn't mentioned it.

"I don't regret the trip," she said quickly. "I've lived more in the weeks since I left Saint Louis than I have in all my twenty-five years. I've seen the country, the towns, the people. You know, Sam, some people in Saint Louis think all people west of Missouri are savages or uncouth misfits. They're not. They are open and friendly and caring and strong. Good, solid people settled this land."

"Some are also mean, cruel and shiftless, as I'm sure I don't have to remind you. Those two men we just left were harassing Jim Two-Horses at Haggerty's, and I stepped in. To them it was reason enough to kill me—and you, too. This country breeds hard men. The winters are long and cold, and the summers are short and hot." He talked as if doing all he could to disillusion her. "Some people can't stand the isolation. I love it. I don't want someone breathing down my neck all the time."

"We've been through a lot together, haven't we, Sam?"

"To you it may seem a lot, but to us out here it's nothing out of the ordinary. Well . . . maybe a little." As he looked at her, the devilish grin spread over his face. "I've not had to lance a boil on a tony lady's sit-down place before."

"Then I'll have a special place in your memory?" Her eyes caught and held his. She watched the grin fade from his face.

"You bet," he said fervently.

It was growing colder. Large flakes were drifting from the gray sky, faster and thicker. Sam saw a snowflake settle on a curl on Elizabeth's forehead and stay there. Her nose was red, her cheeks rosy. The blanket over her lap began to whiten.

"Are you cold?"

"No."

"You're the stubbornest woman I've ever met," he growled. "If you were freezing to death you'd not say so." He reached across her lap to tuck the blanket more firmly around her.

Elizabeth had no idea if it was noon or afternoon when Sam stopped the buggy to allow the horses to drink at a spring coming from a rock formation beside the road. The sky was full of snowflakes. The wind whipped the white fluff across the road, making it impossible to see very far. Since she had expected Sam to ride his horse, she was pleasantly surprised when he got back in the buggy. He sat closer to her. And as if he expected her to do it, she lifted the blankets, covered his legs and snuggled against his side.

He started the horse, prodding her until she settled into a trot. They were alone in a wonderland of drifting snowflakes. Elizabeth's thigh was snug against Sam's. His big shoulder pressed hers against the seat. There was no world outside, just the two of them alone in the vast whiteness. She was so happy that she was surprised when Sam tilted his head to look at her and ask, "Scared?"

"Scared? Why would I be scared?"

"We're a good ten miles from shelter, and if I'm not mistaken, we're in for a ripsnorting blizzard."

"Is this the Bitterroot you were talking about?"

"This is it. It's about thirty miles across and the meanest place in the world for a snowstorm. It kills two or more travelers every year. They get lost up here in the snow and freeze to death."

"I'm not worried, Sam. I'm hungry."

He grinned, and before she realized it, she was holding his arm with both hands, and she was sure that he hugged her hand to his side.

"So am I. I'd like to have one of those apricot pies you made."

"Sam Ferguson, you've got a sweet tooth. Did you know that someone has discovered sugar can rot your teeth?"

"There's nothing wrong with my teeth." He snapped them at her.

"What else do you like?" She loved it when they could talk like this.

"Dumplings. Amanda cooks big, soft dumplings in the broth of rabbit or prairie hen or pheasant—"

"Who is Amanda?"

"Jessie's mother. She had a boardinghouse, and I eat there a lot."

Elizabeth was quiet for a while. She didn't want to talk about Jessie or think about Jessie. She didn't want Jessie intruding on the time she spent with Sam on this mountain road with snowflakes all around them.

A soft sigh escaped her lips. "It's pretty, isn't it? And quiet—"

"You wouldn't think so after four or five months of it."

"It's so peaceful."

"It would be boring after a while."

"Is it for you?"

"Lord, no. I have so much to do, I hardly have time to think."

"I wouldn't be bored. I'd—"

He cut her off with sharp words. "Yes, you would. Believe me, you would."

Silence. He had withdrawn from her again, not physically, but mentally. She was still snuggled to his side and she could turn her face into the shelter of his arm, but it was different now. Glancing at him, Elizabeth saw that he was peering ahead intently, trying to see through the driving snow. He was so sure that she would be bored and unhappy because his mother had been. She prayed for a way to convince him that being with him would be all she would ever want out of life.

The storm intensified steadily until they could see no more than a few feet ahead of the mare's ears. Even then, Elizabeth didn't worry. It didn't occur to her that she and Sam could become lost and fail to find shelter.

It had, however, occurred to Sam. As the minutes turned into an hour, he began to wonder if he had missed the small homestead where old Slufoot lived and tended the horses for the stage company. Sam had never heard the old man called anything but Slufoot. One leg dragged when he walked, and his tracks in the snow were unmistakable. Someone had pinned the name on him, and it had stuck.

Sam could see tree trunks on the left. There would be a break in the trees when they reached Slufoot's place. If they didn't come to it soon, he'd have to start thinking about what to do. A shelter of pine boughs in the thick woods would be the alternative. Even this early in the year the temperature could dip to below zero here on Bitterroot, and a howling blizzard could last for days. Sam cursed himself for not staying at Underwood's, for risking Elizabeth's life on the bridge and in this blizzard.

Then, there it was, the break in the trees. Lord! He had thought for sure he had missed it. Sam pulled on the reins, and the tired mare stopped.

"I think this is it," he said, getting out of the buggy. "Sit tight."

He walked, leading the mare, his head tilted against the wind. Straining his eyes to see through the curtain of snow, he found the path to the house. Finally the log house loomed before him. He rapped on the door.

"Slufoot," he yelled.

All was white and still. He rapped harder. Only then did he see the square of paper stuck in the crack of the door. Turning his back to the wind and holding the paper close to his eyes, he read:

Gone to Petersons till the stage runs. Eat if you've a mind to but clean up the mess. No whiskey. If'n I had some I'd stay. No money. I took it to buy whiskey.

Randolph Higgenbothem

Sam chuckled. *Randolph Higgenbothem*. Who would have thought old Slufoot would have such a fancy name?

He lifted the latch and the door swung open. He closed it and went back to the buggy.

"The owner is gone, but he left a note." He reached for Elizabeth and lifted her down.

"Do all homesteaders leave notes on the door when they leave?"

"Most people leave a message of some sort. You may find it hard to believe, considering some of the people we've run into on this trip, but most folk in this country respect another man's property."

Elizabeth was glad to get out of the wind even if the cabin was dark and cold. Sam unloaded the buggy, and she stayed at the door to help. He carried things as far as the door. She took them and set them in the room out of the way. After he brought in her trunk, he went to unsaddle his horse and bring the saddle and saddlebags inside.

Sam struck a match, found a candle and lit it. The room was small and sparsely furnished, but there was fuel in the wood box and a fire was laid in the hearth. He adjusted the damper so the smoke would go up the chimney, then held the candle to the tinder and fanned it with his hat until the blaze caught.

After Sam went out to put the horses in the shed, Elizabeth looked around at the crude furnishings. Two bunks were built into the wall opposite the fireplace. There was a table, two chairs, a wash bench, a cabinet of sorts and a cook stove. And it was clean.

Elizabeth hung her coat on a peg beside the door and, shivering with the cold, set about starting a fire in the stove. Sam would need something hot. The water bucket was empty, so she poured the water from their canteen into the coffeepot that sat on the back of the stove. Then she lifted a round lid on the stovetop and set the pot directly over the flame. She couldn't be unhappy about being in this place. For the short time they were here, she would make it a home for Sam.

Sam came in and stamped the snow from his boots.

"It's getting bad. By night you'll not be able to see your hand in front of your face. I ran a line from the shed to the house just in case it's this bad tomorrow."

"Will the horses be all right?"

"Yeah. They've got shelter. I see you've got the cook stove going. I didn't know you knew how."

"I didn't learn to cook on a cold stove." Her eyes twinkled merrily. "I used the water we had in the canteen—"

"Give me the bucket, I'll get some."

They ate cornmeal mush. Elizabeth dropped in the last of the raisins while she was cooking it and found a jug of sorghum for sweetener. They sat at the table with the candle between them.

"Will that hold you for a while?" she asked after Sam had finished the second bowl.

"For now. I'd rather have had pie."

"Oh, you! We don't have anything to make pie. Too bad Mr. Slufoot doesn't have chickens. I'd make you some dumplings."

"How about rabbit?"

"We don't have a rabbit."

"We will by morning. I'll set a couple of snares."

"Oh, Sam. Don't go out again in this weather."

"Don't worry. This is my country. I've been through as many blizzards as you have garden parties." His grin was back, and she basked in it.

"There wasn't much danger of my getting lost and freezing to death at a garden party, but I did almost choke at some of the maneuvering that went on. Sam, you wouldn't believe the things a mother with a fat, bucktoothed daughter approaching the age of twenty will do to get her married off."

Sam's grin widened as he watched her eyes light up.

"I thought a garden party was when women got together and planted potatoes and onions."

"Far from it! They dress in their best and go to see and be seen. I'll have to tell you about the time Netta had a dress sent all the way from New York for a certain party, and old Mrs. Bloomington, who weighs over two hundred pounds, showed up in a dress identical to the one Netta wore. Netta almost had apoplexy. She was cross as a bear for days."

Laughter bubbled as she looked at him. Sam thought she was delectable enough to grab a man's heart right out of him.

"It was that important to her?"

"Oh, yes. It was very important."

Sam's eyes were on her frequently, softly dark and intent, but Elizabeth, unsure of why he should gaze at her so, stared back questioningly. He didn't look away, but rather studied her openly.

"What would we have done if we hadn't found this place?" she asked, not wanting to think about her life in Saint Louis.

"I would have built us a shelter in the woods out of pine boughs, covered it with the canvas and built a fire. We would have snuggled in the blankets and survived, although we'd have been hungry as hell."

"You are so capable, Sam, and so self-reliant. It would be nice to be a man and not have to depend on anyone," she said wistfully.

She turned away then and, anxious to be busy, tidied up after the meal. While she worked, she thought carefully about Sam, about their kisses...their needs. He was certainly keeping his distance, still afraid of being hurt. If only she could tell him that all she wanted in the world was to be with him, that she would never leave him.

Sam went to the shed to check on the horses, and Elizabeth quickly changed into a flannel gown and heavy robe. She was sitting in a fireside chair, brushing her hair, when he came in carrying an armload of firewood. He closed the door quickly against the rush of cold air and put the wood in the box beside the fireplace.

"Snow's piling up," he said. He hung his coat and added another stick of wood to the fire, squatted on his heels and held his hands out to the flames.

Elizabeth filled her eyes with him, the broad shoulders, the narrow waist, the lean hips. *I'll always love him,* she thought. *How could I possibly love another man after knowing him?* She continued brushing her hair in order to have something to do with her hands. This could be her last night alone with him. The thought tortured her.

He sat in the chair opposite her and stretched out his long legs. Because he was so still, she thought he was looking into the fire, and dared to look at him. His brown eyes were staring at her. She held his gaze for a moment, then dropped her eyes, the color coming into her cheeks as she remembered the night in the other cabin when he had brushed her hair.

"It's cold in here. Are you warm enough in that thing?"

She recalled what he had said in the buggy about her freezing and being too stubborn to admit it.

"All except my feet. They feel like two clumps of ice."

He moved his chair over beside her, lifted her feet to his thighs and began unlacing her shoes.

"Hmm. It seems I've seen these shoes somewhere before." His smile was beautiful. Elizabeth couldn't take her eyes from his face.

With his big hands he held her stockinged feet and rubbed them until they tingled.

"Ah... That feels good." She leaned her head against the back of the chair.

Abruptly he set her feet on the floor, got up and went to the bunks where she had spread the blankets. He took a blanket from one bunk and spread it on the other, tucking it in at the foot.

"Go to bed, 'Lizabeth."

Elizabeth looked at him dazedly, her trembling fingers working on the end of her braid, tying it with the ribbon she took from her pocket. With bowed head and shaky legs, she stood.

"You'll only have one blanket."

"It's enough. I'll keep the fire going." He went to the mantel and stood with his back to her, kicking at a log that had rolled off the grate.

Elizabeth was on the point of tears. Why was he being so abrupt? If the storm let up, this would be their last night together. An ache settled in the pit of her stomach and a pain in her heart. She was desperate for him to love her. She yearned to give him all her woman's sweetness and to know the joy of being one with him. She knew with a certainty that he would not make an overture toward her. She would have to do it.

Eleanor had said that someday a man would come into her life who would fill it with his presence. She would love him, he would cherish her, she would give him children. When the time came, he would be an extension of her. Elizabeth wasn't sure if Sam loved her, but she needed sweet memories to take with her into a loveless future. She had to reach out if she would have those memories.

Tension held her very still. Then her decision was made.

Sam turned to her as she dropped her robe onto the chair. His dark, questioning eyes traveled her up and down.

"Sam?" Fear of rejection kept her from saying more.

"Go...to bed," he said huskily, barely moving his lips.

"Sam..." she started again bravely. "Stay with me. Sleep with...me." Holding her chin steady with an effort, she went to him, leaned against him and lifted her hands to his face, feeling the drag of new beard. As her palms held his cheeks, her thumbs stroked the soft hair of his mustache. She trembled with unbelievable tension. "I want to be with you...tonight. I'll not hold on to you. You'll be under no obligation afterward."

"Do...you know what you're saying?" he rasped out hoarsely.

"Yes! Yes, I do. I'm almost twenty-six years old—no longer a girl. I want to know...you."

"'Lizabeth...I can't!" The words were torn from him. It was hard for him to take a deep breath. He could see that she was desperate and uncertain and near tears.

"I love you." She pressed her face to his shoulder. "You don't have to love me back."

"Ah...sweet woman..." His hands on her shoulders pushed her away from him.

Green eyes flooded with tears looked into his. "You don't want me...like that?"

"Dear God! I want you so bad it's tearing my heart right out of me, but there's no future for us, 'Lizabeth.

No future at all! You should save yourself for the man you'll share your life with.''

''There will not be another man. Never,'' she whispered. ''Give me tonight . . . please.'' Her voice vibrated with emotion. Her barriers were down, and her pride was gone.

''But . . . Stephen loves you!''

''Stephen loves me like a sister! Please believe me!''

''Sweetheart, I want to. It's been hell being with you, knowing you were his.''

''I'm yours . . . all yours, if you want me.''

''I want you! Oh, Lord, how I want you—''

He wrapped her in his arms, lifted her off her feet and buried his face in the curve of her neck.

She trembled with unbelievable happiness.

Chapter Eighteen

God help me—but I can't resist you! Sweet woman, I'll despise myself tomorrow.''

"Oh, no! Please don't. I love you so much," she whispered into his ear between kisses. "Are you afraid I'll try to hold you? I won't! I promise, I won't!"

"Wanting you is . . . killing me!"

"I don't want you to hurt!"

His mouth moved over hers, soft then hard. She felt the tremor that shook him when her lips opened to him. His hand moved to her hips, and he pressed her against the rock-hard part of his body that had sprung to life.

"Love me, Sam," she gasped. She tore her lips from his and looked earnestly into his face. "For a few hours let me be your lover."

The emotional plea came from the depths of her heart, bringing a mistiness to her eyes and a tightness to her throat. Her arms closed around him with desperation, and her innermost thoughts leaped to her lips.

"I love you. You fill my eyes with beauty, my heart with joy."

"Oh, love . . . oh, my sweet love . . ." His answer was a groan that came from deep inside him.

Her mouth was trembling and eager against his as he lifted her and carried her to the bunk. He sat her on the edge and knelt. She stroked his head while he rolled her stockings down and pulled them off. The bed was cold when he laid her in it and covered her, but she scarcely noticed. Sam went to the fireplace and set a small log on the grate. Then he blew out the candle.

Scarcely breathing, she watched him in the flickering firelight as if she was in another world and this was happening to someone else. He took off his boots, his shirt and pants and came to stand beside the bunk in a suit of long underwear. He undid the buttons to below the waist, then pulled the garment off his shoulders and over his lean hips. Seconds later he slipped beneath the blankets and gathered her to him.

He was warm flesh, hard muscle. She was warm flesh and sweet-smelling softness.

"My...sweet, beautiful woman, you're too elegant for a rough man like me. But, God help me, I can't help myself...." He buried his face in her hair and quietly held her as if he was holding something far more precious than life. After what seemed like an enchanted eternity, he tilted her face to his and kissed her lips softly, tenderly, again and again.

Sam had no experience with *good* women. The women he'd known had been eager and willing and far more experienced than he. He had placed money on the table beside the bed when he left them and within hours could not recall their faces or names. *Go slowly,* he cautioned himself. Her body was tender and sweet and virginal. He would go where no other had ever been.

Then her soft hands were on his flesh, soft breasts against his chest, long, strong thighs between his, and her mouth…dear God—she was driving him crazy. His body flamed and hardened and began to quake.

"I don't want to frighten you," he muttered thickly.

"Nothing you could do would frighten me." She cupped his cheek with her hand and turned his lips to hers. "I love you," she whispered into his mouth.

Sam's heart was drumming so hard that his breath came jerkily. He was too stunned with happiness and joy of her to utter a word. His hand moved slowly under her gown to stroke her thigh, her hips, and then his hand was at her breast. She moved slightly away to give him access. The need to feel her soft flesh against his caused him to pull at the gown until it was above her breasts.

She slipped the gown over her head and wound her arms around him, pressing every inch of herself to him— her breasts to his hard chest, her soft belly to the taut muscles of his, the soft, furry mound covering her femininity against the maleness that stood hard and firm, a monument of his desire for her.

"Ah . . ." A sound of pure pleasure escaped her.

She burrowed into the haven made by his arms, tasting the clean moisture that dewed the skin of his throat, stroking the crisp hairs of his chest and running her hand over his hard, muscled back.

"You feel so good, my darling. Sam . . . oh, Sam, you are my darling tonight and forever. This…this is the most wonderful night of my life."

Her hands fluttered over his smooth, muscled shoulders and down along his rib cage to his narrow flanks with a freedom that was new and wonderful. A half-choked cry came from him as her fingers touched his quivering flesh. He had not expected this sweet willingness, the astounding passion that lay slumbering beneath her innocence. She was more, far more than he had ever dreamed a woman could be.

"This is the mysterious part of a man I've heard about. Oh, my," she said with wonderment in her voice. Her fingers moved over his aching hardness.

He moaned and murmured, "Ah . . . love—'

"Does it hurt you like it did—the other time?" she asked against his mouth. "Tell me what to do. . . ."

Her mouth trembled against his as his hand cupped her hips and moved them so that the silky down between her thighs teased his hardened flesh. In a frenzy his heated blood raced, swelling him even more. An inarticulate sound escaped from him.

"Oh, sweet, sweet, you tie me in knots."

"Do you love me . . . just a little?"

"Dear God! How can you ask?"

"I love you. I love you." The words were wrung from her, accompanied by fevered kisses on his mouth.

His murmured reply was lost in her kiss. He kissed her hungrily and murmured endearments during the brief intervals when he was not taking the lips she offered so eagerly. "Sweet, sweet, darlin' girl . . ."

His hands moved over her, touching her from breast to thigh. She tangled her fingers in his hair as he made small nibbles across her shoulder and down her neck to her breast. The drag of his rough cheeks and the brush of his mustache sent a powerful tug of desire pulsing between her thighs, where his fingers seemed compelled to go.

He rolled her onto her back and raised himself on quivering arms to hover over her. He kissed her lips, feasted on her lips, then with his hand beneath her breast, holding it up, he buried his mouth in its softness.

Unable to restrain himself, he slid his muscular body over hers. He positioned himself between her thighs with firm but gentle insistence. With new, sweet freedom, she opened her legs to welcome him when she felt the first firm, velvet touch of his probing flesh at the moist opening in her body. The gentle nudging started a fire that surged through the seat of her femininity, causing involuntary shudders of delight. Wholly caught up with the sensations trembling from that secret place, she spoke to him in snatches of almost inaudible words.

"My love . . . my wonderful man . . ."

"Ssh . . . darlin'. Be still and let me love you."

Holding her buttocks in his hands, he slowly slid into her until he felt what he had never felt before, the membrane guarding her virginity. It was a once-in-a-lifetime moment for both of them, one that both of them would hold in their memories like a secret treasure for as long as they lived. He held himself there for endless seconds while little spasms of exquisite pleasure rippled through her.

"Liz, honey . . ." Her name was a caress on his lips.

"Sam?" There was uncertainty in her voice, and she began to kiss his face frantically and thrust upward. "What's wrong?"

"Nothing's wrong, love. It's all so perfect, so damn perfect!"

A low, growling sound came from deep in his throat as she rose to meet the driving shaft of pleasure. Then suddenly, unexpectedly, there was a pain so intense that she cried out his name. Then she was floating on a mighty wave, seeking more and more of the delicious pleasure of being filled where before there had been emptiness. An unending moan rose in her throat with every surge of his magnificent, probing flesh. Her arousal intensified to so great a pitch that fire ran along her nerves and her eyes flew open. She had the strange sensation of not knowing where his body ended and hers began.

"Oh . . . oh, my—"

When gratification came, it split her body into fragments, each alive with vibrant sensations. The explosion sent her rising, gasping upward, spinning her into the warm, misty darkness. The only thing holding her was the glorious spear that pierced her very soul.

Sam's bursting body writhed in the sweetness he had entered. He felt himself enveloped in a sheet of flame that ignited his every nerve. He was enclosed in sweet softness, pillowed in a warm and silken place where an irreversible tempo built to a consuming release. Then his mind and his body separated, and he was floating, flying and drowning all at once. He felt his soul reeling somewhere above his body, which erupted and filled her with his life-giving fluids.

Reason returned. He turned with her in his arms. They lay, their arms wrapped around each other, breathing deeply. When he finally stirred, it was to pull the blankets more snugly around them. Still cradled in the loving folds of her body, her belly tight against his, he solemnly kissed her forehead, her eyelids one after the other, and smoothed the tangles of hair from her face with gentle fingers.

"What happened?" she whispered in a low, husky rasp. "It was as if I left my body and went to this beautiful place." Tears trickled from her eyes and rolled down her cheeks and onto his shoulder.

"Did I hurt you?" he asked anxiously.

"Oh, no! I didn't want it to end. It was so beautiful."

"It was for me, too."

"You've . . . done this before. You knew what to expect."

"No, love, I've not done *this* before." His voice was a shivering whisper. His hand stroked her hair gently, as though she was fragile and infinitely precious. "Not like this," he repeated with a world of meaning in his voice.

"Are you warm?" she asked, feeling along his back to see if it was covered.

"Uh-huh."

The completeness of their lovemaking had left her exhausted. She fell asleep almost immediately. Sometime later she was drowsily aware of a hard body pressed to her own, of the hand that cupped and fondled her breast. With tender eagerness she turned her face to his and accepted his hungry kisses, gently shifting her hips to welcome him to her most private self. The feel of him was exquisitely pleasurable. His heart thundered against hers, and she moved her hand down to his taut, driving buttocks.

"Sweetheart!" he whispered helplessly, and with a long breath he thrust with frenzied urgency.

She held him tightly to her when his body jerked repeatedly, filling her with a healing warmth. From some far-off place she heard a soft, triumphant, "Dear God!"

"I love you," she whispered.

Feeling wonderfully loved and relaxed, she cuddled in his arms and was almost instantly asleep.

Sam sat in the fireside chair, his hands clasped over his stomach, his booted feet stretched out to the fire. The storm had intensified. Snow, driven by a gale-force wind, had sifted in under the door and onto the windowsills. He looked across to the bunk where Elizabeth lay sleeping. He had covered her with all the blankets and his heavy sheepskin coat.

He stared into the fire, assembling and sorting out his thoughts. He had not meant for the intimate, soul-stirring, gut-stomping experience he'd shared with Elizabeth to happen. His intentions had been to take her to Stephen, then head for the logging camp where he hoped to get her out of his mind, if not his heart. He admitted that every night since he'd met her he had fantasized about holding her, warm and naked, in his arms. What man in his right mind *wouldn't* want to hold her? He was a man with the same desires for a woman as any other, and hunger for her had torn at his groin.

She had said she loved him. Did she? He wondered if she had been only carried away by thoughts of a romantic interlude. Yet she had given herself openly, completely, and had been more loving than any woman of his dreams. He recalled hearing that physical love was distasteful to the so-called *refined* women. This glorious creature had taken uninhibited pleasure in their mating, and the thought of parting from her brought on acute despair.

Sam reached the conclusion that this was a woman he could give his heart to, but with whom he could not share his life. A man needed a woman who would share the hardship as well as the joy. Living with her would be like living with a keg of powder that could erupt at any moment. She would vanish, leaving his life shattered.

In the quiet of the night, with only the sound of the wind lashing the cabin, he reflected on his future. He would build his house amid the tall pines. In a few years he would find a steady, quiet, undemanding woman who would give him children. He in turn would give her a home and security. Elizabeth would find a man to love her as she deserved to be loved.

Sam was so lost in his thoughts that he didn't know Elizabeth had gotten out of bed until she was beside him. She stood there in her long white gown, her bare feet on the cold plank floor.

"'Lizabeth!" He drew up his legs. "Go back to bed. It's cold in here."

"Why did you get up?"

"I . . . had to tend the fire."

She took his hand. "Come back to bed with me."

"No. I'll sit here a while."

She turned and sat on his lap, then wrapped her arms around his neck and snuggled against him, bending her knees to place her feet on his legs.

"Let me stay with you." She turned her face into his shoulder and nuzzled the warm flesh of his neck.

"'Lizabeth . . ."

She raised her head to look at him. He was so close she could see every detail of his face: the dark half-closed eyes, the strong nose, the sensual curve of his mouth, the darkened cheeks, the silky hair on his upper lip, the sweep of his brows. *Oh, please, God, don't let that be regret in his eyes!*

He drew her close against him, her breast against his chest, her head on his shoulder. She curled her arm around his neck. He pulled her feet up and covered them with with her gown. She felt his fingers in the mass of hair that had come loose from the braid. He stroked it for a long while. The sigh of the wind and the crackle of the fire were the only sounds she heard above the beating of his heart.

"You're sorry, aren't you, Sam?" She gnawed on her lower lip, refusing to acknowledge the tears that gathered behind her eyelids.

"It would be better for both of us if it hadn't happened. But what's done is done."

"Why do you say that?" He was silent for so long that she brought her hand up to his face. "Tell me."

"We both know why, 'Lizabeth. We have no future together. We would make each other miserable."

"I'm not trying to tie you to me, Sam." Swallowing the lump that clogged her throat, she tried to speak naturally.

"Someday when you're back among your own kind, you'll be glad."

"Thank you for giving me a wonderful memory." Thank God her voice didn't reflect the misery that covered her like a black shroud.

"You've given me a cherished memory, too." He murmured the words in her hair.

She held her lips tightly between her teeth. Tempestuous feelings were threatening to overpower her. She was at life's crossroads; one road would lead her to heaven, the other to hell. Only her strength of character kept the inner misery hidden.

Later, when Sam carried her to the bunk and covered her with the blankets, she lay there and cried silently. Then the weight of her wretchedness hit her, sending her into the black pit of despair that not even tears could reach.

Elizabeth was awakened by the sound of the door closing. Drugged with sleep, she raised her head to see Sam lowering an armload of wood into the box. When he straightened, he glanced at her, and their eyes met briefly.

"Storm hasn't let up one bit."

Elizabeth wanted to say she was glad. Instead she said, "I smell something cooking."

"I caught two rabbits in my snares. One is in the pot." He went to the door. "I'll bring in more wood."

"You don't have to leave so I can get dressed. Just turn around." She laughed nervously.

He went to the wash bench and poured water in the washdish from the teakettle and carried it to the bed. His eyes caught hers as he set it down on the floor.

"Thank you."

"I'll be out for a while," he said, and went out the door.

Elizabeth used the chamber pot and washed herself in the warm water Sam had so thoughtfully provided, then dressed hurriedly. In the light of day it was hard for her to believe that she had lain in the narrow bunk wrapped in Sam's arms and that they had done the dreadful *thing* she had heard discussed by her friends. There had been nothing dreadful about it. It had been wonderful, glorious, and she would not let herself think that it would never happen again.

Sam loved her. Otherwise how could he have been so sweet, so gentle, so loving? He had admitted his love at the bridge. Now he was afraid to commit himself. She had to find a way to convince him that, although she and Eleanor came from the same background, she was not Eleanor.

A rush of cold air swept across the floor when Sam came in. His mustache was frosty, his face red with the cold. His eyes caught hers the instant he came in the door.

"It's below zero."

"How can you tell?"

"By the way the twigs snap and the snow crunches under my feet."

He hung up his coat. She poured coffee for him and set it on the table. With a rag she lifted the lid on the iron kettle where the rabbit was simmering and poured in more water from the teakettle. These were the things she would be doing, she thought, if they were married and living in a home of their own. She would see to her husband's comfort, pour his coffee, cook his meals. At night he would hold her in his arms and they would whisper intimate things for only each other to hear. In the morning, over breakfast, they would talk about everyday things like the weather.

"I wonder if it's blizzarding in Nora Springs," she said while refilling the teakettle from the water bucket.

"Could be. These quick blizzards hit the mountain ranges, and usually they move on down into the valleys before they play out."

Elizabeth poured coffee for herself and sat across from him. She looked into his face, but he looked everywhere but at her.

"Do you work outside all winter?"

"Sure. It's sheltered up in the woods. It gets colder than hell, but as a rule there's not much wind."

After that Elizabeth couldn't think of anything to say. The silence in the cabin was deep. They were like two polite strangers. Elizabeth squirmed inwardly. She felt a desperate desire to plunge into the subject uppermost in her mind.

"Sam, will you listen to what I want to say?"

Although he finally looked at her, he waited so long to speak that she was not sure he was going to.

"Say what you're determined to say." His dark eyes raked her face searchingly while remaining inscrutable themselves.

"Please let me tell you about your mother. Don't you want to know what kind of person she was? How she lived? What she did?"

"I figured that was what was on your mind." His unreadable scrutiny sent an icy chill through her body. "You forget that I *know* what kind of a person she was."

"But—"

"And I don't give a damn about how she lived or what she did, just as she didn't give a damn about how I lived or what I did. She is dead to me and has been for the past twenty-two years."

"Sam…please. What harm will it do if I tell you about her?"

One brow lifted, and his dark eyes glinted with anger.

"Leave it be, Elizabeth. You're meddling in a family matter that is none of your concern."

For a heart-stopping moment she sat there, her face slowly turning scarlet. Her green eyes misted. This couldn't be happening—not after all that had transpired between them. She looked into his face and realized things could not possibly get any worse between them. It was too late to turn back. She took a deep breath and plunged in.

"You're a lonely, bitter man. Your mother didn't die for you twenty-two years ago. Deny it if you will, but she's been in your heart all this time—"

"Enough!" Sam slammed his hand on the table.

Elizabeth refused to be intimidated by his loud voice. It was now or never, she thought.

"You loved her so much. Eleanor had a way of making people love her."

"Oh, yes," he sneered. "She was a sweet, delicate little thing with the soul of a viper!"

"What she did to you and your father was wrong," Elizabeth went on determinedly, "but I knew her. I know that she loved you, Sam."

"Did she tell you that, Miss Prissy-tail Caldwell?"

"No, but—"

"Did she mention me at all?"

"No, but—"

Sam got up so fast his chair tipped over. He bent over the table and glared into her face. His eyes were cold, his words clipped when he spoke.

"I don't want to hear another word! Not another damn word about that bitch!"

Elizabeth stood. "You love her still."

He jerked his coat off the peg and slammed his hat on his head. "I despise her!" he shouted, and pulled on his coat.

"You love her. She was your mother. She gave you life—"

"I'll show you how much she means to me." He went to his saddlebags and pulled out a packet of letters. "Stephen brought these letters from my *dear mama*. I've not read them. I will *never* read them." He flung them into the fireplace and stomped out, slamming the door behind him.

"No! Oh, no!"

Elizabeth grabbed the poker, raked the packet from the fire and stamped out the flames that burned along the edges. The four envelopes were tied together with a blue ribbon. She recognized the handwriting and the stationery. Eleanor had written to Elizabeth regularly while Elizabeth was away at school. Elizabeth held the letters in her hands and read the name on the envelope through a blur of tears: "Samuel Ferguson."

Oh, Eleanor. How could you? You not only have made your son a bitter man, you have ruined my life!

Elizabeth took the letters to the table and sat. She looked at them for a long time. As far as Sam was concerned, the letters had been destroyed. What harm would it do if she read them? Knowing she shouldn't but compelled to do so, she opened the first letter and began to read.

After she read all four letters, she folded her arms on the table, buried her face in them and cried. She cried for Eleanor, for Stephen and for Joe Ferguson. But most of all she cried for Sam.

Chapter Nineteen

The storm of weeping passed.

While Elizabeth washed her face and tidied her hair, she mulled over every word that had been said between her and Sam up until he slammed out the door. She had seen him angry before, but never this angry. He was a man of changing moods: fierce and cruel when he was angry, sweet and gentle when he was pleased. He was also honest and straightforward. The anger that flared so suddenly was the result of deep and lasting hurt. Last night he had said that they had no future together. He sincerely believed that to be true. She had understood his feelings perfectly and had asked, even begged him to take her to bed.

Sam didn't want a future with her even though he cared for her. A man like Sam wouldn't blurt out his love as he had done at the bridge without meaning it. That he chose to ignore his feelings was his way of shielding himself from hurt.

She would not, could not make another overture as she had done the night before. Where had all that courage come from? She had read someplace that love had no pride. She was beginning to believe it.

Sam was going to know what was in the letters regardless of how angry he became. She would do that much for him, and then it would be up to him. He could live with his bitterness or he could put it behind him.

Elizabeth straightened the bunks and swept up the snow Sam had tracked in; the plank floors were so cold the snow had not melted. She searched their supplies and those in the cabin and found what she needed to make dumplings, all except for sage, which she decided she could do without. Grateful for something to do, she stirred up the batter. When the rabbit was tender enough to fall from the bone, she dropped large spoonfuls of soft dough in the boiling broth and covered the pot with a tight lid.

Time went by, and Sam hadn't come back. Elizabeth moved the kettle to the back of the stove. She went to the window to look out. It was still snowing, but the wind had died down. The world outside the cabin was a white wonderland. The ground, covered with a foot of the fluffy white snow, was a sharp contrast to the deep green of the evergreen trees that surrounded the cabin. Elizabeth watched tiny brown sparrows flit from the trees in search of food. Nothing else stirred.

Sam had been gone for a long time. It hurt her to know that he would rather be out in the cold than inside with her where it was warm. Worry for his safety set in. She began to pace the length of the small room. She was so nervous that when a burning log fell from the grate, she jumped and her hands flew to her throat in fright.

Something could have happened to him. His rifle was in the corner, but his gun belt was missing. At least he was armed ... but he had been armed the night the one-eyed man slipped up on him. Had the one-eyed man and the fat man come looking for Sam? Fear knifed through her, and she decided to take the rifle and go looking for him.

She was reaching for her coat when the door opened and he came in. She was relieved yet angry at him for the worry he had caused. He hung up his coat and hat before he looked at her.

"Your dinner is ready," she said quietly, but was unable to keep the chill out of her voice.

Without waiting for him to say anything, she dished up a generous helping of meat and soft, fluffy dumplings. She set the plate on the freshly scoured table, poured coffee in a cup and set it beside the plate.

"Are you going to eat?" he asked when she made no move to fill a plate for herself.

"No. Not now."

"Why not? You didn't have breakfast."

"I'm not hungry. I'll eat something later." She found herself looking directly into his eyes and watched his gaze fall away and become fixed on the plate before him.

"Suit yourself." He shrugged his shoulders and sat down.

Elizabeth went around the table to the fireside chair. The emotional strain had taken its toll on her strength and knotted her stomach, making it impossible to eat. As her fingers clutched the letters in her pocket, she wondered where in the world she would find the courage to bring up the letters. But bring them up, she would.

When Sam finished eating, he came to the fireplace and added several large split logs to the those burning in the grate.

"The dumplings were good."

"Thank you."

"You should eat something."

Elizabeth washed the plate Sam had put in the pan and covered with water from the teakettle. He was a man used to doing for himself. He didn't need a woman to do for him. She forced herself to look directly at him as she dried the dish and wiped the crumbs from the plank table.

He was watching her. She refused to be moved by the shadow of hurt she saw in his eyes. She was hurting, too, and unless she acted, she would go on hurting for the rest of her life. When she finished the meager chores, she hung the wet cloth on the oven door handle to dry and sat at the table.

Sam sat in the fireside chair, his forearms resting on his spread thighs, his clasped hands dangling between his knees.

She felt both pity and irritation. Pity for the small boy who had been hurt, and irritation at the man who had refused to try to understand his mother.

For a long time Elizabeth stared at his broad back and bowed head. The silence that enveloped them was utterly complete. Taking a deep, trembling breath, Elizabeth pulled the letters from her pocket, opened them, took out one and placed it on top of the others on the table before her. She closed her eyes tightly and said a silent prayer that when she began to read he would not explode into a rage.

Then, into that continuing stillness, she began to speak in a not quite steady voice.

My Dearest Sammy,
Today is your fifteenth birthday. Are you as tall as your father? You were well on the way when I saw you last. I can still see you strutting proudly into the woods with your little ax on your shoulder, doing

your best to be like him. Joe was so proud of you,
our firstborn.

Elizabeth dared a glance at Sam's back, surprised that
he hadn't jumped to his feet and snatched the letters from
her. Encouraged, she read on, slowly now, pronouncing
each word distinctly.

I have written to you on each of your birthdays,
knowing that you may never read my words, but
taking comfort in writing because it made me feel a
little closer to you. I don't suppose a young man
wants to read that his mother loves him, but, oh, I
do love you, Sammy. If only I could turn back the
clock. But if I could I don't know if I would do
anything differently, feeling as I did at the time. I
was so frightened that summer five years ago, so
frightened that I feared for my sanity. You see, my
dearest Sammy, I thought by leaving you, I was
doing what was best for you and for my precious
Joe, whom I loved with all my heart.

I am taking pen in hand on this fifteenth anniver-
sary of your birth to tell you why I left you, not to
offer any excuses for myself.

When I was growing up, my mother's sister,
Clara, lived with us. She was a sweet, gentle person. At age twenty she suffered from a sickness unknown to the doctors. She lost the use of her hands,
then her legs. Her muscles seemed to dissolve. In a
year's time she was completely helpless, unable to
move except to swallow the food put into her mouth.
She had to have constant care during the three years
she lived. Thankfully my parents were able to af-
ford that care. All that the doctors could tell us was

that they believed it a weakness in the females of our family.

Can you imagine my fright that summer when at times I became so weak that I sank into a chair because my legs wouldn't hold me and I was unable to raise my arms above my head? There was not a doubt in my mind that I had Aunt Clara's sickness and that soon my husband and my boys would be burdened with a helpless woman. To me it was unbearable to think of my Joe having to take care of me. How could he work and support a family with a helpless wife on his hands? I had to come home to my parents.

Dearest Sammy, I couldn't take both of Joe's boys from him. You shared his love for the woods. Stephen was so young. I was selfish enough to want one of my sons with me during what I considered my last days. So I sneaked away like a coward. Your little tear-stained face has haunted me every night for the past five years, and I'm sure it will haunt me until the day I die.

At the time I comforted myself with the thought that I had saved you and Joe the agony of seeing me die a useless pile of flesh and bone, bedridden and helpless.

The irony of it, sweet Sammy, is that I didn't die. When I arrived home, I took to my bed, a total wreck of a woman who believed her life was over. After a few months I was stronger. The doctor said I had suffered from exhaustion. I didn't believe him at first. Finally I had to, but it was too late. I knew in my heart that you and Joe despised me. I had told Stephen his brother and father were dead because the poor little boy grieved so for you both. How

could I tell him otherwise? He is happy here, while
I am locked into a nightmare.

There you have it, my dearest boy. I hope someday to have the courage to mail this to you. Never,
never think that I left you because I didn't love you.
Happy birthday, darling. You are in my heart now
and always.

                                              Mother

Her voice cracking, Elizabeth finished reading the letter. With tears in her eyes she looked at Sam. He sat
hunched over, his head bowed. There was no way for her
to tell if he had heard the words she had read to him. She
looked at the next letter. It was written on his twentieth
birthday, and the next one when he was twenty-five years
old. The last letter had been written two years ago, when
he was thirty. In the last letter there were also four yel-
lowed pages that recorded a line or two written on each
of Sam's birthdays. All the pages had smears from what
surely must be Eleanor's tears.

Sam sat as still as a stone. Elizabeth sighed deeply. She
had done what she could to bring him peace. The rest was
up to him. She placed the letters in their envelopes and
got up from the table. She went to his side and held the
letters out to him, fully expecting him to snatch them
from her hand and to throw them in the fire.

He didn't move.

Elizabeth waited. Then her eyes moved to the clasped
hands hanging between his knees. *They were wet!* She
bent to see his face and saw tears falling from his eyes like
drops of rain. *He was crying!* Not a muscle moved, but
he was crying. Her shock held her immobile for a dozen
heartbeats before she slipped the letters into her pocket
and dropped to her knees between his spread legs. She

put her arms around him and pulled his tear-wet face to her shoulder.

"Oh, Sam! Oh, please try to understand and forgive her."

In a quick movement he grabbed her to him as if she were a lifeline in a storm-tossed sea. He crushed her in an embrace and buried his face in the curve between her neck and her shoulder. His large frame shook with great, silent sobs. Elizabeth held him and stroked his back.

"My dearest, my love, your mother suffered a living death knowing you and your father were lost to her forever."

With tears rolling down her cheeks, she offered him what comfort she could.

"Eleanor didn't leave because she hated this country or the hardships. She told me many times how beautiful the trees were and how clear the mountain streams. She said the sky was bluer than blue here in Montana. The reason she never mentioned you or your father was that it was so painful. She kept you all to herself, locked in her heart. She didn't want to share you with anyone. Not even Stephen."

Finally his arms loosened, and he raised his head. He looked into her face unashamedly. His thick lashes were spiked, his brown eyes glistening with tears. Elizabeth lifted the end of her apron and wiped his face, then cupped his cheeks with her palms and kissed his eyes, then his lips.

"I'm so glad you can cry, Sam. My father told me that only strong men feel deeply enough to cry."

He pulled her off the floor and onto his lap. She snuggled in his arms. He nestled his warm mouth against her forehead with a gentle reverence that turned her heart over.

"Thank you for fishing the letters out of the fire," he whispered huskily.

"You were hurting, hurting so badly." She lifted a trembling hand and stroked his cheek.

"I've lived with it for a long, long time," he murmured.

"The other letters will tell you more about her. The one I read explained her leaving."

"I'll read them . . . later."

"The Eleanor I knew was sweet and gentle, and her eyes were always so sad. I don't think I ever heard her laugh."

"I thought for a long time that I had done something to make her leave us." His voice was strained, husky. "Later I convinced myself that she just wanted to go, that she liked the easy life and didn't love us enough to stay and make a home for us."

"She must have been desperate. I remember my father talking about Clara and how someone had to be with her day and night. She couldn't talk or turn her head. Eleanor didn't want the ones she loved to see her like that."

"Pa loved her so much. It tore the heart right out of him when she left."

"Poor lonely man," she whispered, and moved her face so she could place kisses along the line of his jaw. "Will he let me tell him about her?"

"He never said a word against her. He loves her still."

"Your mother wrote to you on each of your birthdays."

He started to speak and failed. They were silent for a long while. He slowly stroked her back in silent communication. Finally he lifted her face with a firm finger beneath her chin.

"What about us, Elizabeth?" His eyes met hers and held them steadily.

"You know how I feel. I love you. I want to spend the rest of my life with you, be your wife, your lover, have your babies. You said we didn't have a future together. I know you were afraid to depend on me for your happiness. Let's depend on each other and build our future together."

In an instant his face changed as if an inner light had been turned on. He turned the full impact of a coaxing smile on her upturned face.

"You're willing to spend the rest of your life with a hell raiser?"

"Well—" she pretended to be in deep thought "—I guess I can live with a hell raiser if you can live with a tony prissy-tail." Her eyes, made all the greener by the dark smudges beneath them, sparkled happily into his.

He lifted his hand to push a strand of hair behind her ear; there his fingers lingered, their tips against her earlobe. He watched her face in fascination as her eyes changed from sparkling with devilry to being soft with love.

"I'm in love with you, pretty little prissy-tail." His voice shook with emotion. "I want to spend every day of my life with you. When I come home from a day's work, I want you there waiting for me. At night I want you in my bed loving me." His hand moved up and down her arm. She didn't know she was crying until his fingers brushed the tears from her cheeks. "Darlin'! Don't cry!"

"I'm crying b-because I'm so h-happy, you...big p-pea-brained—"

"Then hush up your bawlin' and kiss me." His last words were a mere whisper against her lips.

Her arm slid around his neck as she surrendered her mouth to his. His kiss was sweet, gentle, one of deep dedication.

"Liz...Liz, you're sweet...so sweet," he whispered, his lips moving to her eyes. "You were sweet before...but now that you're mine..." His voice was no more than a sigh. His mouth returned to hers, and his tongue gently stroked her lips, the moist, velvet caress sending spasms of delight down her spine.

She gently stroked the soft hair above his lip.

"Do you like it, love? I'll grow a beard if you like." The words were said between nibbles on her fingers.

"No beard. I love this." She angled her head so that their noses were side by side and rubbed her face against his mouth. A soft sound came from his throat, and she felt the trembling in his body when she wiggled against hardness that was suddenly pressing against her hip.

"Keep that up and I'll carry you over to the bunk and have my way with you," he threatened.

She leaned back to look at him. "Do decent people do *that* in the daytime?" Her fingers combed the hair at his temples.

He chuckled softly, his eyes moving lovingly over her face. "Some do."

"Will we do it after we're married?"

"Why not...before?"

"Ah... Samuel Ferguson, you are an extremely smart man." Her voice was soft and beautiful, and her eyes were achingly anxious. "Come to bed and love me. I can't think of a nicer way to spend a cold, blizzardy afternoon."

"Oh...sweetheart, I don't deserve you." He buried his face in the side of her neck.

"Hmm. That sounds familiar. I think you said that when you met me in Missoula."

He groaned. "I was as dumb as a stump!"

"You're a fast learner," she teased between pecking kisses.

"Get in the bed," he whispered anxiously. "I'll stoke up the fire and drop the bar across the door."

Elizabeth shed her clothes and climbed between the cold blankets on the bunk, shivering in anticipation more than from the cold. Her eyes feasted on each part of Sam's body that was revealed to her as he undressed. He stood before her on muscular legs, and where they joined she saw the thatch of dark brown curls that enclosed the root of his maleness. For the first time she saw the male body ready for love. His member stood firm and hard. She stared at him with the fixed expression of the hypnotized before her lips parted and the air escaped from her lungs with a pleasurable sigh.

He lay beside her. She pressed her body's full length to his. He felt her satiny breasts crush against his chest, felt the down covering her mound brush his hardening body and the warm writhing skin of her slender thighs interlace with his. He gathered her close to his long, muscular body with a sigh.

"I love you, my pretty little prissy-tail," he muttered thickly between kisses, and stroked the thick, dark curls from her face.

Her arms held him closer, her body strained against his. He covered her face with kisses, releasing his pent-up desire with each touch of his lips. He stroked her breasts, bent to look at them and caressed them with his eyes, then his mouth. His hand moved between her thighs, stroking her soft inner skin, moving upward. She gave a muffled, instinctive cry as his fingers found her wetness and probed gently inside.

After a prolonged, delicious discovery of each other, they were interlocked and breathlessly surrendering to a voracious hunger that found her as impatiently eager to receive him as he was to insert himself into her yielding warmth. And then they were one fierce flesh, seeking the peaks that could not be found alone. He was deep inside her, and she gloried in the delicious invasion. Soon they were swept beyond the limits of return, into a private, mindless tilting world. When it righted again, she was holding him tightly.

"I love you, love you . . ." She held his head pillowed against her breasts until his breathing audibly calmed.

"I love you, darlin'."

"Is it getting easier for you to say?"

"Much easier. I'm going to tell you every day of our lives."

"I'll never leave you—"

"It . . . would kill me if you did."

"Oh, love . . ."

He placed a kiss on her breast and laid his cheek on it with a long, gusty sigh. "I could stay here forever."

"You're tired. Rest, darling."

"Am I too heavy for you?"

"No! Heavens, no!"

He lay quietly. She stroked his head. Love for him filled her heart. Now that she knew of this pleasure she could give him, and he her, she would banish that lonely, love-starved look from his eyes and fill his life with love. She needed him. He needed her. Oh, it was so wonderful to belong to him. She would take care of him always.

She reached to secure the covers over him, delighting in the sensation of his warm body against hers. They were in their own little private world. Never had she felt so safe, so loved, so complete. And never had she been more determined that nothing, and no one, would take this happiness away from them.

Chapter Twenty

The sun shone brightly on a countryside cloaked with white. The world was glistening snow, green trees and a wide expanse of blue sky. Elizabeth's laughter rang out in the still morning air as she pelted Sam with a ball of snow when he came from the shed, leading his horse.

"I'll get you for that," he shouted, and hurried to tie his horse behind the waiting buggy.

She let fly another missile that missed him completely and struck Old Buck, causing him to dance sideways. She hurriedly formed another ball as Sam came toward her. She rushed her throw, missed him again and began to run, her laughter trailing behind her.

Sam caught her easily, whirled her around and received the fistful of snow she had secreted in her hand.

"You little devil! I'll wash your face..."

She broke away while he was wiping the snow from his face. "Sam, Sam, catch me if you can!" she chanted.

He caught her after a dozen yards, as she knew he would. An expression of warmth and laughter shining on his face, he wrapped her in his arms just as his feet slipped out from under him. They fell into the snow with her on top of him. He lay there, holding her, staring in fascination at her sparkling green eyes, rosy cheeks and pink, parted lips. She lay between his spread thighs and laughed at him. Then she propped her elbows on his chest.

"Shouldn't you be looking down at me?" she asked seriously, then laughter rang out as she grabbed another handful of snow.

"Not always and...no, you don't," he said, and grabbed her wrist.

"Kiss me and I'll let you up," she murmured sweetly.

Sam was still chuckling as she lowered her head and tantalizingly caressed his lips with her tongue while he pressed her tightly to his groin. She ended the kiss and lifted her nose with prim confidence.

"That will teach you not to get smart with me."

Laughing, Sam stood and brushed the snow from her coat and skirt. With their arms around each other they went to the buggy. Sam settled her on the seat and tucked the blankets around her before he climbed in beside her.

"I read the note you left for Slufoot," he said as he put the mare in motion. "'Your cabin is beautiful,'" he quoted, and snorted.

"It *is* beautiful. I'll remember it forever," she said defensively, and tucked her hand under his arm.

When they reached the road, it was a sea of unbroken white. Sam put the mare into an easy trot as they rolled silently over the snow.

"When we get home, I'll put runners on the buggy and take you for a sleigh ride."

"With sleigh bells?"

"Sure. I've got several strings."

"I love you."

He looked at her and saw that the laughter had gone from her face.

"What brought that on?"

"I'm scared. I'm afraid your father and your friends will disapprove of me. I know Mr. Owens will."

"I don't care if anyone approves of you or not, sweetheart. Why is it important to you?"

"Mr. Owens said everyone expected you to marry Jessie. He said Jessie loves you and that the two of you are suited to each other."

"Burley talks too much."

"Mrs. Underwood said—"

"She talks too much, too."

"But would you have married her?"

"Maybe someday. You would have married Stephen."

"What will you say to Jessie?"

"About us? Nothing. I've known Jess and looked out for her since she was knee-high to a grasshopper. I've never given her any reason to think I was going to marry her."

"She'll hate me if she's in love with you."

"If she is, she'll get over it. I hope the two of you can be friends." He chuckled and shook his head as if what he was hoping was impossible. "You're as different as night and day."

"Oh..." Elizabeth didn't know whether to be hurt or not.

"You'll be good for Jess. I've not see her in a dress for a good ten years. She needs someone to take her in hand and show her how to act like a lady. I'm afraid that she'll end up an old maid unless she settles for some man like Frank Grissom, a logger who works at the mill."

"You don't like him?"

"He's a good worker, but—"

"Not good enough for Jessie."

"No. Jessie needs a man with a firm but gentle hand."

Elizabeth felt a surge of pity for the unknown girl. If she was in love with Sam, she was in for a letdown.

"Where will I stay when we get to Nora Springs?"

"I've been thinking about that. I'll take you to Amanda's until we're married." A worried frown puckered his brow. "Stephen is the one I'm worried about. He didn't want you to ride the stage because you'd come in contact with toughs. He said you had been sheltered and would be unable to cope. What's he going to think about you marrying me and living here?"

"I guess Stephen didn't know me very well if he thought I was so helpless," she said slowly. "But he is a gentleman," she said quickly. "He'll release me from the engagement when I tell him I've fallen in love with you."

"I would rather he approve, but if he doesn't, it's not going to make any difference," Sam said firmly.

"Glad to hear it, Mr. Ferguson," she said pertly.

They reached Peterson's Station in the late afternoon. The wind had blown the snow off the road in places, and they had made good time. Sam introduced Elizabeth as his fiancée. Everyone was friendly and congratulated them. Sam told the story about Vernon and the one-eyed man and how Elizabeth had buried a hat pin in the fat man's rear end. Then he told about the two drifters trying to kill them at the bridge, and much to her surprise, Elizabeth was looked upon as a heroine. She basked in the warmth of Sam's proud smiles.

The next morning they left the station with invitations to hurry back ringing in their ears. Mrs. Peterson had been especially friendly to Elizabeth after Elizabeth had offered to help her with the evening meal and had stayed to clean up after the others had left the long table. They had talked of many things, and Jessie was not mentioned, much to Elizabeth's relief.

"I missed you last night," Elizabeth said the minute they were alone. "How long until we can be married?"

"I missed you, too. One more night, sweetheart. We'll be married tomorrow. I'd like Pa to be there, and Stephen, if he wants to come."

"He'll want to come. I expect he and Charles are eager to get back to Saint Louis. Will you invite Jessie and her mother?"

"Would you mind? They're like family."

"Of course, I don't mind. Oh, sweetheart, I'd love to make this same trip again someday—without the...complications, of course." They both laughed heartily.

"...and Vernon and the men at the bridge," Sam added, and his face turned serious. "It scares the hell out of me when I think of what could have happened."

"But it didn't. We handled things together, didn't we?" Her green eyes begged him to smile again.

"Remind me, honey, to hide your hat pins."

"I'll do no such thing," she replied sassily. "I never know when I may need one."

"Lordy! I've got a little fighting cat on my hands!"

"Do you know, Sam, I've not worn my corset since that day you told me that no one out here cared if my waist was an inch smaller? I think I'll wear it only on Sunday from now on."

"I'm going to get rid of those damn corsets," he growled, then added firmly, "and you'll not have to remind me."

Elizabeth began to giggle uncontrollably. "What would people think if they knew you had seen my bottom before you even thought about kissing me?"

"Honey, give me due credit as a hell raiser. I had thought about it." His eyes, brilliant with laughter and love, held hers. "Did I ever tell you that you've got the prettiest little bottom I've ever seen?"

"How many little bottoms have you seen, Mr. Ferguson?" she demanded sternly.

"Whoa." He laughed. "I shouldn't have mentioned it."

"You bet your life you shouldn't. Just for that I'm going to tell Stephen you practically puked on me. He'll probably challenge you to a duel."

"Oh, sweetheart, don't mention *that*, ever!" He tilted his head so he could look into her eyes. His face was wreathed in smiles, and his eyes shone with happiness.

She laughed, hugged his arm and rested her cheek against it. His heart swelled with pride and pleasure. Knowing they would reach Nora Springs that day, she had worn her maroon suit under her heavy coat and had pinned her hair back before she carefully covered it with the shawl.

"Sam . . ." They had started toward the valley.

"Yes, love."

"When will we get there?"

"In an hour or so. It isn't far from Peterson's Station."

"Did I understand you to say the afternoon we spent in the bed that you were going to keep me in that position for a week after we are wed?" Under the blanket that covered their legs, she moved a caressing hand to the inside of his thigh and stroked upward.

"I said I'd like to. Ah...honey, don't!" He took a deep breath.

"You said you were going to. Promise." Her fingers inched up and spread out.

"You little . . . devil! Stop that, or I'll—"

"Are you threatening me with bodily harm, sir?" she exclaimed in a horrified tone, and squeezed, then burrowed her fingers beneath his thigh.

"I'll do more than threaten if you don't behave." He bent and kissed her lips, then slapped the reins against the mare's back to hurry her along.

In the middle of the afternoon they came onto a shelf that overlooked the town. Sam stopped the buggy.

"This is it, honey. That's the mill at the far end of town. The church with the white cross is where we'll be married tomorrow. See that piece of land on the other side of the mill pond? That's where we'll build our home. The spring is there. Nora Springs, Pa named the town. He always called my mother Nora."

"Eleanor would be so happy to know that. I wish she could see it."

"I wish she could, too," Sam said wistfully. "I wonder if Stephen told Pa why she left us."

"I don't think Stephen knows."

From within the circle of Sam's arms Elizabeth gazed at the town that would be her home.

"I'll be a good wife to you, Sam. It will take time for me to learn everything I'll need to know about living in this country, and no doubt I'll make you angry at times."

"I know a good way of making up," he whispered, kissing her on the nose.

"We won't have to wait for a blizzard, will we?" she asked with hope, her eyes shining.

"Sweetheart, we won't even have to wait till dark."

Sam stung the mare on the rump with the end of the reins, and the buggy moved down the slope toward town.

* * * * *

You'll flip . . . your pages won't!
Read paperbacks *hands-free* with

Book Mate · I

The perfect "mate" for all your romance paperbacks

Traveling • Vacationing • At Work • In Bed • Studying • Cooking • Eating

Perfect size for all standard paperbacks, this wonderful invention makes reading a pure pleasure! Ingenious design holds paperback books OPEN and FLAT so even wind can't ruffle pages – leaves your hands free to do other things. Reinforced, wipe-clean vinyl-covered holder flexes to let you turn pages without undoing the strap . . . supports paperbacks so well, they have the strength of hardcovers!

Pages turn WITHOUT opening the strap

SEE-THROUGH STRAP

Reinforced back stays flat

Built in bookmark

BOOK MARK

BACK COVER HOLDING STRIP

10" x 7¼", opened.
Snaps closed for easy carrying, too.

Six exciting series for you every month... from Harlequin

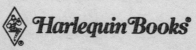

**TWO NEW COMPELLING LOVE STORIES
EVERY MONTH!**

Pursuing their passionate dreams against a
backdrop of the past's most colorful and dramatic
moments, our vibrant heroines and dashing heroes
will make history come alive for you.

**HISTORY HAS NEVER BEEN
SO ROMANTIC!**